A MAN LIKE ALL OTHERS

When Shanna first saw Yui, she thought he was different from all the other Seminoles she had known. He had rescued her and her sister from certain death in the trackless swamps. He had offered them food and protection. He had spoken to her gently and looked upon her with gentle eyes.

But now, in the night, all gentleness had fled. "Be still, girl," he said, and his voice was more of a growl, an animal utterance, than human speech. His hands were on her breasts, her hips. His mouth sought hers, his lips pressing against hers, bruising her lips against her teeth.

Shanna felt fury building. She opened her mouth, and bit down savagely through Yui's lips, tasting his warm, salty blood. He fell back, holding his mouth. Then he laughed, and came to her again . . .

He is the same as all the others, Shanna thought. But even as she furiously fought his overwhelming strength, her own body's response told her it was not so. . . .

SEMINOLE SKIES

Read all the titles in
THE INDIAN HERITAGE SERIES
by Paul Lederer

☐ **BOOK ONE: MANITOU'S DAUGHTERS**—These were the tribes' chosen daughters: Crenna, who lost her position when she gave herself to the white man; Kala, who found her perfect match in the Englishman as ruthless as she; and Sachim, the youngest who was ill-prepared for the tide of violence and terror that threatened to ravish their lands . . . All facing the white invaders of their land and their hearts. . . . (138317—$3.50)

☐ **BOOK TWO: SHAWNEE DAWN**—William and Cara Van der Veghe raised by their white father and Indian mother deep in the wilderness, had to choose sides on the frontier. Brother and sister, bound together by blood, now facing each other over the flames of violence and vengeance. . . .
(138325—$3.50)

☐ **BOOK THREE: SEMINOLE SKIES**—Shanna and her younger sister Lychma were fleeing the invading white men when they fell into the feared hands of the Seminoles. But Shanna would not be broken . . . until she met the legendary warrior, Yui, the one man strong enough to turn her burning hate into flaming love. . . . (156862—$3.95)

☐ **BOOK FIVE: THE WAY OF THE WIND**—Born a Cheyenne, and given by her mother to the whites, she became Mary Hart. But in the arms of a great warrior chief, she became Akton, the name of her birth, educating her people, and loving without limit as she was born to do. . . .
(140389—$3.50)

☐ **BOOK SIX: NORTH STAR**—A brave beauty—fighting for her threatened people, and risking all for a forbidden love. Against the injustice of the white world and the darkening dangers of the Indian world, Heavatha had to find a way to tear down the barriers both worlds put between her and the man she loves. (147405—$3.95)

☐ **BOOK SEVEN: FAR DREAMER**—A woman's vision and a man's courage join in the fight for their people's survival. Beautiful and spirited Sachim could see into the future and through the web of deception woven by the white intruders. Only the brave and brilliant war leader Black Horse could help her save the noble tribe. (150406—$3.95)

Prices slightly higher in Canada.

BOOK 3

SEMINOLE SKIES

THE INDIAN HERITAGE SERIES

Paul Joseph Lederer

A SIGNET BOOK

NEW AMERICAN LIBRARY

Prologue

The war had become an eternal, marauding beast. Sweeping out of the east, it reached bloody probing fingers into the Ohio Valley, and the Shawnee nation began its long fight for survival against those who had come. They were British or French or Americans, but all were under the spell of the war spirits.

The Kata Shawnee had made their war. When they had seen finally that they would not win, that the clouds of destruction would continue to roll across their land, Cara, the wife of Ousa, sent her children away, away from the evils of war and the humiliation which would follow a white victory.

They were given to a Creek woman and taken south, away from the flames of battle to search for a peace beyond the ravaged land.

❋ 1 ❋

Shanna lay still, her heart hammering, her eyes wide. The Creek woman had told them to lie still, and so they did. Lychma was beside her, and Shanna, who had her arm around her younger sister, could feel her shivering.

This was a beautiful place. Of all the camps they had had since leaving home in the Shawnee lands, this was by far the prettiest. They were in a small green glade which was guarded on three sides by great ancient pines, red spruce, white birch and cedar. Before them stood a gray granite cliff. From its heights fell a sheer, silvery waterfall which fed the calm, mirror-bright pool at the base of the cliff. There they had bathed their weary feet. There they had swum with brother, Kokii, who had black eyes much too old for him and was proud of his maleness. Kokii, who was proud of being the son of a Shawnee war leader, which he was.

There had been mockingbirds and orioles singing in the wind-swayed spruce trees. Now they were silent, and Shanna again felt Lychma tremble.

She turned her head slightly and smiled at Lychma. Lychma, who was not strong like Kokii, like Shanna. Lychma, who had blue eyes like her Dutch grandfather. Shanna's arm tightened a little, trying to reassure her sister.

Where was the Creek woman?

"Hide. Stay hidden," the Creek woman had shouted. Then she had lifted her buckskin skirt and gone running toward the woods beyond the clearing where Kokii had gone to explore.

"Shanna . . ."

"Shh!"

"Shanna." Lychma would not be still. Perhaps she did not remember the other times. Times when they had hidden from the white men. Long ago when their father, Ousa, was still

3

alive. Then their mother had whispered to them that they must be as still as stones, quiet as the lake. If their muscles cramped and ached they must pay no attention at all to the pain.

That was long ago and very far away, when Ousa was still alive, when their mother Cara was . . . no, Cara was still alive! They had to believe that. She had told them always to remember that one day she would come for them and that for now they must be good and mind the Creek woman who was taking them south, away from the war.

"What was that?" Lychma's whisper was nearly a shriek, and Shanna clapped her hand over her sister's mouth.

She whispered, "Be still, little one. Do not be afraid. Just be still."

Lychma's blood pounded in her temples. Two small hammers. She was frightened. She was very young, but she had learned already that the world is a place where evil exists and that evil destroys.

Now she lay still, but she could not keep her shoulders from trembling, could not hold back the small birdlike sobs which rose from her throat. She was not her mother, was not Shanna—she was only herself and she was frightened by know-not-what.

Kokii was also afraid. He was glad the girls were not there to see how frightened he was. The sun fell through the forest like gold spilled from the skies. It lay in mottled pools across the mossy earth. The wind whispered in the trees.

Dark things walked the woods.

Kokii had a stick in his hand, and it was reassuring and pathetic at once. He wished he had his father's bow and arrows, but they were back in the camp, in the sheltered cove beneath the tall spruce.

Kokii had been moving silently through the forest, and now he threw himself to the earth again, listening to the small sounds, as soft as the soughing of the wind. Yet it was not the wind and he knew it.

There were footsteps behind him, and he rolled onto his back.

The Creek woman. She looked old, frightened. Her sturdy thighs flashed beneath her uplifted skirt. She rushed toward him, her feet too loud on the humus-matted earth.

Kokii squinted into the sunlight, which shifted and flickered with the movement of the trees. The woman rushing toward him out of the sunlight appeared now as a dark, bustling shadow. A soulless, onrushing creature.

"Kokii!" she shouted. Her arms were uplifted. She tumbled to the earth, and when she rose again there were pine needles clinging to her hair. Her dress front was stained with dark soil and leaf litter. There was blood on her forehead.

"Kokii. Come, we must run."

He did not want to run, and he fought as Dava swept him up into her arms. He did not want to run, and then across her shoulder he saw them.

Other shadows, other specters rushing out of the forest, fragments of shadow against the sunlight, and Kokii's pointing finger lifted.

The Creek woman had him in her arms, and she was running. They wove through the trees. A branch hit Kokii on the back of the head and made his skull ring. The Creek woman was panting heavily as she ran. Her mouth hung open.

At the precipice she stopped, skidded, and nearly fell.

She turned around frantically. They were still there, and a war whoop filled the air as they came out of the trees swinging war axes overhead.

Kokii wanted to fight them and he struggled in the Creek woman's arms, but it was useless. She was strong. The arrow made a dull thump in her back when it hit her, and the Creek woman's eyes opened wider.

Kokii tried to leap free, but although one of the Creek woman's arms was waving wildly in the air the other held him in an iron grip that forced the air out of his lungs, and although he beat his small fists on her shoulders he could not get free as the Creek Woman staggered and toppled forward.

They fell through the emptiness at the edge of the precipice, and Kokii, resigned to his fate now, no longer struggling, could only notice that the sun through the trees was still quite beautiful, that the dark ones still stood on the lip of the precipice, watching them fall.

"I heard Kokii yelling!" Lychma said, and Shanna, who had taken her hand away from her sister's mouth, clapped it over her lips again.

5

Shanna buried her face in the soft humus in frustration. There, in the packed layers of leaves and pine needles, earth and grass left from a hundred summers, Shanna could smell life and death alike. The scent was rich, stirring a wealth of memories. The sun of other years seemed to be locked into the humus. The clean, hard scent of frosts long ago melted. A scurrying dark beetle with pincers trailing behind his hard-shelled body ran across her hand.

Lychma suddenly went rigid and writhed beneath her arm, and Shanna's head came up as they came from the forest. Lychma just lay there, tears filming her blue eyes. Shanna could only sit up and then rise; there was no point in running.

They were big ugly men with their arms and legs covered with ornate tattoos. Their hair was pulled up into a topknot. Their blue hands were wrapped around the handles of their war clubs. Shanna's legs gave out. She sagged to the earth again.

They spoke, and Shanna could not understand them. Eyes seemed to examine her budding breasts, her narrow hips, and discount her.

One squatted and then with astonishment fell back after looking into Lychma's eyes.

Blue eyes.

Hands yanked Shana to her feet, threw Lychma beside her. One of the men wanted to tie her, but the others laughed. It was true. What could she do?

"Who are they?" Lychma whispered. "Where are they taking us? What's happened to Dava and to Kokii?"

Shanna could answer none of those questions but the last. She knew already what had happened to their brother, what had become of the woman their mother had given them to. Where they were going now, what would become of them, she did not know. Perhaps she did not want to.

They went southward at a hectic pace. The air seemed close, stifling. The days were clear, but at night low, sinister fog crept in along the river bottoms. It was impossible to breathe or to sleep.

"Where are they taking us? Where is Kokii?"

Lychma was close to her sister. They shared a single broadly striped blanket which was infested with small bugs. Lychma's breath was close and damp against Shanna's ear.

6

Shanna did not answer. If they spoke too much the tallest of the men, the one who carried a long cane, would whip them into silence.

"Why don't they kill me?" Lychma said, her breath hissing from between her teeth. Her hands gripped Shanna tightly. Shanna lifted her hand from beneath the blanket and stroked Lychma's soft dark hair until she heard her sister's breathing slow, until Lychma was asleep.

There were tall trees with waxy leaves and great white flowers along the river. There were oppressed cypress trees weighed down by tethers of Spanish moss. Twice they saw alligators, and each time Lychma screamed until the man with the cane hit her.

They moved through a swampy, noisome land inhabited by strange creatures. They were waist-deep in scum-darkened water much of the time.

There were no mountains. The water was not clean. At night Shanna could hardly sleep. Her body was always damp and sticky.

"They are taking us to the end of the world," Lychma said. Perhaps they were.

Gone were the rolling hills and the deep-green meadows of their home, gone the clean-scented pine forests. Gone was Kokii.

Gone—she could admit it now, to herself if not to Lychma— was their mother, Cara, who had gone out to fight the white men and their cannon. There was only Lychma, and Shanna held her tightly, murmuring to her.

Another dawn would come and they would rise again, be tossed scraps by the tattooed men who squatted by the campfire eating. Then they would again move southward.

The sky was a brassy dome throughout the day and at sundown a crimson bowl. The stars seemed to swelter in the night skies.

Three days after they had started one of the men began yelling and they all had to rush from the water to kill the leeches which were clinging to them. Black, slimy things with poisonous little mouths. Now Lychma did not scream, she simply sat and stared.

Now and then one man, younger than the rest, would give them sweet water from a skin sack he carried across his shoulder. He would speak to them in words they could not understand, and his eyes would be sad. The others caught him doing this once and they laughed. Then he did not speak to them again.

When they had been on the trail for a week, Shanna heard a sudden hiss from the man who was leading the party. She saw his hand go up, and then she and Lychma were knocked to the ground and held there.

A canoe drifted on the lake, and in it were three men. Creek. Shanna knew they were Creek Indians. She had seen them many times before.

Through the long grass before her she could see the tattooed men slip into the water and swim beneath it without making a ripple.

The scent of the grass was sweet, nearly sickening. The sun was hot on her back, and a snake shuttled away somewhere near at hand. Great cypress trees hung out across the water.

The Creek men pulled in a net heavy with fish and began congratulating each other.

But the tattooed ones came up out of the lake, and Shanna closed her eyes. She heard a sound like a melon being split, heard a terrible scream, and she did not look. She knew what she would see if she opened her eyes, and so she did not. She simply lay against the earth, clumps of grass squeezed tightly in her hands, until the sounds all died away, until there was not even the rippling of the lake to disturb the silence.

Far away a bird cried loudly, mockingly, and Shanna was yanked to her feet by a man with a bloody hand. They traveled on and had fish for dinner that day. Shanna could not eat any of it.

The forest became so deep and tangled that Shanna could not find the sun. The smell of rotting vegetation and dying lakes was everywhere. Great canopies of trees overhung their path.

They came upon the village quite suddenly.

The men were given a hero's welcome. Women in bark skirts came to greet them, and old grizzled warriors with tattoos nearly covering their skin. Naked boys frisked around, screeching and poking at Lychma and Shanna.

The houses these people lived in were on stilts. They had

straw or grass roofs and no walls. The people wore bone necklaces and bone or shell earrings. Fish racks were everywhere, and flies swarmed over the drying fish. A girl whose job it was to keep the flies off with a fronded switch was chased back to her duties as the warriors and their trophies were discussed and pored over.

It was Lychma who astonished them. Lychma with her Dutch blue eyes, and they poked at her, mocked her, and put their faces next to hers until Lychma began to cry again.

Eventually they were led away. The warriors went to their houses or to celebrate, and a woman with rough hands and a tight mouth took Lychma and Shanna to a small house which was unlike the others. It was built on the ground, had four walls and no windows. The floor was covered with rotting dry grass.

The woman gave a shove between Shanna's shoulder blades, and she staggered forward into the darkness, which was nearly complete although the sun was high outside.

"Well?" The voice came from the corner of the hut. It was a woman's voice, not young and not friendly. "Are you Cherokee or not? Who are you?"

Shanna sat against the floor, her hand on her sister's shoulder.

"We are Shawnee."

"Shawnee! Cousins, eh?" The Shawnee and the Cherokee were related distantly, and their tongues were not dissimilar. "Me, I'm Cherokee." The woman's accent was difficult for Shanna to understand. Some of the words made no sense. As Shanna watched the woman scooted forward to sit beside them. Shanna could not make her out. Except to see that she was middle-aged, that her face was round.

"Where are we?" Shanna asked.

"Where are you?" The question was almost mocking. "In the camp of the Seminole. The camp of Potaqua. A terrible man. A bloodthirsty man. He hates everyone who is not Seminole. I think he hates everyone in the world. What's your name?"

"I am Shanna, the daughter of Cara and Ousa, the Shawnee war leader."

"Never mind all that." She waved an impatient hand.

"Just your name. And what is this you have brought with you?"

It was a moment before Shanna realized what the woman was referring to. "This is my sister, Lychma."

Lychma sat up, rubbing her eyes. The woman unexpectedly patted Lychma's head with a rough fondness.

"Lychma. Shanna. My name is Corta. I am Cherokee. The wife of the man Hasha, who was once a warrior and is now a man who tills the land."

"Was he shamed?" Shanna asked. A warrior content to till the land and grow crops like a woman?

"Shamed?" The woman's voice was puzzled, then she laughed. "I see. I forgot you come from a wild northern tribe. The Cherokee have made their peace with everyone. Everyone except Potaqua, the Seminole who makes peace with no one. The white leader Madison sent us a treaty of peace. He promised us our land forever. The white leader Madison sent us implements to farm with and seed and animals. The Cherokee do not make war anymore. Nor do the Creek nor the Choctaw."

"They have made peace with the white man?" Shanna could hardly accept it. Her mother had said there would never be peace for any Indian, only for cowards. Were the Cherokee cowards?

"Peace, yes!" Corta said vigorously. "Why not? Our leaders are wise. Not like this Shawnee firebrand, this Tecumseh."

"I do not know him."

"No?" Corta shrugged. "Why not make peace? There is much to be learned from the white man. I wanted to see my babies grow up. I was happy when peace came. Now we live well. Our land is ours. We are free and the war is gone."

"But not for the Seminole?"

"Some Seminole. Not for Potaqua. He hides himself in the swamps and kills all those who have made peace. He hates the Creeks especially for making peace. But that is a family quarrel. The Seminole were once part of the Creek nation. That was some time ago. The name 'Seminole' means 'runaway' in the Creek tongue—that is because the Seminole ran away into the swamps to fight instead of making peace."

10

"What now?" Lychma spoke for the first time. "What will happen to us? We are not Creek, we are not Cherokee."

"But you are not Seminole."

"What will happen?"

"The same as happened to me, to everyone they bring here," Corta said. "We are slaves. We work."

"We work." Lychma's voice was a numb echo. "I do not wish to be here. I wish to go home."

"You will not go home." Corta's voice was softer. Perhaps she was thinking of her own babies, who could have been the age of the Shawnee sisters. "You must do what they tell you. You must work or they will beat you. You must not run away, for if they catch you it will go hard. No one but a Seminole can find his way out of the swamps anyway. You saw. You traveled here."

Shanna nodded her head in the darkness. She had seen. Seen the limitless swamps, the alligators, the quicksand, the water thick with water moccasins.

"For how long?" Lychma asked. Her hand sought and found Shanna's in the darkness. "How long must we stay? How long must we be slaves?"

"What?" Corta laughed sharply. "How long! For all of your life, small one. But do not worry—your life will not be that long."

There was nothing to do then but wait. Shanna gathered straw together, ignoring the small thing which scurried away. She made a bed and a pillow for herself and Lychma and then they lay back to try to rest.

They were exhausted, but they could not sleep. They could only lie in the humid, airless hut and stare at the darkness, listening to Corta wheeze, listening to the distant sounds of unintelligible voices.

Shanna thought of a distant place. Snow drifted lightly through the air. Endless ranks of blue spruce clotted the hills, and a silver rill ran through the valley, which was carpeted with deep green grass. There deer drank; there life was different. People breathed the air and found it tasted sweet. People laughed and there was no harshness in their laughter. It was cool!

Darkness fell across her thoughts like descending veils. And there was blood and twisted bodies and faces drawn with

11

pain. And Shanna reached out for her mother before she realized she had been sleeping, that she was now awake in the sticky night. That Lychma was sleeping fitfully beside her and they were slaves.

Daylight came early. A pair of women, burly as men, and as rough, opened the door to the hut, jerked the girls to their feet, and took them out. Corta was already gone, Shanna noticed.

They were led across the Seminole camp, and dogs yapped at their heels. The sun was a pale-red glow in the east. It was still sticky and hot. There was a salt scent to the air.

They were taken to a large chickee, as the straw-and-stilt houses were called, and a woman clambered down a ladder to examine them.

She was slender, pinched, wearing necklaces of shells. She walked around them, poking at their bodies. She said something rapidly and then climbed back up the ladder.

Her name, if Shanna had understood correctly, was Tohope. She was a powerful woman, obviously.

"Who was she?" Lychma whispered as they were hurried across the camp again in the opposite direction.

"She is our mistress," Shanna answered.

"What do you mean?"

"She is our owner," Shanna explained to her sister.

"No one owns a Shawnee," Lychma said with a dignity which surprised and pleased her sister.

Except a Seminole.

They were taken to a collection of shacks built of bark and crooked poles. A pot of white manufacture stood in the middle of a clearing, and the smell of fish stew was strong in the air. Around the pot squatted or stood a dozen ragged, weary people. Slaves.

No one spoke. Shanna and Lychma were given bowls of the chowder, which seemed to be mostly fish heads and a sort of tuber Shanna did not recognize. They were half finished when the burly women returned, carrying cane poles which they whished around menacingly, and the women were herded out in different directions.

Shanna and Lychma were returned to the large chickee. Around in back there was a stack of fresh hides. Deer, otter,

12

muskrat. An older woman sat there diligently scraping the hides with a bone tool.

Shanna and Lychma were left in her custody.

"Work," she said through the toothless gap which was her mouth. She too, it seemed, was Cherokee. "Work. Do you understand, girls? Work or they will come back and beat you."

They sat cross-legged on the ground and followed suit. This was the sort of work the wife of a hunter did. Yet this woman Tohope did none of it. Her husband was rich or powerful if he could keep three slaves to do his wife's work.

"Who is Tohope?" Shanna asked the old woman.

"Tohope." The old woman's head jerked from side to side with some nervous disorder. She was ill. There were boils on her back and arms. "Tohope is the wife of Potaqua. Second wife. The first wife is Caal. She is an old woman. Caal birthed many children and then she could bear no more. Caal walks the everglades. She speaks to many spirits and prays for death." The old woman went on in her dry, rambling voice. All the while she scraped at her hides. She worked sedulously, her bluish tongue protruding slightly from her weathered lips.

"Tohope is our mistress? Tohope owns us?"

"Tohope is very bad. A bad woman. You must work and not waste time talking. She does not like anyone. She is worse than her husband, who hates when his eyes first open in the morning."

They scraped.

The sun rose higher, and their fingers grew numb and bloody with the work. The old woman chanted under her breath. Her hands were horny and crooked, her neck like a tortoise's. The sun seemed to bore a hole in Shanna's skull. She was grateful for the bit of shade which stretched out and touched them.

She turned suddenly, realizing that it was someone's shadow. Tohope was standing over them, hung with shells and stone beads. Her face was pinched into a tight repellent mask. She said nothing.

Shanna continued to work. The old woman's eyes were worried. Lychma looked up, and Shanna heard Tohope hiss. She crouched down peering at Lychma—at her eyes. At those

13

sky-blue Dutch eyes. She remained that way for a long time, and then she muttered something and left.

"What did she say?" Shanna asked the old woman, but she received no answer except a quick shake of the head.

"What is it?" Lychma wanted to know. "Why was she looking at me? What does she want?"

"It was nothing," Shanna replied. "She just wanted to see our work."

"No." Lychma shook her head quite definitely. "It was more than that. I know it."

They were not fed again until sundown glazed the skies above the everglades with pale colors. Then it was only the fish chowder again. Shanna could barely keep her eyes open long enough to finish her bowl.

They staggered back to their hut to find Corta sagged against the floor, her head hanging. Lychma lay down and was asleep in minutes. Mosquitoes buzzed and dove around them.

Despite her exhaustion, Shanna could not sleep.

"Is the work too hard?" Corta asked. Her voice again was a strange mixture of what might have been both concern and mockery.

"It is something we are not used to."

"If it is too hard you will die. If it is not too hard you will live and wish you were dead."

"Do you wish you were dead, Corta?"

"All slaves wish they were dead," she snapped.

"They wish for freedom."

"There is no freedom. You cannot run from this camp. Where can you go?"

Where could she go, in fact? Home was distant; perhaps it no longer existed. The army of the white men had come. Their own village had been burned, the forest bombarded by cannon. Their mother, Shanna knew, must be dead. Cara would be dead because she would not run from the army which had murdered her husband, Shanna's father.

Where would she go? Into the swamps where the trails were hidden, known only to the Seminole. And then—nowhere. There was nowhere to go. Perhaps things would not be so bad here. There must be a way of becoming accepted. She said as much to Corta.

14

"Become Seminole?" Corta laughed out loud. "If you could, why would you want to? They are savages."

"I am here," Shanna said simply. "As you say, slaves die, or live as the dead. Can you teach me their language?"

"I speak their language. But what has it gotten me?" Corta was hostile and bitter. Shanna scooted closer to her in the darkness.

"At least you know what they are saying. You know what is happening."

"Do I? They do not speak in front of me. Only 'Do this, woman,' or 'Get out of the way, crone.' "

"I would like to be able to speak their language," Shanna said.

"You are a strange girl, Shanna. Strange and foolish. You would do better to learn how to be a good worker. Learn to weave baskets and mats, learn to mend nets, learn to do everything that they ask of you and be the best at it. That is the way to security. The best slaves are not beaten so much."

"Then I will do that as well," Shanna answered. "Why can I not do both? But I must learn their language."

"All right. What I know of it. Most of that is concerned with work. It is all anyone ever spoke to me about. It is all they will every speak to you about. I will teach you what I know."

With that Corta curled up and went to sleep. Perhaps she was dreaming of her husband and his land, of the soil where corn grew tall and sturdy. The Cherokee, Shanna thought again, must be cowards to live like that. The Seminole at least were free.

She lay back, hearing Lychma's soft breathing, and she too fell asleep, dreaming dreams of distant wandering. Of great swamp alligators and headless men. The everglades were filled with wandering people, walking silently as shadows, passing each other without seeing. And slowly, one by one, the swamp devoured them as Tohope, floating like a necklace-hung sun in a bleak sky, glared down approvingly.

The following day was no different from the first. They worked building a thatched roof for a chickee under the stern and unhappy gaze of a woman named Takal who was a Catawba slave. At sunset they ate the same chowder and returned to their hut, where Lychma fell immediately to sleep. Shanna stayed awake, speaking with the Cherokee woman, learning the Seminole language until her head buzzed with weariness and her eyes felt hard as stones, until she could no longer speak with her thickened tongue.

Then she slept and again the dream came. Wanderers. Blind slaves, endless swamp.

The next day was the day Potaqua returned.

A low murmuring buzz passed through the village. The sound was not one actually heard, but one intimated. A knowledge, a premonition. And then the people began to come out of their huts, to come up from the river where they had been fishing, to gather.

A runner came in, and as he reported the sound became audible. It was "Potaqua, Potaqua," a sort of chant, a Seminole communal voice which expressed love and fear, warmth and awe at once.

"What is it?" Lychma asked.

"Potaqua. Their war leader."

"Tohope's man."

"Yes." Shanna continued to work, weaving the grass to form a section of roof for the chickee. But her eyes were on the villagers.

Their bodies were rigid with anticipation. They leaned forward, straining to hear, to see, to sense the warlord's coming.

They must love him, Shanna thought. Her fingers continued to work, and her pulse quickened. The excitement in the air was palpable.

A shout went up, and they saw the people of the village rushing toward the far side of the clearing. Someone had begun beating a deep-voiced drum. Children shrieked. A woman called out from a chickee.

And Potaqua entered the camp.

Fifty warriors all fiercely tattooed, their bodies carrying the records of their valor. They carried bows and muskets. War bags were slung across their copper shoulders.

Children danced around them, were scooped up. Women cried and wailed and laughed—the sounds mingling.

And the big man strode through them.

Potaqua, it must be. Men bowed away deferentially. He was a big-shouldered man with a deep chest. There was no inch of his body uncovered with tattoos except his face. His hair was pulled tautly into a topknot, tied with a red ribbon. Huge stone earrings had lengthened the lobes of his ears.

"He's terrible!" Lychma gasped.

He was terrible. His nose was flat, broken. His eyes were dull with no redeeming, humanitarian gleam. He looked upon his people without warmth.

Shoving them aside, he strode toward his own house—the house where Lychma and Shanna were working. They were watching with awe, and in Shanna's case, with disgust.

Potaqua walked past his wife without speaking, and motioned to a warrior who strode behind him. Shanna looked down from the roof, wondering. The warrior carried a long stick with six gourd-shaped objects hanging from it. Potaqua said something, laughed without humor, and pointed to the roof of his chickee where the two young Shawnee worked.

"Heads!" Lychma shrieked, and she nearly slid from the roof.

They were heads. Severed trophies which hung from the stick Potaqua's lieutenant carried. All the heads of Indians. Shanna could not guess their tribe.

"Who are they?" Potaqua asked, his voice powerful, low.

"Two Shawnee girls," Tohope answered. "Immokalle brought them to us. I have kept them, my husband. If you do not want them . . ."

"It does not matter." Potaqua threw his weapons to one side, and there was a boy there to snatch them up and run with them to the chickee. "You, girl!"

Shanna hesitated. She knew Potaqua was talking to her, he must be, yet she could not answer. She touched her breast, and Potaqua nodded impatiently.

"You, girl. Place these on the corner poles!"

Shanna bent low and reached for the pole. The warrior was grinning. Potaqua was watching her closely. Shanna took the pole and raised it to the roof.

"That's right, you stupid thing. Put them on the corner poles."

Shanna looked for Lychma, but her sister had her head turned away and bowed to the roof. Shanna got to her feet and walked along the ridgepole as the warriors below watched.

She looked at the ridgepole, at the sky, at the everglades, but not at the heads which spun and leered. There was a sour smell about them, like old rotted leather.

"Right there."

Shanna nodded. The upright pole at the corner of the chickee was before her. She tried to fit one of the heads on the corner without touching it, tried to jiggle it free of the pole.

"Not like that!"

She knew what they wanted her to do, what she must do, and kneeling, Shanna put the pole onto the woven grass roof of Potaqua's chickee. The men watched her, hands on hips, black eyes glittering.

Shanna took the nearest head without looking at it. Her hands went around it and she felt stickiness, dried leather, hair. Shuddering, she slipped it from the pole and impaled it on the upright pole to leer and gape at the villagers, who cheered.

The second was easier, although she had to do it quickly to keep her stomach from turning over. Finished finally, she dropped the pole to the ground. Potaqua already had his attention elsewhere. The girls were left alone on the roof with the dead ones.

They seemed to be peering up over the edges of the roof, watching as Shanna and Lychma tried to work. Once Lychma backed into one as she worked her way toward a corner. She did not scream, but her mouth fell open and she clung to the roof as if the force of her vertigo might hurl her off into space.

"Savages," Lychma said. "Savages. I hate them. I hate them all."

Shanna shushed her. Lychma looked at her sister with hurt eyes and nodded. She said no more, but as she worked her lips continued to move in silent censure.

Shanna kept her eyes down. The sun was hot on her back. Her fingers were raw and sore as she wove new grass into the roof. The shadows flitted across the roof. Hoarse cries broke the silence.

Shanna looked up to see them. A raven was perched on one of the severed heads, and in its mouth was a strip of flesh.

18

The other birds fought for it, tried to tear their own meal free of the skull.

Shanna rose, screaming, and chased them away. The ravens took off with a fluttering of black wings and circled, cawing angrily.

"Shanna." Lychma's voice was weak and shaky, and Shanna went to her sister. "Don't let them come back."

"I won't," she promised, holding her close to her breast.

"Please. You must not let them come back."

"I won't."

They knelt together, their arms around each other, as the ravens continued to circle. Shanna, looking across her sister's shoulder, saw the woman on the ground watching, her mouth pursed, tight.

"Come on now," Shanna said. "Let's finish this work and then we can get down."

"Yes. I'll work as quickly as I can," Lychma said, wiping back a long strand of black hair. They returned to the job, and when Shanna looked again she saw that Tohope had gone away. The ravens had not given up so easily. They wheeled through the clear blue sky, mocking and shrilling, and when Shanna and Lychma finally climbed down from the roof of the chickee they came in like a green-black cloud and settled, cawing triumphantly, to strip the skulls to the bone.

Shanna's dreams that night were dark and tumultuous. They came from out of the sky on iridescent wings and tore at her hair and eyes until she sat up panting in the darkness, her eyes wide, heart palpitating like a rabbit in a snare.

Reality, consciousness, was less frightening, but no brighter, no less solemn. She sat staring at the darkness, listening to the hum of mosquitoes, the night wind lifting the thatching of the roof, the uncertain breathing of Lychma. Then she turned and lay on her stomach, pounding her fists against the earth in frustration.

She awoke a second time that night, with violence around her.

"Get up. Run!"

The woman at the door shouted again and then was gone. Beyond the entranceway Shanna could see people rushing past, their arms burdened with their belongings or with small children.

19

"Get up!" Corta was gathering her few effects—a blanket, a straw basket with needles, a second pair of moccasins, a few mismatched beads, an awl, a rabbit skin.

"What is it?" Lychma had gotten to her feet, and she stood crouched like a wild animal.

"We are being attacked." Corta broke for the doorway.

"Who is attacking us? Who? Why?" Shanna called after her.

"What is it?" Lychma asked, her voice rising with fear.

"I don't know. Come, sister."

Shanna took Lychma's arm, and they ran out into the night. People rushed past, scarcely glancing at them. A dozen warriors, still naked, ran the opposite way, hastily snatched-up weapons in their hands.

"Run!" Shanna said, pushing her sister's shoulder. Lychma did run, not knowing where she was running, what she ran from. There was danger. The herd moved. Shanna was at her side, her bare feet carrying her forward, into the swamps as the Seminole dispersed.

Shadows moved everywhere. Faceless, voiceless people. Far away Shanna heard the sudden sharp report of a musket being fired. Only one.

They ran into the cypress grove, the ground soft and boggy underfoot. The Seminole were into the lake already, wading into the dark waters as the pregnant moon glared down.

They held their possessions high. The children sat on their shoulders, silent and motionless. Another musket was fired, and then a dozen shots sounded, all nearer now.

Lychma stumbled as they entered the lake, and Shanna grabbed her arm, yanking her to her feet. The water was warm. It closed around them as they waded toward the distant shore.

They ran on through the night, finally reaching a clearing deep in the mangroves. There people sat collapsed against the earth. There was a warriors' council, and after a minute a dozen of the men slipped off into the night again. The rest of them sat together, muddy, weary, smelling of the swamp.

"What is it?" Lychma asked. Her face was against Shanna's shoulder. "Why are we running? Why are we always running, Shanna? Where are we going?"

Lychma's teeth bit into Shanna's shoulder. It hurt, but she

said nothing. Why were they running? Because people ran. Because men came and there was war. Their names, their reasons, their faces were always different, but they always came, wanting war and blood. They said they wanted peace. That was a lie. None of them wanted it. They liked war, the glory of it, the destruction. And so they ran.

There was no food, no sleep that night. With the dawn they rose and stretched the stiffness from their muscles while flights of sea birds, pelicans and terns, glided westward through the smoky orange skies above the mangrove swamp.

They waited. It was another day and a night before Potaqua returned.

"Everyone up," the Seminole warlord said. He said it only once, and they all rose, Seminoles and slaves alike.

"Where are we going, Corta?" Shanna asked. The woman picked up her belongings and said nothing.

It was another day's travel to the new campsite. The old camp had been destroyed. By Creek warriors, they were saying. Creek warriors and Americans. They had come to avenge the heads.

The work was more difficult now. All of the vegetation had to be cleared from the new campsite. New chickees had to be built. New fields where pumpkins and cane and maize could be planted.

Lychma grew haggard. Her eyes were glazed, her hands wrapped with bloody rags as they worked, digging in the fields. At night she could not eat and had to be helped to their half-completed hut.

"I am ill," she told her sister. Her blue eyes looked up pleadingly at Shanna. Her hand clutched her sleeve. "It is the air in this place. Still and heavy. The spirit who lives in the swamps is a bad creature. His hands stretch out to drag us down, to smother us."

"The little one will not survive," Corta said after Shanna had talked her sister to sleep.

"She will survive!" Shanna's voice was angry. "Why should she not survive? Don't say such things."

"I will not speak if you do not wish me to." Corta rolled up in her blanket then, her back to Shanna, and Shanna herself lay back, biting down hard on her wrist to keep from crying out. Because she knew already. She knew that what Corta had said was true.

There was a spirit in these swamps which hated them. Hated these women from the north. It would not let them breathe or smile or have a future. It held them in its oppressive, remorseless grip and slowly crushed them.

"It shall not kill you," Shanna whispered to the girl who slept at her side. "I will not let it. When you are weary I shall work for you. When you are hungry you shall have my food. When you cannot sleep I shall sing to you, and when you need someone to comfort you, to reassure you, I shall whisper the little lies you need to hear."

He was young and brown and dark; unkempt hair sprouted from his head in wild profusion. He smiled, flashing white, even teeth, as he watched Shanna straighten up from her work to hold her back.

He was no older than Shanna, perhaps fifteen. When she looked away he grinned again and squatted down beside the pumpkin patch, watching the Shawnee girl work.

The air was stagnant, humid. The sun a fierce yellow ball. Shanna felt perspiration trickle into her eyes, run down between her breasts. When she looked again the boy was still watching her, still smiling.

"Don't you have any work to do?" she said in annoyance.

"I am Seminole. A warrior," he said, holding his smile.

Shanna muttered to herself, holding back the replies she thought of.

"What is your name, girl?" he asked.

Shanna looked up, sat back on her haunches, and shook her head. She did not like this boy. *A warrior.* She returned to her work, turning her back to him. A row away Lychma worked, glancing apprehensively at her sister and the youth.

"They call me Apopkakee," the boy said. He was in front of Shanna again, and he bent over to peer up at her face. "Apopkakee. Understand?" he asked.

"Yes, I understand, boy. Go away, leave us to our work. You are not supposed to talk to slaves anyway."

"I don't care about that," he said flippantly. He sat cross-legged before Shanna, a blade of yellow grass between his lips. "My father is a priest. His name is Tukakee. You must know his name."

"No."

"No? He is a very powerful man. I will be a powerful man one day as well, but not a priest. I am supposed to be a priest. That is my clan. But I wish to be a warrior. You see—I do not care for convention. And so I speak to slave girls if I wish."

"Are you a crazy boy?" Shanna straightened up and wiped her hair from her forehead with the back of her hand. "Go away. I must work or be beaten."

"No one would dare! Who owns you?"

"Tohope."

"Oh." The smile fell away. He brightened again. "I do not fear her either. You don't, do you?"

"Yes. I fear her. Her and her cane. Go away now, boy."

"Apopkakee," he said.

"Apopkakee, go away," Shanna said, and she turned her back again.

When she glanced up he was gone, and despite herself Shanna looked around for him. He was behind her, still grinning, and he waved as Shanna's eyes found him. She turned away, her face growing hot.

"Who was that?" Lychma asked.

"Only a stupid boy," Shanna said irritably.

"It would be nice to have one friend," her sister answered.

"We cannot have friends, Lychma. We are slaves."

"Ah," Lychma said, and a sly smile crept over her lips.

"*Ah*? What does that mean?"

"It means nothing, sister. I am just happy that you have met this stupid boy."

"Will it mean more food for us? Less work?" Shanna demanded, but her sister, humming to herself, returned to her work. Across the field Shanna saw Tohope. The sun glinted on her clamshell necklace. She held her cane across her body. Shanna bent her back to her work, feeling angry, happy, and apprehensive at once. "Stupid boy," she muttered again, and Lychma laughed out loud.

Twice they had to leave this camp, both times in the dead of night, as Potaqua's enemies attacked. Neither time was the village destroyed, however. There were new heads to be hung on the upright poles of Potaqua's chickee.

The maize grew tall, and the pumpkins began to turn color

and swell. One morning Shanna awoke to find that it was hours past dawn and still no one had come to awaken her, to herd the slaves out into the field.

"What is wrong?" she asked Corta.

"Wrong?"

"There is no work. Are we moving again?"

"It's Boskita," Corta said. She was putting on the little hat she had made out of her rabbit skin and the necklace she had strung out of old beads and bits of shell.

"What is that?" Lychma asked. "Boskita?"

"The festival. The holiday. Even the slaves will celebrate. The corn is ripe, the crops are good. The spirits are pleased with the Seminole. There will be food and games and drink and singing and dancing." Corta spun in a circle, her heavy breasts bobbing as she danced.

"Boskita."

"Yes. It is the beginning of the new year. The women put out the fires in their houses and throw away all that is worn out. New tools will be made. We are rejuvenated. Sins are forgiven."

Shanna thought dourly that if Tohope threw out all of her old things they would have to make new ones for her. Lychma was on her knees, eyes alight.

"No work!"

It was enough for Lychma on this day. When had they last had a day without work? Long before they came to this camp. Long ago and far away when they had not been slaves but the children of a Shawnee war leader and the shaman Cara.

"Help me comb my hair, Shanna," Lychma pleaded. "Will there be food for us?"

"All you can eat," Corta promised.

"I will stuff myself until I explode. And games?"

"Not for the slaves."

"No work!" Lychma said again excitedly.

"Hold still!" Shanna slapped her sister playfully on the head and ran the tortoiseshell comb through her long dark hair. She noticed the small sores on Lychma's scalp, noticed that the hair combed out too easily, but said nothing. Lychma was happy. She lived still in a child's world. One festival day was enough to erase the memory of a thousand days of labor, of running through the swamps with fear constricting their throats, of the constant threat of Tohope's cane.

"Hold still!" she said again, and as she laughed her eyes were stinging with tears. She kissed Lychma's head and squeezed her tightly for a moment.

Outside there was much activity. Venison was being roasted over open fires. Women were happily throwing away old furniture, household articles, and tools from their chickees.

Priests in paint strode through the village, and behind them was a cortege of men who had fasted throughout the week and were now praying for forgiveness. The women were picking young corn for the feast. Husbands ceremonially lit new fires to signify the rebirth of the year, of the soul, of the Seminole people.

Visitors were beginning to come into the village from out of the everglades. Men from other Seminole tribes with gifts of venison and fish, of duck and wild pig. The younger ones were beginning to clear the field to the west of the camp in preparation for chunkey, a form of lacrosse, organized mayhem in which two tribes competed with as many as fifty men on either side.

Above this all, on the porch of his chickee, stood Potaqua in his holiday raiment. He wore white linen with a striped sash and a striped cap. His hair had been freshly oiled and braided, woven with bright cloth. He looked dour, but then perhaps Potaqua cared nothing for festivals, but only for war.

The drums and pipes had been playing since dawn. Now the cymbals joined the refrain, and dancers moved through the camp in a sinuous procession, wearing their finery. The women wore togas of linen; those of high rank wore feather cloaks. The men had oiled their bodies, cleansing themselves. Cane baskets filled with new corn and dried fish, with beans and turtle meat, with pumpkin seeds and millet, with duck eggs were carried to the communal dining area, where rows of cornhusk mats had been spread on the ground.

Boys carried watermelons to the feast. Lychma saw a man carrying four turkeys, holding them by their necks. The dancers wound past her hut, and she watched them with bright eyes.

"I've never seen so much food."

"There will be much at our feast," Corta said. "The

25

slaves too celebrate. Behind the council hut they have made a place for us.''

''Shanna. Let us go and see.''

''Go on,'' Shanna said. ''Go with Corta.''

''You must come too.''

''After a bit.''

Lychma finally left, dancing arm in arm with Corta as the drums continued to play, as a shout went up from the field where the first chunkey game had begun. Feathered dancers walked past Shanna, heading for the ceremonial fire where they would perform.

Shanna turned away. She wanted nothing to do with this. What was there to celebrate? She could not explain it to Lychma, to Corta. What they were celebrating was the feast itself, not the meaning behind the feast.

Rebirth. New life. A cleansing. And what rebirth was there for a slave? Shanna walked slowly from the camp. No one seemed to notice or to care. It was cool among the mangroves. A soft breeze off of the sea rustled the broad shiny leaves and stirred the water of the inlet. The trail was overgrown with a tangle of snakelike roots, and Shanna had to watch her feet as she moved through the trees, and so when he suddenly appeared before her it was as if he had risen out of the ground.

He was a man of twenty summers with broad shoulders and chest muscles like slabs of oak. His sinewy arms were decorated with broad tattooed bracelets. His eyes were dark and piercing. His nose was uncommonly straight, and his mouth was even and expressionless.

He carried a rifle. A hatchet was tucked into the waistband of his loincloth. Red and yellow feathers waved from his topknot as the breeze stirred.

He looked at Shanna with eyes which seemed not only to see through her toga but to strip her flesh from her bones, to see into her soul.

He threw back his head and laughed.

''Stand aside, little one,'' he said in a rumbling voice, and she backed away, her heel catching on a mangrove root. She waved her arms for balance and just prevented herself from toppling over.

He laughed again.

Then the laugh died away and he strode past her, quiet and

26

competent in his movements, a panther in the everglades, a silent deadly man. Shanna's head barely came to his shoulder, she noticed as he walked by.

She watched him for a moment, watched the shadows of the trees paint moving images across his muscular back. Her heart was thundering in her ears and her legs wre trembling. She seemed unable to catch her breath. Was that fear she felt?

It was fear, she decided, of a primitive sort. She had met a panther face to face. It had twitched its tail and fixed savage eyes on her and then passed her by, its fluid body a menace and a fascination at once.

"That was Yui," the amused voice behind Shanna said, and she spun to find Apopkakee leaning against a convoluted mangrove trunk, shredding a leaf between his fingernails. He was dressed in a white linen garment. His hair had been gathered on this day. He wore the paint of a priest.

"Yui?" Shanna barely managed to get the word out. She hoped the fear, the excitement, didn't show in her eyes, but she knew it did. Apopkakee's smile was knowledgeable.

"I see you are dressed in the priest clan's paint," she said, changing the subject.

"Yes." Apopkakee frowned and threw away his shredded leaf. It landed in the dark water beside the tree and bobbed away. "I suppose it is true. They say I am a boy with many words and few actions. My father says I am to be a priest, and so I am." He shrugged as if it were of little importance. "Still," he added quietly, "I would like to be a warrior."

His face was suffused with excitement for a brief moment. Imagined triumphs lit up his eyes. "Would you like to walk to the sea with me, Shanna?"

"To the sea?"

"It is not very far. Haven't you smelled it, felt the wind? It is this way. Not a mile. Come along if you wish. I am supposed to be with the other acolytes, but I don't care."

"Won't you get in trouble?"

"My father will beat me until he raises welts," Apopkakee replied. All the same he started walking westward, toward the sea.

"Who is Yui?" Shanna asked after they had gone a way.

"I knew you would not forget him so quickly!" Apopkakee said.

Shanna flushed. "I only wondered."

"He is a great warrior. The kind of man I will become. He is chief of his people, their war leader. He is not so powerful as Potaqua, but no Seminole is except for Osceola."

"He does not fear Potaqua?" Shanna was walking with her hands behind her back. She ducked to clear an overhanging branch.

"Yui fears no man!" Apopkakee looked around as if to assure himself he hadn't been overheard. "But he does not like our war leader. He does not like the Spanish men either."

"Who?"

"The Spanish men. They give presents and guns to Potaqua. The Spanish men say that they own all of this land, but that they are friends to the Seminole, unlike the Americans."

"Where are these Spanish men? I have never seen any."

"They come sometimes. To trade." Apopkakee stopped suddenly as if he had been about to say something Shanna should not hear. She looked at him with curiosity, but he only shook his head.

After a time he went on. "Yui doesn't trust any of the whites—Americans or Spanish. He refuses to ally himself. He says that any alliance will only weaken the Seminole, shackle him."

"What does Potaqua say?"

"The opposite. He says we are made strong by alliances. He shows the warriors guns to prove it. I think he only likes to get presents from the Spanish men. . . . Come, let's run. There is the beach."

There it was. A splendid white crescent glittering in the sunlight. A long line of brown pelicans winged southward over the azure sea. Sandpipers on stilted legs raced behind the lapping ribbons of dying surf, plucking sand crabs from the white hem of the ocean's skirt.

Apopkakee had thrown off his toga, and now he was running across the silver sand, the birds fleeing before him as he waved his arms and plunged into the sea, sending up silver fans of water.

He swam through the breakers, ducking low as they broke over his head, and by the time Shanna reached the water he was far out, behind the surf line, waving merrily.

Shanna walked along the beach, letting the water rush up

over her feet, feeling the tugging of the coaxing sea as it ran back into the depths, leaving the sand gray and glistening.

She found a sea-carved, twisted mangrove on the beach, and she perched on the fallen giant, watching Apopkakee swim. Beneath the tree salmon-colored crabs scuttled in their odd sideways motion, their protruding eyes rolling irregularly as they searched for prey and predator alike.

Long ranks of wind-tilted palm trees lined the beach, and their fronds rustled pleasantly in the soft sea breeze. The sea ran out to a sandy, barren key and beyond, to the ends of the earth. It was a massive, pulsing thing. Alive and indomitable.

Behind Shanna lay slavery. Close jungle and brutality. There—ahead lay freedom, limitless and clean. No stain marked the indigo horizon. No drifting heads floated above the surf to mock and leer. She only watched it. Watched it pulse and move, shifting from blue to green and back again, sparkling in the clear sunlight, flexing its might as it hurled foaming breakers against the beach, softening as, spent, it crept away in silver rivulets.

"Shanna?"

How long had he been standing there? Apopkakee was watching her intently, almost with concern. His body was beaded with rapidly drying jewels of water. He crouched down, his dark hair plastered to his skull.

"What is it?" he asked. "What's the matter?"

She told him. Told him what it felt like to be a slave and feel that even the air you breathed belonged to someone else, to feel suffocated and diseased, to have no moment to dream, to be—herself—and not some withered appendage of the tribe which would be useful so long as it still functioned, and when proved too weak, too great a burden, would be severed from the body and cast aside to rot in the mangrove swamps.

"I did not know you felt so strongly about it. I should have known, but I did not. I am a stupid boy, as you told me. Stupid and blind. Shanna . . ." He hesitated. "Suppose someone could help you. Suppose someone could help you to get away. Do you have somewhere to go?"

"No one can help."

"Where would you go? If it were possible?" Apopkakee was poking at an obviously annoyed crab with a stick.

"There are still many Shawnee people," she said. She

29

sighed as she spoke. "My people were the Kata Shawnee. They are gone. But there are others. Relatives of ours. We would go north again. Go home. But it is foolishness to talk this way. You yourself told me no one can travel through the everglades but the Seminole."

"No." Apopkakee stopped annoying the crab, and it crawled away. "From here you could not make it. But sometimes the tribe travels farther north. When the bad weather comes. At such a time—if there were someone to guide you—perhaps you could escape."

"What are you saying, Apopkakee?" Shanna leaped from the log to squat beside the boy, to look into his eyes. "What are you telling me?"

"I will take you. When it is possible. When we have gone to our northern camp."

"The swamps . . ."

"No one knows them better than I. We would be miles away before anyone knew you were gone. We would travel quickly."

"You—" She shook her head. "You would do this for Lychma and me?"

"Yes." He stood, hurled the stick away, and grinned. "When it can be done. I will do it. I swear to you that I will."

"But your life . . . you could not come back to the Seminole camp."

"No." He brightened. "But perhaps the Shawnee would allow me to become a warrior!"

Sunset gilded the ocean, The sands were pink and pale mauve. The sea continued to pulse, its constant eternal rhythm unchanged, unchangeable. Shanna sat on the sand, her legs drawn up. The boy's dark head was against her knees. He was thoughtful, silent.

"When?" Shanna asked abruptly.

"What?"

"When can it be done? When will we travel to the northern camp?"

He shrugged in response. "When the weather changes. When the rains come. A month perhaps, perhaps more."

She rested her hand on his head, feeling the sun warmth there. She watched the rim of the red sun touch the margin of

30

the sea. She watched the endless waves roll in, and she felt hope stirring for the first time in a long while. Freedom. No one who hasn't lost it can know what freedom is worth. Shanna knew, and she thirsted for it. Hungered! A month. She watched the wild sea darken and her heart pounded like the rolling surf.

She looked again at the slender smiling boy and felt doubt. Doubt was a poisonous emotion; she let the sea breeze waft it away, and she sat, arms wound around her updrawn legs, her head leaning against Apopkakee's, watching the day of festival grow dark.

Lychma felt light-headed. They had given her black drink. The slaves had somehow obtained this terrible concoction from the communal pot. Made from the ilex plant, it was used in the purifying rituals of Boskita.

There were two immediate and unhappy results of drinking it. First of all, Lychma had vomited up all of her large meal. In shame she had staggered off into the forest, laughter ringing in her ears. Then the second effect had become obvious. She was intoxicated. Spots swam behind her eyes. The night seemed gelid and deep. The trees thrust out long black arms. One of them very definitely winked at her with a hidden eye.

Lychma stumbled and fell over an unseen root. There was an accusing moon drifting through a cloudless sky, the sounds of echoing laughter, the writhing mass which was the forest. She buried her face in her hands, smelling her own stink.

For a while she laughed, not knowing why, and then she began to cry. She crawled off the path and up into the mossy undergrowth, listening to the distant drums which had not stopped their insistent thudding since dawn.

Lychma lay on her back, her heart beating too rapidly. She peered through her lashes at the moon, at the dark canopy of trees. Her stomach gave one last convulsive leap.

Lychma sat up suddenly. There were wild beasts in the mangroves. She heard them. Panting softly as they crept toward her. She rolled to hands and knees, eyes wide, forgetting all of the sickness.

Panthers. It had to be panthers. She looked around, realizing she was lost. The trail which had been beside her was gone, spirited away by mischievous swamp ghosts.

"They have left me to the panthers."

She got to her feet, finding her knees weak, her vision still blurred and uncertain. Crouching, she listened. She could hear them in the underbrush. A small growl. More panting.

The drums had summoned them; the scent of food had kept them near. Lychma began searching for the trail, the blood in her temples beating with the rhythm of the drums from the village. Her toga was stuck to her breasts. Her knee hurt, and pausing to touch it, she found that it was bloody.

"Panthers."

She crept farther ahead, finding the undergrowth thicker yet. An owl perched in a cypress tree studied her with moon-bright eyes. Something small scurried away through the long swamp grass beneath the black trees.

She had reached the inlet and knew this was not the way to the trail. Black water moved slowly with the impetus of the distant sea. A water rat floated past, turning tiny black eyes toward her. A night hawk darted low, and Lychma jumped.

She turned back, holding up her arms to fend off the low-hanging branches. She stopped suddenly and crouched again, looking around her at the tangled shadows spun by the moon.

The sounds came again, and they seemed to be nearer. The panthers prowled, and the night closed around her. The dizziness behind her eyes was growing worse instead of better. They had given her black drink and sent her to meet the panthers. She was to be the sacrifice.

It is because I have blue eyes, she thought solemnly and with the tinge of guilt she always felt when she thought about that. They would devour her.

Still, she felt her fear waning. It was something she could not explain. When one dwelt among Seminoles long enough they no longer struck through the heart with terror. When one was long enough among the evil trees, the dark spirits, they became less fear-inspiring.

She crept forward on hands and knees, drawn by the wheezing of the panthers. Parting the long grass, she saw them.

She drew back suddenly with surprise more than fear; curiosity more than anything else caused her to return and peer through the grass.

32

They made small growling noises. Purring sounds. She knew him by his back, by the profusion of tattoos. Potaqua, the Seminole warlord, lay there, and beneath him was pressed a naked, slender woman. He was mauling her, biting her throat and shoulders, while she fought back, her hands digging at his back.

Lychma did not recognize the woman. She saw moonlight on her teeth as her slack mouth hung open, saw her writhe and slump. And then sudden fearful knowledge burst upon Lychma.

She backed away, shamed and enlightened.

She crawled away rapidly, tearing her hands and knees. Her heart pounded fearfully. When she had gone far enough she got to her feet and began to run.

She ran into Tohope.

Tohope stood in the trail, her cane in hand, her eyes stonelike and lifeless. Lychma bowed down, turned away, and in a desperate lunge ran past the wife of the Seminole chief, expecting to feel the crack of the cane on her back.

There was nothing, and when Lychma looked back Tohope was still standing there, arms folded, staring at her with a gaze more terrifying than any panther's cold appraisal.

❀ 2 ❀

The weather grew stormy and the rains came in from off of the broad gulf. Days were dark and hot and weary. The work did not abate with the worsening weather; it grew more strenuous. Now all of the crops had to be brought under shelter as quickly as possible. Corn had to be picked, pumpkins lugged to the hut where three women working quickly with razor-sharp bone knives cut them into strips and hung them up to dry.

The rain did not even slow the warring. Potaqua was gone with two hundred warriors, fighting the Creek and the Americans, the Cherokee and Catawba.

Shanna sat in the flimsy hut with three other women shelling beans, which were then placed in great straw baskets to dry. Her fingers were sore and stiff, but she hardly noticed. The weather had changed. Perhaps soon they would break camp and travel northward. As soon as the food had been brought in, perhaps.

Northward lay the swamps, but beyond the swamps was freedom, and Apopkakee had promised to help. He was only a boy, it was true, but there are few men who know the secret ways, the hidden paths, as a boy does. It was only a matter of waiting, of biding her time, of finishing one more day's work and then another. It may be another week, a month—perhaps tomorrow—but freedom would come.

It would come. It must come.

Lychma was not well. She moved unsteadily, carrying the huge burdens she was given. Fifty-pound pumpkins, great split-cane baskets filled with wild rice and millet. The rain beat down on her back and the footing was treacherous.

The rice had to be carried from the shallow inlet across a narrow spit of land studded with palmetto and marsh elder.

There were wild orchids, stunned by the heavy rains, Spanish moss hanging from thickets of live oak, wild fig woven through the gaps in the black mangroves.

Above it all hung the leaden sky. Lychma plodded on, the basket on her back cutting her shoulder blades.

She stopped abruptly.

The woman stood there, arms folded, watching.

"You move too slow, girl."

"Forgive me, Tohope."

The last word wasn't out of Lychma's mouth before the cane, whipping through the air with all the menace of a rattler's buzz, landed on Lychma's cheek. She dropped the basket she carried, and brown rice spilled over the muddy earth.

"You clumsy girl!" Tohope clubbed her again with the cane. "Pick it up. Every bit."

"Yes, Tohope." Lychma got to hands and knees and began scraping the rice together. Mud clung to the rice, and Tohope bellowed:

"Do you think anyone will eat that? What are we, savages like the Shawnee?"

"No, Tohope."

The cane whished through the air again, landing on Lychma's buttocks with a blow which seemed to cut her to the bone. Lychma turned to protest, her hand going up defensively. The cane rang off her skull, and she fell, the handfuls of gathered rice spilling again.

"Pick it up!" Tohope's voice was shrill and broken. "There. There's more. Can't you see?"

"Yes, Tohope." Lychma could not, in fact, see well. Her eyes were blinded by tears and by a thin trickle of blood.

"There's more," Tohope said impatiently. "Scrape that up too. Wash it all, you lazy girl. Can't you see that rice over there?"

"Yes, Tohope." Lychma's throat was knotted with fear and pain.

"Right in front of you. It is your eyes, girl. They are useless. White eyes. You see nothing. Perhaps they should be put out."

Lychma was scraping up the spilled rice as rapidly as she

could. The rain washed over her. The gusting wind chilled her, but it was not so chilling as Tohope's threat.

"You are a stupid girl." The cane fell again, landing on Lychma's neck with enough force to stun her, to cause her to lurch forward on hands and knees, to gasp for mercy.

"Please do not hit me again, Tohope. I will do as you wish."

Tohope did not hit her again. Instead she stood there, hands on hips, cane dangling, laughing! She laughed as the rain drove down, obscuring the forest, as the day went dark and cold.

"I know you, girl," Tohope said at last. "I know you and I know what you have done. I would kill you, but the body does not suffer enough when it dies. It suffers only when it lives. You will live, Lychma." She wrenched Lychma's head around and stared into those blue eyes. "You will live, child, and you will suffer."

Then she was gone, and Lychma collapsed against the sodden earth. She lay there, feeling the rain on her cheek, the ooze beneath her, staring at the grains of rice which drifted away on the rivulets of water.

"You would do better to kill yourself." The voice was old and cracked, and Lychma turned her head to see the gray-haired woman, stooped and palsied, standing near her, just off the trail in the scant shelter of a palmetto.

"Who are you?" Lychma asked miserably.

"Caal. Caal! You hear me? Potaqua is my husband too." Then she laughed, a wheezing, empty laugh. "Potaqua was my husband. He was my husband and this cunning one came to marry him. Now I live here. I live here!" She waved a scrawny arm around her, indicating the forest, the swamp. "I live here because if I return Tohope will beat me as well. She came . . ." The old woman got down and hung over Lychma, her eyes bird-bright. "She came and she took my husband with her young body. She came, and when she was secure as Potaqua's second wife she began to beat me. She would give me nothing to eat. She would call me terrible names. Now she knows about you. Now she knows that the same thing could happen to Tohope. Now she knows that Potaqua might take a third wife and Tohope would either have to serve the new wife or take to the swamps as I did."

"I don't understand any of this," Lychma said.

"No?" Caal looked at the girl oddly, her old eyes penetrating. The rain had softened. It drifted past like curtains of strung glass beads. "Maybe you do not know," Caal said at last, straightening up. "Maybe there is something I do not understand. I have been told . . . well, maybe it is all wrong. But it will not matter to Tohope, girl!" The gnarled finger pointed again. "It will not matter to her! Take to the swamps. That is what I did. It is the only hope, the only security."

And then she was gone. Caal turned her bent back and was gone, shuttling off into the rain-heavy forest. Lychma stood, shaking her head with exhaustion and confusion.

"What do they want of me?" she asked the skies. A lazy, rolling peal of thunder came to her from the distances. It was an insufficient answer.

Lychma shouldered her basket. Carefully she trampled all of the remaining rice into the mud so that it could not be seen. Then, glancing fearfully across her shoulder, she set out to wash the rice again.

It was a private place, one she had discovered on her own. Great cliffs rose up from some ancient stony ridge and shaded the earth. Here the sea rushed in through deep grooves cut into the pocked stone. It rushed in and passed beneath the stone, spouting up in geysers through dozens of head-sized holes.

The sea gurgled and withdrew. Then again the tide would urge the water landward and the gray water, flecked with foam, would roar through the clefts in the rock. Again the geysers erupted, salty spray jetting into the rainy sky. Withdrawing, the sea hissed and gurgled in the hollows beneath the stone.

At times it sounded as if spirits were imprisoned beneath the rock. Lychma heard what sounded like the deep-throated moaning of men, the shrieking of women. The heavy panting of interlocked panthers . . .

She knelt and held the split-cane basket in one of the sea-carved channels, letting the rushing water flood it. The current tugged at the basket and the muddy sediment was carried off.

Lychma stood. She placed the basket to one side. She

37

looked up at the great cliff and she listened to the grumbling spirits beneath her feet. Behind her the sea raged. She remained there a long while, letting the geysers spout over her, letting the falling rain drench her. She did not wish to return to the village. Ever.

Tohope was there, and that dreadful cane. Lychma touched her face where the cane had stung her, and felt the tenderness.

She did not want to return, and yet there was no place else to go. Finally she shouldered her basket and turned away from the waterspouts, from the taunting voices of the stone spirits.

She did not go into the village until it was full dark. Then, soaking wet, shivering, she slipped into the hut and stripped off her clothes, crawling in beside Shanna.

"What happened?" Shanna asked.

"I thought you were asleep."

"How could I sleep with you out there in the storm? At night!"

"It was Tohope," Lychma said with a small yawn. The blanket and the proximity of Shanna's body were warming her quickly, and despite the lingering anxiety, she felt safe and sleepy. It was as it had been when she was tiny, sleeping between Shanna and their mother, listening to the night birds sing, knowing that morning would bring exuberant games, joy, peace.

No, it was not quite like that. It never would be again. But it was enough for now to be warm and near to Shanna.

"What happened, Lychma?" Shanna demanded, poking her shoulder.

Lychma told her. "But I don't understand the cause of it all. Why is she suddenly violent? Her eyes. It is nearly panic I saw there. Panic and a mad menace."

"I understand," Shanna said. "Think of what Caal told you. Think of what you saw on festival night. Did you not meet Tohope that night as well?"

"Oh, no!" Lychma put her hands to her mouth. She shook her head heavily. "She thinks that Potaqua favors me. That it is I he meets in the forest. That it is I who might displace her as Potaqua's favorite wife. I have to tell her that it is not so, Shanna!"

"She would not believe you."

38

"Then Potaqua." No. Lychma looked helplessly at her sister. Who would dare approach the Seminole chief? A slave asking for favors. The very best one could hope for would be to be laughed at and sent away. With his black temper he might very well beat her himself.

"He might encourage the idea," Shanna said. "It might amuse him to have Tohope believe you are his lover."

"What can we do then?" Lychma's head was throbbing. Her body ached from the lashing Tohope had given her. What was there to do except to run into the swamp as Caal had done?

"It will pass. She must see eventually that she has made a mistake. Do not leave the camp alone."

"She hates me, Shanna." Lychma's voice was low and urgent. "I am afraid she will kill me. I am afraid!"

"Go to sleep," Corta said from her corner. And there was nothing else to do that night, and so they tried to fall asleep. It was impossible. Lychma ran naked through the swamps in her dreams, pursued by hundreds of mad Seminole women who screamed out obscenities and cried for her blood.

Finally when she had given up on sleeping, when she lay awake in the night, her eyes moving restlessly, searching the darkness of the hut, Lychma heard her sister whisper.

"Endure a little while, sister. There is a way. Perhaps soon this will be over. Perhaps soon we shall be free."

"Shanna? What do you mean?"

She shook her sister's shoulder, but Shanna would not answer. Lychma lay back again feeling small and cold and afraid. *There is a way.* What way could there be? What way could there ever be as long as she lived among the Seminole?

The following day was the day Shanna saw the white man.

She was gathering in the forest, walking beneath the tall somber manchineel trees, placing her bare feet carefully. Both the sap and the sharp husked fruit of the manchineel are poisonous. At times Potaqua's men gathered sap to poison their arrows.

Shanna rested, sitting on a moss-covered log, watching sleek blue dragonflies flit past and hover motionlessly in the air. Through the deep ranks of trees the sun sparkled. Fine dust motes danced in long shafts of sunlight. Beneath the trees greenbriar vines wove intricate patterns.

She was aware suddenly of the interrelationship of all of these manifestations of Manitou's dream. Decay and growth; organisms warmed by the sun nudging aside the deep, rich humus and emerging green and tender into the air to crawl across the earth or to shoot up, becoming mighty columns of forest timber. Fed by tendrils ranging wide beneath the soil, they reached maturity, aged, fell to the earth, and became life-giving humus themselves as bark crumbled and rotted into minute, still-living particles. The insects fed the darting birds which fell prey to the hunters which themselves would pass into earth.

All of it a part of Manitou's plan. She became aware suddenly, intimately, of her own part in all of this. She too was earth and water and sunlight. A small strand on an endless bead necklace. She frowned.

She had never thought of herself in that way, thought of her body as a part of this whole, of this vast continuum. She was a whole within a larger unity. What fed the forest fed her, and when she was no longer here she would still live, as a part of the forest and the swamp grass, of the mangroves and strangler fig.

"I am eternal," she said with the sort of awe such new thoughts induce. Slowly, thoughtfully, she rose from the log and resumed her walk.

She was suddenly face to face with him. A big man with yellow hair, he wore a blue uniform with a broad red sash. He carried a musket and wore a long knife on his hip. His beard was a massive tangle of yellow hair. His eyes were a startling green, lidded heavily, thickly. His lips were parted in an expression of surprise or triumph or lust. Yellow teeth showed between his fleshy lips.

His face was wide, nearly round. A jagged scar ran across one eye and down across his cheekbone into the mat of beard.

Shanna screamed.

She flung her basket aside and ducked away, feeling a grasping hand tear at her shoulder. She knocked it aside and ran wildly into the forest, hearing the heavy footsteps behind her.

She darted through a close-growing thicket and along a game trail which she knew. It wound among the century plants and marsh elder where there was barely room for a woman to pass as the thicket closed in tightly, fighting back intruders.

Ducking low, she scooted beneath the undergrowth of live oak, feeling the branches and leaves scratch at her face and exposed arms. Behind her was the crashing of a massive body forcing its way through the thicket.

Shanna crouched, panting, her mouth open, eyes flickering from point to point. It was still. Nothing moved. A mockingbird squawked somewhere nearby and took to the air on white-banded wings.

Shanna listened to her own heart beat. She watched and listened, scenting the air, every muscle taut, her nerves leaping and tingling.

He burst from the underbrush, and Shanna took off at a dead run, rushing through the restraining thicket, heedless of the thorns and grasping vines, the menacing tangle of briars.

She ran until she reached the inlet, then she dived headlong into the black waters and swam, her lungs filled with fire until she reached the far bank.

She ran on into the village, her arms uplifted, her voice raised to a manic pitch.

"White soldiers! White soldiers!"

The warrior Immokallee grabbed her arms as she tried to run past, and she was yanked around. He shook her and demanded: "Where?"

Shanna could only point. Her arm trembled as she lifted it and gestured northward.

"How many?" Immokallee demanded. "How many?"

Shanna stared at him, her eyes wide and blank. Immokallee slapped her face so hard that her knees buckled. He shook her again until Shanna's teeth clacked together.

"How many were there?"

"I don't know," she managed to sputter. "That way. White soldiers."

Immokallee let go of her, and she nearly fell. A dozen Seminole warriors were already on their way, running toward the inlet, rifles or bows in hand. A dozen more were racing for their chickees, calling for their weapons.

Shanna stood alone in the middle of the camp.

"Young fool."

The voice was Corta's, and she repeated, "Fool," standing

41

before Shanna with eyes as black as obsidian, accusing, sharp-edged, angry eyes.

"Corta . . ."

"Young fool. Why did you say anything? We could have been free! The whites are the friends of the Cherokee. The enemy of the Seminole. We could have been freed!"

"Corta . . ."

The Cherokee woman turned and walked away, her lips compressed, her back rigid with anger and frustration. Shanna watched her go. Her arms dangled limply.

Why? Why had she called out? She had simply been frightened. Corta called the white men friends. She did not know. Shanna had seen the white man's friendship before.

Fear, instinct, had prompted her to take to her heels at the sight of a white face, but now as she stood alone in the center of the Seminole camp, as a trailing warrior sprinted past her toward the inlet, Shanna wondered if Corta was not right.

It could have meant freedom for Lychma, who was being tormented by Tohope. It could have meant escape for Shanna if the whites had come to Potaqua's camp. Or would they have become slaves again? She had heard that the whites too kept slaves in conditions no better than those they now endured.

Yet Corta had seemed sure. Corta had lived among them. The Cherokee, she said, were friends of the whites, treated fairly, allowed to keep their own land.

Freedom was becoming an elusive, uncertain thing, an ideal and not a reality, a dream which frustrated with its evanescence. Had she failed to grasp it just now?

That night old Takal came, bringing scraps of cloth for Corta. She told them what had happened.

"There were only three white men, all Americans. Searching for Potaqua's camp, no doubt. But the warriors ran them down."

"And then?"

"And then?" Old Takal cackled, her single eye searching out Shanna, examining her minutely as if she were some alien form of life. "Are you stupid, girl? Potaqua himself was with the war party. The men were hung upside down from a cypress tree and slowly their skin was peeled from their bodies, slowly they were opened up so that their entrails

42

could spill upon the earth. And then they were killed." Takal laughed.

Lychma looked as if she were going to throw up. Shanna closed her eyes briefly. I have done this, she thought.

With the morning came the news that they would have to move again. There was a possibility that there had been four white scouts, or perhaps an Indian allied with the whites. This man who left almost no tracks might even now be carrying word to Boggs, the American warlord.

The chickees were left to stand empty, and again the Seminole were on the move. The slaves were heavily burdened, and they sank deeply into the marshes and bogs. Potaqua set a terrific pace. They were on the march from well before sunrise to well after sunset.

Shanna did not care; they were heading north! Northward lay freedom, and she once managed to exchange glances with Apopkakee. The boy was traveling with his clan, the priests of the village. Usually these people stayed well away from the slaves, since their law forbade touching these unclean ones. Yet that once Shanna saw Apopkakee. That once he smiled, and his slow, reassuring nod told Shanna that he had not forgotten his promise.

They traveled northward, the forest steaming as the white sky reclaimed the recent rain. A Seminole warrior was bitten by a water moccasin on the third day. His leg swelled to nearly twice its normal size. Gradually it turned black.

"Let the priests dance over him," his woman begged.

"Let him lie," Potaqua answered. And he was left to die alone. The Seminoles did not look at the dying man as they walked past him. When Shanna looked back he was still watching them, propped up against the bole of a palmetto, his warrior's mask in place, hands clutching his leg.

Potaqua would stop for nothing. A child was lost in quicksand at a river ford. The distraught, wailing mother was not allowed to have a proper funeral ceremony.

"I must think about the tribe," Potaqua told her angrily. He hovered over her, fists bunched as if he might strike her down. "Many others will die if we do not keep moving." He glanced around as if measuring the effect of his words on his people. Then he led off again, the pace increased still more. Five minutes later Shanna heard Potaqua laugh.

"No one is behind us," Corta said. She was walking beside Shanna, her shoulders burdened with a heavy blanket-wrapped load. "I heard the runner report to Potaqua. No whites are coming. No one follows. He is not rushing northward to save his people. He is rushing to make war."

"To make war?"

"To the north are the Cherokee and the Creek. The Americans. Potaqua seeks vengeance. Tukakee has told him that blood is required to pacify the spirits. Tukakee tells him this because he knows that this is what Potaqua wishes to hear."

"Then Tukakee is that powerful?" She had thought that Apopkakee had exaggerated the power of his father, the head priest of Potaqua's Seminole.

"There is no power but Potaqua's," Corta said. She shifted her burden and wiped the perspiration from her eyes. "Your sister is ill." Corta nodded her head, and Shanna, looking behind them, saw that Lychma, staggering beneath her burden, was indeed ill. She was not strong, never had been. This march was taking its toll.

"Lychma?" Shanna touched her sister's forehead as they walked. Her face was grim and sallow, strained. "Are you all right?"

"They will not leave me to die," Lychma said determinedly.

"Of course not."

"That is what Potaqua would do."

"I would not let him."

Lychma smiled, her top lip curling under. Perspiration beaded her forehead. "He would not stop for a slave. He would stop for nothing."

"I would make him stop."

"He would not let you."

"I would stay with you. If you were so ill."

"Then we would die together."

"Give me a part of your burden, Lychma."

Lychma did not argue. She let Shanna shoulder the smaller of the two packs she carried—packs filled with the pretty personal belongings of Tohope.

"I cannot go on."

"You can," Shanna said cheerfully.

"I have been walking all my life! I have been running all

my life!'' Lychma shrieked so loudly that the other slaves turned to gape at her. She lowered her voice. ''Where are we running, Shanna? To what? From what? Is life only war and escape? I do not want to live anymore if this is to be all we live for.''

''I do not want to hear you talk like that. I do not want to hear you speak of death or surrender or hopelessness, Lychma!'' Shanna's voice was stern and bordered on anger. Lychma looked stunned for a moment. ''You are my sister. My only friend. I will not have it!''

''You will not have it,'' Lychma repeated. She shifted her pack as they forded a quick running muddy stream. ''That does not mean it cannot happen, Shanna. You will not have death. You will not have illness. You will not have slavery. It is all around us! All of it.''

''I will not have you giving into it.'' Shanna gripped her sister's shoulders, stopping her in midstream as the expressionless slaves splashed by them.

''Endure,'' Lychma said.

''Yes!''

''Endure so that more may be endured,'' Lychma said tonelessly. ''Endure endlessly.''

''Perhaps there is an end to it,'' Shanna said, and Lychma's eyes brightened perceptibly, briefly, before blankness returned to them.

''What end?'' she asked warily. ''Let us walk before someone beats us.'' They continued across the stream and entered the magnolia and mangrove forest.

''I did not want to tell you anything about it,'' Shanna whispered. ''But there may be a way.''

''A way? A way to what? How?''

''Be quiet, sister. A way to escape, a way to make our way north again.''

''North,'' Lychma said coldly, ''to the old war.''

''We would not be slaves. Is that of no importance?''

It was all-important. Lychma nodded. The air was humid. Waist-high fern clotted the path they traveled. There was no sound but the calling of mourning dove in the cedars and mangroves.

''How,'' Lychma asked, spacing her words cautiously, ''could this be done?''

45

"A friend. We have a friend among the Seminole, one who knows the hidden ways, the swamps and the forests."

"A friend?" Lychma nodded her head slowly. "What friend is that, Shanna? What friend have we except the one small one—your admirerer?"

"That is the one," Shanna said, objecting mentally to Lychma's term.

"Apopkakee!" Lychma laughed out loud, from deep in her throat. The slaves in the caravan turned disapproving heads. "Apopkakee," Lychma said, touching her sister's arm, mirth dancing in her blue eyes. "He is a boy, a child. Worse, he is a dreamer."

"You liked him well enough before," Shanna replied stiffly.

"Yes! As a friend. But not as a savior, sister, as a guide and protector."

"He is willing. He knows the way," Shanna answered.

Lychma started to answer, but she was suddenly racked by a spasm of coughing. Her face was flushed, and touching her cheek, Shanna felt an unhealthy clamminess.

"You are sick."

"It is the swamps! The damnable swamps and the fevers, the unhealthy spirits which live here."

Lychma's voice was overloud again, and the slaves around them objected.

"Be quiet, Shawnee! If there is trouble we shall all be beaten."

"What is the matter with you, girl? Are you mad? Do you want Potaqua to beat you?"

She was ill. Shanna watched her sister closely. Ill and weary and heartsick. They had been walking forever, as Lychma said, walking toward nothing, but always *away*. Away from evil and despair, never managing to leave these quick-darting dark specters behind.

They trudged on. The air was heavy, sticky. It seemed to weigh on Lychma's shoulders. She didn't care about escape any longer. There was no escape. There was only endless swamp. Moss, vines, bogs, scummy mosquito-infested ponds made up all of the world. Manitou had turned his head and dark forces had crawled across the land.

There was no air fit to breathe. The body which cloaked

Lychma's soul was only a worn-out, damnably heavy, useless bit of fleshy equipment, unsuited for its work, for any purpose.

Save trudging onward.

"Give me your pack. Lychma."

"You already have a part of my burden."

"Give me your pack. Lychma!" Shanna was angry, angry not at Lychma, but at all of the universe, at the Seminole chief, Potaqua, and at all of the Seminole. At war which would not be eradicated.

War. They went on trying to kill war with more war. Let the people die. We must have our war, and so they had it. And so new tattoos were proudly worn, new feathers adorned the topknots of the proud, strutting warriors. And another fell by the wayside.

Lychma, with a sense of shame, handed her pack over to Shanna, who staggered momentarily under the double load. Yet she walked on, throwing her shoulders back. Nothing would stop her. She swore it. Nothing would stop her or blunt her determination. Hopelessness was a state of mind. Slavery was illusion.

Lychma stumbled and fell against Shanna. She went to her knees and looked up with fevered eyes at her sister.

"What will you do now?" Corta asked harshly. "Carry your sister as well? I told you she was weak. I told you she would die."

Shanna, stooping cautiously, the weight of her load pressing her down, helped Lychma to her feet.

"She is right. I will die."

"You will not die. I have told you! We are going north. Soon the burden will be put down and we shall run to freedom."

"Freedom!" Lychma's voice was a broken sob. "I do not remember what it is."

Shanna compressed her lips. Holding Lychma's arm tightly, she struggled on. They had fallen back until they were the last slaves in line, and now they were prodded on by the Seminole woman Nokatak.

"Fall aside if you cannot keep up," she said. Her cane jabbed at Shanna. "Fall aside, Shawnee girl. I will miss my supper."

Shanna did not answer. She walked faster, drawing her

47

energy from her spirit alone and not from her bodily resources. She propelled Lychma along the swamp trail.

They reached night camp exhausted and parched. Corta had been carrying their water skin, and she had moved far ahead of the lagging Shawnee sisters.

There was something odd about the camp, and it was a moment before it occurred to Shanna in her present weary state.

"Why are there no fires, Corta?" she asked.

Corta stood over Lychma, who was trembling and feverish, barely able to lift her head to drink.

"I don't know. Potaqua has ordered it. We must be near the enemy."

"The enemy!" Lychma's eyes widened. Corta, in one of those inexplicable moments of softness, reached down and petted Lychma's hair.

"Don't worry, Shawnee girl. We are not going to fight. Not with the women and children in camp."

"But we might be attacked. There might be no choice."

"Potaqua will have sentries out. No one will slip up on us tonight."

Lychma seemed reassured. She handed the water skin back to Corta, who shook it and handed it to Shanna.

Shanna drank deeply. The water was tepid and acidic, but her body craved it. The sun was low, silhouetting the moss-hung cypress which surrounded the camp. A distant lake seen through the trees gleamed golden. Across the crimson skies a long flight of blue heron winged softly homeward.

"Thank you, Corta."

Shanna handed the water skin back to the Cherokee woman. Corta stood holding it for a moment, her face reddish in the sunset light.

"You know I am not such a bad woman, Shanna," she said.

"No, Corta, of course not. You have been a help to us."

"I tried. I am angry at times. Angry because I have been a slave. Because I have not seen my husband, Hasha, for a long while. Hasha, who must bring in his crops alone and sleep alone because of the Seminole."

"I know that, Corta." What in the world was she getting

48

at? The evening was going gray rapidly. It was difficult to make out Corta's expression.

"Here." She tossed Shanna the water skin. "Keep this with you. The little one will need it."

Then she turned and was gone, and Shanna crouched beside her sister, touching her forehead, which was hot and extremely dry.

"Drink all of the water you wish," she said.

"Yes, Shanna," Lychma answered in a child's voice.

Shanna folded a blanket to make a pillow for her sister. She lifted her head and placed it beneath her. Then she rose, wiping back her hair.

There was only a rose-colored line seen indistinctly through the black ranks of trees to mark the grave of the dying sun. The rest of the world was dark and silent. Restlessly Shanna walked through the slave camp, seeing the women tired, hungry, sick, sitting together in small silent clumps, or lying exhausted alone against the bare earth.

In the Seminole camp it would be better. They would at least have plenty of food and water. But there too women would be weary, men hungry, children sick. None of it mattered to Potaqua, apparently. He must continue this mad chase, this dirty war.

Shanna had walked away from the camp, moving soundlessly through the trees, her spirit restless despite her body's fatigue. She crested a low hummock where long swamp grass grew and a scraggly bay cedar etched itself against the darkening skies.

She stopped abruptly, her breath catching.

She knew why Potaqua's camp was dark and silent, why there were sentries posted.

The answer was below her.

The settlement she saw was large, perhaps five miles square in all. Tall corn grew in geometric patterns across the rich bottomland. Fifty fires glowed across the valley. It was time for the evening meal. Time to stretch weary muscles and warm the stomach.

Cherokee.

Shanna knew that by the houses in which the farmers dwelled. They were Cherokee, thriving in their peace. The land was rich and broad. Their lives appeared to be good ones.

Beyond the most southern of the lodges was a log building which had to be of white construction. Looking more intently, Shanna decided that it was a fort of some kind. There were American soldiers living side by side with these Cherokee. In *peace*!

Peace. An insubstantial notion, a dream, a child's wish. And yet it was there before her.

The scream rippled through the night. A long ululating pathetic sound. The sound of a wounded rabbit, a dying animal of the night. Shanna stiffened, her head jerking around compulsively in the direction of the sound.

Lychma!

She thought first of her sister, and she was running through the night, down the hillock, the long grass swishing around her knees, before she realized that it could not be Lychma, should not be. Lychma was sick and she was tired. She was asleep in the Seminole camp, and this sound was not from that direction.

She slowed her pace, watching the night shadows warily. No animal had made the sound. It was a woman in distress, a woman in pain, a woman crying out with the anguish of a crushed and defeated soul.

She nearly ran into the Seminole sentry.

"What do you want?" he demanded.

"I heard a cry."

"Yes."

"Well, what has happened?"

"Return to the camp, slave. Nothing has happened that concerns you. Nothing at all."

He gave Shanna a shove and laughed as she stumbled. Nothing had happened. Nothing at all. Women screamed in the night for no reason. Nothing at all.

Shanna reached the slave camp in ten minutes. Despite her certainty that it could not have been Lychma, she obeyed the compulsion to bend over and touch her sister as she slept, to place her fingers beneath Lychma's nostrils to assure herself that she breathed.

Shanna let out her breath. She had not been aware that she was holding it, had been holding it for long agonized minutes.

She sagged to the ground beside Lychma. She was all right. She was sleeping. Nothing had happened.

Nothing at all.

They were shaken awake before dawn, and Shanna rolled stiffly from her blanket, pawing at her eyes, which seemed to be filled with sand. Lychma sat blinking at her as if for the moment she had forgotten. Forgotten who she was, where they were. As Shanna watched it all seemed to come back to her. She stiffened perceptibly, and her shoulders seemed to sag.

They got wearily to their feet, arranging their packs. Corta's water skin and bundle still lay there. Where on earth . . . "It was Corta," Shanna said slowly.

"What?" Lychma looked around in confusion.

"It was Corta, who wished to go home to her husband and help him with his crops. Who wished to see her children again."

"I don't understand you, Shanna."

"It does not matter."

"Where is Corta? We shall have to carry her bundle as well as our own."

"Then we shall carry it."

With the dawn they were moving. The dawn was a deep golden glow, and the air seemed devoid of oxygen. Glancing seaward, Shanna could make out a long band of horsetail cloud. The wind had begun to blow, and the palms around them rattled their fronds. It would rain.

She thought that briefly, and then returned her thoughts to Corta, to her dash toward freedom. She had died in her attempt to escape this life. She must have known that it was possible that she would be killed, and yet Corta had tried to go home.

Potaqua, the savage, broad-chested, tattooed man, the killer, the beast, walked at the head of the long column of Indians now, and Shanna watched him for a time. She knew now that she too would risk death. It was only concern for Lychma which held her back.

Lychma, who, never very strong, was growing weaker as the days dragged by. Could she run through the swamps, could she endure? Where could they go? Despite her talk about returning north, living with another Shawnee tribe, she was unsure.

There was war in the north. The Shawnee were involved. She knew this through the grapevine. Word had slowly trickled in of great battles being fought in Ohio and around the Great Lakes by this Tecumseh and his British allies as they tried to beat back the American advance.

There was war in the south, war in the north. Everywhere the white man came there was war. She made up her mind to speak to Lychma that evening anyway. To speak to Lychma and then to Apopkakee to remind him of his promise.

The rain drifted in from off the turgid green sea, lashing the palms and mournful cypress. Shanna hitched up her pack and trudged onward. They were traveling north, still north, and ahead somewhere lay freedom. Or death.

They lay that night in the feeble shelter of a hastily constructed lean-to, listening to the wash of the rain, the shriek of the wind. Now was the time for it, now while the eyes of the Seminole sentries would be blinded by the mesh of the falling rain, their hearing subdued by the rush of the wind.

"Lychma," Shanna turned to her sister. "This has been on my mind: to escape. To run northward. I cannot endure being a slave."

"Nor can I. There is Tohope; one day she will kill me."

"This is the night for it. The rain will shield us."

"All right." Lychma stirred. "When will we leave? Where is my pack?"

"Wait, Lychma." Shanna held her sister by the shoulders, and kneeling, looked down at her, seeing only vague outlines through the darkness. "There is more to this decision than we have discussed. Corta . . ."

"Do you think I am a child still, Shanna? Do you think I can be protected? I know that Corta went away and that something terrible happened to her. I know that if we run and are captured Potaqua will harm us, perhaps kill us, as he must if all of the slaves are to be taught that they cannot run away from his camp. I know this."

"And still you wish to go?"

"I will not live as a slave."

Long hours later Shanna crept from the lean-to. The wind slapped her in the face. A pouring rain continued to batter the forest. She moved through the woods toward the Seminole camp. If she could not find Apopkakee, talk to him, then their scheme was no good. The swamps were impenetrable unless one knew the way.

As she moved across a clearing her body was temporarily exposed to the full force of the wind, and it surged over her with enough violence that Shanna had to stop and brace herself. The rain was a cold veil drawn across the world. She glanced skyward and frowned, then crept on toward the Seminole camp.

The clans slept in groups. Warriors to one side, priests to another, and Shanna knew their order. What she did not know was how to find Apopkakee except by slipping into the camp and creeping among the sleeping priests. That in itself could be fatal.

She could discover nothing by standing in the shelter of the trees, peering at the camp. They had all built lean-tos against the storm, and nothing at all was visible except for a foot here or there, a prowling sentry, a shivering dog.

The dog too worried Shanna, but she knew most of the camp dogs and she trusted to that. If worst came to worst she thought she could slip away again through the storm without having been identified.

Maybe.

She crept forward, the rain hammering against her back, stinging all exposed flesh, blinding her with its intensity. Where was Apopkakee?

How could she hope to awaken him and talk to him without drawing attention to herself? The idea seemed suddenly mad. She looked about furtively, and taking a deep slow breath, crept into the camp, which was built in a mangrove clearing.

She moved toward the nearest lean-to, bent down, and drew away sharply, her heart pounding. He was not there. An aged, heavy priest slept soundly through the roar of the storm.

She touched her breast, wondering how long she could continue this mad game before her courage leaked out of her. Crouching low, she continued to move around the camp.

The Great Manitou was with her. The third lean-to she peeked into was the shelter of Apopkakee and his father. They slept side by side.

Shanna pulled away from the opening of the lean-to and looked around, searching the ground. Finding a long, crooked twig, she crouched as low as possible and reached around, prodding Apopkakee's foot with it.

He groaned and rolled over. His father stirred, and Shanna felt her heart drop like a stone into deep water, sending out rippling tremors which shook her arms and legs. She closed her eyes briefly and took another deep breath. Again she prodded Apopkakee's foot, and this time he sat up immediately.

He opened his mouth as if to speak, and Shanna waved her hands in a furious gesture. Apopkakee's jaw snapped shut, and for a minute he simply sat staring at her, his eyes glazed with sleep.

His vision seemed to clear. He frowned, his eyebrows drawing together, and Shanna beckoned to him.

She drew aside and waited, the seconds passing slowly until Apopkakee emerged from the lean-to into the driving rain, wearing only a loincloth and a bewildered expression.

"What . . . ?"

Shanna put her hand to his lips and gestured toward the forest. Together in silence they walked from the camp, no more than two flitting shadows in the night.

Shanna stopped in the shelter of a massive magnolia. Leaning her back against it, she studied Apopkakee's face by the dim light. The youth was shivering, although it was not cold. The rain was warm and heavy.

"What is it?" he managed to stammer, and Shanna had the idea that he already knew. Perhaps he did. He made no immediate response when she said:

"Tonight. We are far enough north now, Apopkakee. Lychma and I are going to leave. We are going to run northward. We need you to show us the way."

"Tonight," he said finally, tonelessly.

"Yes. The storm will cover our passage. Dress and pack a bit of food for yourself. You will have your chance to become a Shawnee warrior."

"Tonight," he repeated, running his hand across his black hair. The rain swirled around him and he looked briefly skyward, shaking his head. "In the storm."

"When better?"

"I know. Only I did not expect it so soon."

"Perhaps you did not expect it ever," Shanna suggested. "Perhaps you thought I was a stupid girl weaving dreams."

54

"No, Shanna," Apopkakee said hastily. "I did not think that. Think you stupid? Never. It is only that I have been sleeping. This is so unexpected."

"Tonight. It must be tonight."

"Yes." Apopkakee looked miserable. "I know that. It must be tonight. I will pack a bundle. Silently. No one will see me."

"Good." Shanna smiled.

"A mile north of here, perhaps more, there is a knob of granite. It is called Eagle's Roost. You will find it if you follow the river. If you wait there for me I will be along."

"You are brave, Apopkakee," Shanna said, and she kissed him, a gesture which startled Apopkakee and surprised Shanna. It seemed to bolster Apopkakee's resolution, and he said more strongly:

"I will be there. One hour. Bring fresh water and be prepared for a long night's journey."

They parted in the storm, and Shanna fought her way back through the wind and increasing rain to where Lychma sat in the lean-to. Her expectant eyes widened as Shanna said, "It is time," and she seemed to shrink with apprehension.

"Then let us go. Now," Lychma said. She snatched up her small bundle.

"Have you water?"

"Yes."

Shanna looked around the dark, low lean-to. Corta's things lay in the corner. Water trickled down through the roof of the crude shelter. Shanna turned and went out into the night, and Lychma followed.

They walked northward through the steady rain, keeping to the trees. After a mile or so they began looking for their landmark, the rock called Eagle's Roost.

"We must have passed it," Lychma said.

"No. He said to follow the river. We have. It must be farther on."

Shanna had to speak loudly to be heard above the howl of the wind. A great cypress tree groaned, and as Lychma watched it began to tilt, its massive root system tugging loose.

"Come on." Shanna took her sister by the elbow and they

hurried on, staying close to the river, peering through the dark of the storm for the landmark.

"We have missed it."

"No. Stop it now, Lychma."

"We will never find it. We shouldn't have come." There was increasing panic in Lychma's voice.

Shanna clenched her jaw and continued on. In the rain they nearly walked into Eagle's Roost. It was all of a hundred feet high, polished smooth by centuries of wind and rain. Apopkakee was not there yet.

Thunder rumbled through the skies, and almost immediately a flash of bone-white lightning illuminated the night, showing Lychma's face to Shanna. She was frightened. Well, she had a right to be, Shanna thought. That was no reason to stop. They had made their choice and it must be now.

"Where is he?"

"He will be here," Shanna said.

They stood waiting, the rain increasing its tempo until it was a lashing fury flailing the dark, shuddering earth. Boughs clacked together in the forest; from time to time a branch broke, the snapping sound loud and demonic. To Lychma it seemed that the Stone Giants roamed the dark forest, trampling the trees with their great feet.

"When is he coming?"

"He will be here," Shanna said tightly. "Be still and wait. He will come." He must come, she thought. They could not go back to the camp even if they wished it. There was the chance their absence had already been discovered. Shanna wiped the rain from her eyes. They huddled together at the base of the great stone monument. The rain poured down.

"Come on," Shanna said.

"We are going back?" Lychma asked, almost hopefully it seemed.

"We are going on. Northward."

"Without Apopkakee?"

"He will not come," Shanna said. She knew now. Knew that Apopkakee was indeed a boy who spoke much and did little. He was a priest and would remain a priest. He was Seminole and would remain Seminole. He could not pull up his roots, roots so much deeper and stronger than those of the cypress they had seen toppling in the storm. He was a boy, a frightened boy. Shanna could not even feel disappointment. Perhaps she had expected it.

"Shanna?"

Lychma touched her sister's arm. Shanna turned to her and hugged her tightly. It was more reassuring than words. Promises.

They started off through the inky, raging night. Northward. Beyond the storm somewhere lay freedom. Beyond the darkness and the swamps.

They walked on, two small, impudent creatures, into the face of an angry nature. And out at sea the hurricane continued to build.

It rained throughout the night and the wind continued to build. Farther south and west, great waves lashed the shore. The fishermen of the Calusa and Tekesta tribes, men of the sea, dragged their boats onto higher ground and lashed them to the trunks of ancient trees which had withstood all the storms of a lifetime. Then, taking their few belongings, they led their families to the highlands. The Mococos, on the eastern Florida coast, sank their cane canoes in shallow coves, weighting them down with stones. With luck, no more than half of their canoes would be lost as the big tides surged in. The Mococos had seen hurricanes, and they simply abandoned their village, already resigned to a month's work rebuilding their chickees and storehouses, their smoke racks and cribs.

At dawn the skies held a bluish glow and the rain seemed to lighten temporarily, as if nature had compassionately decided to restrain the dreadful coup. It was all illusion.

Shanna and Lychma worked their way northward, finding all the inlets along the way glutted with rainwater. Fully grown palm trees bobbed past, carried along on the foaming rivers created by the storm.

At midmorning the air grew warmer yet, stultifying. The light of day altered, dimmed, becoming yellow and then pale green. Minutes later a deep-purple twilight settled over the swamps.

They found themselves gasping for air. They filled their lungs and it was as if they had filled them with cotton. Conversation became impossible. All of their energy was needed to ford the rivers which days before had been stagnant sloughs. What had been riverbank was now a foot under water as the rivers became arms of the sea and the sea rose, pushing its way inland, crawling across the world as the wind rose and shrieked and the rain fell across purple slate skies.

"There!" Shanna cupped her hands to her mouth and yelled. Lychma did not hear her. It was impossible to hear anything as the full force of the storm roared across the land. The noise alone was incredible. Banshee shrieks, deep-throated, explosive rumbles, chattering sourceless gabbling, and as the storm increased, an ultrasonic whine which seemed to pierce the eardrums and cut through the bone of the skull, driving out all ability to speak, to hear, to think, to do anything at all but lie down in the frothing, silt-laden water and surrender.

"There!" Shanna tried again, tapping Lychma's shoulder, pointing to the low sandy hummock which rose up across the freshet before them. Lychma's pale face turned blankly toward Shanna. Her blue eyes were empty. Her lips moved, making no sound which could be heard above the roar and whip of the wind, the battering pandemonium of the rain.

Shanna waded into the river, holding her bundle over-head—as if anything in that bundle could now be kept dry—and immediately lost her footing. The current was awesome. Rain, funneling into narrow channels, carrying away the soil and forest detritus, stormed seaward, gaining velocity with each foot traveled as thousands of freshets joined the frenzied chase. Shanna was knocked to her knees, and she stood sputtering, searching for her bundle, which was already lost, carried away on the current.

She fought her way to the far bank and sat down, trying to breathe. The force of the storm seemed to suck the air out of her lungs. The palms lining the creek bowed low in submissive obeisance as the hurricane raged across the world, staining the skies, flooding the land, poisoning the air. Stalking, killing, destroying.

Lychma was at the river's edge, and she looked uncertainly at Shanna, who waved a frantic arm. They must get onto higher ground, must climb the sandy hillock behind Shanna. The water in which Shanna now sat, which swirled and eddied around her, was already two feet deep.

It would grow deeper.

Lychma opened her mouth soundlessly, her eyes filled with dread as she studied the rising river where sawyers and fallen palms bobbed and writhed past, showing themselves first here and then there as lightning, twisting across the skies, ripped open the belly of Manitou's heaven and the rain spilled out.

Shanna stood, waving an arm frantically. The water was rising with every minute that passed. Soon there would be no river at all, but only a sea spread across the dark and trembling earth.

Lychma plunged into the river, waving her arms, twisting her body, looking first ahead and then back toward the safety of the shore. But there was no longer any safety, no longer any shore to be seen as the murky waters spilled out across the land.

The water was warm, dirty, frothing. Lychma trudged slowly onward, to her waist now in the white current, her skirt hiked up for freedom of movement.

Shanna was standing, waving, beckoning, her smile an encouragement. Thunder rolled across the land like the echoing of far distant cannon. Lightning spread itself across the violet skies in weird, fiery concatenations. The thing wrapped itself around Lychma's leg, and she screamed, screamed in defiance of the smothering storm's vast crescendo. It was as if she had opened her mouth and spent her lungs, emptied herself of oxygen, of air, of her soul, but nothing at all emerged from her throat. No sound could make itself known above the splendid fury of the hurricane winds.

She began to dance, to wave her arms, to kick out and leap as her soundless throat repeated its futile gesture. The water moccasin had wrapped itself around her thigh.

Swept away by the driving rain, the cottonmouth had been carried downstream until it met Lychma. In its own desperation the snake had wrapped itself around the first solid object it happened to meet. And now the cottonmouth, deadly poisonous, dark and sinuous, wound itself more tightly around Lychma's thigh, seeking the security of this mooring.

Lychma held her arms out toward Shanna and staggered on, face ashen, eyes wide with revulsion and fear. Shanna watched her wade through the river, not understanding what could produce the loathing and terror she saw in her sister's eyes until at last Lychma was near enough that Shanna could identify the terrible black coil around Lychma's thigh.

Shanna fought her way to the oak grove behind her. Her own heart was drumming like the rain, her own eyes must have been wide with terror. She tore a branch from the oak and waded through the water to the point where Lychma would emerge from the river.

Lychma, moving woodenly, her tongue lolling from her soundless open mouth, waded to shore and stood helplessly watching as Shanna prodded the water moccasin lightly with the branch.

The snake enjoyed the warmth of Lychma's body; it seemed to its dull intelligence to be a warm, secure place to wait out the hurricane. But it did not enjoy the prodding, and it dropped away from Lychma's leg.

Lychma lowered her skirt and fell into Shanna's arms. She whispered small, disgusted sounds of loathing and fear. Shanna had to push her away, to pry her sister's interlocked fingers from her neck. There was no time to be afraid, no time to tremble and grow weak, no time for soft reassurances. The water was rising and the wind was a roaring menace.

"Follow me. Take my hand," Shanna said. Lychma could not hear her; she could not hear herself. She gripped Lychma's wrist and moved off through the oak grove toward the low sandy knoll.

The water rose throughout the day. By late afternoon the knoll where they had sought safety was one of a few scattered islands protruding from an oily, debris-strewn sea.

The sky had calmed temporarily. It hovered over them pink and deep orange, a yawning silence in the heart of the storm. Shanna sat where she had wedged herself when the wind had reached its terrible zenith, between two massive, squat oaks which alone of all the trees in their sight had survived the winds. Lychma sat with her knees tucked under her, her head against Shanna's breast, trying like a small animal to sleep the danger away.

Shanna shifted slightly, felt Lychma stir and placed her hand soothingly on her head. The world had been swept clean. Forests had toppled, the land was now a sea. No one would be pursuing them now. With sudden hope, Shanna realized that.

The Seminole camp had been made on lower ground. If they had not all been able to make it to a place of safety, many would have been lost. Many would be missing. Potaqua would not even know they had gone. If he did know he would have other troubles than two missing girls.

The wind began to build again, and the bright skies overhead gave way to the slowly encroaching clouds. The eye of the hurricane had passed, and now they must endure the storm once more.

"We shall endure it, Lychma," she said, and her sister's hands clenched in response. "We shall endure. No one will find us after this. We shall make our way north. We shall endure!"

The night was a terrible shrieking maelstrom of wind and water. Twice hurtling branches slammed into the sheltering oaks, and the water rose until their small island had shrunk to half its original size.

Yet morning brought clearing weather. The world leveled and flooded by an angry Manitou was a bizarre, wretched spectacle. But the worst had passed. They would wait until the waters had receded. They had enough food, enough clean water. They would wait and gather their strength.

And then they would leave this terrible land, leave it to the Seminoles, to Potaqua and his descendants. If there were to be any. Perhaps the storm in its fury had destroyed all of Potaqua's people. Perhaps the white armies had been washed into the sea. It would be a fitting end to their bloody war.

It was three days before the water had withdrawn enough for them to begin. Their food was nearly gone, but the rest had done wonders for Lychma.

She was bright, alert, and eager to be traveling. She chattered on about the life which lay ahead of them, of becoming Shawnee again.

The reality of the journey soon dulled her optimism.

The swamps were thick with tangled debris. Trees lay scattered everywhere. The water was high in the bogs. Snakes swam the ponds and hung from the cypress trees, and Lychma went rigid and trembled at the sight of each one.

The days were hot, hotter than ever, and steam rose in thick blankets from the swamps. They waded dark rivers and fought their way through deep jungle, resting wherever they could.

"We're lost."

"We are not lost, Lychma. We are still traveling north."

"We are lost."

She hung her head, and Shanna looked at her sister closely. Lychma's legs and her skirt were coated with greenish slime. Her arms were covered with red welts from the leeches. Her eyes were feverish. She shook.

Shanna said roughly, "We could not find our way back if we wanted to. We cannot remain here. We will go on, Lychma. Do you understand me?"

"Yes, Shanna."

That afternoon they found a trove of turtle eggs along a shady bank beneath a massive mangrove tree. They got to their knees and ate them on the spot, six eggs apiece, raw and warm and superb.

Dusk brought no cooling. The skies went to a red-violet, and long shadows stretched out from beneath the trees.

"Lychma!"

Lychma, who had been picking her way through the fallen timber in their path, turned her head in time to see Shanna lunge toward her.

"What is it?"

Shanna grabbed her arm and spun her around, throwing her to the ground. Lychma was sprawled against the damp earth, watching Shanna, who backed away slowly from the pile of timber.

Then Lychma too saw it, and she screamed.

The alligator had been resting among the fallen logs. Now its mouth gaped, revealing long rows of sawtoothed yellow teeth, and with amazing quickness the ancient reptile turned and placed its front feet on a log. Then it slithered across the barrier and waddled toward them. Moss-backed, horny, primeval, it was all of fifteen feet long.

Shanna yanked Lychma to her feet, and they took off at a dead run through the swamp forest. They ran long after any danger was past. They ran heedless of the stones which tore at their feet, of the shattered branches which slashed at them.

When finally they collapsed to the earth, arms around each other, their hearts pounding, their lungs fiery, their sides aching as if filled with jagged glass, it was a complete collapse. Their bodies would recover. Rest and be strengthened.

"How long, Shanna?" Lychma asked, putting into words the dread, the confused and bitter emotions in Shanna's heart.

"How long can we continue? The swamp is an endless thing. Malevolent and angry. Cruel. How long can we go on?"

Until we are through it, Shanna wanted to answer. As much for Lychma's sake as anything else. She wanted to form the words, to be strong and reassuring as she always had been since the day so long ago when she had taken her young sister's hand, bravely kissed their mother goodbye, and trudged off southward in the care of the Creek woman. She wanted to say that, but could not.

She did not know how long she could go on. She bent her head to Lychma's, holding her hand. She was thankful that the dusk had darkened to night and Lychma could not see the tears which tracked across her cheeks.

Morning brought fresh resolve, old weariness. They rose and without eating began again their journey. The sun rose, a red eye winking above the low line of trees to the east.

The ponds were briefly gilded, shot through with crimson fire. Jays and cardinals sang in the trees still black against the fire of the coming sun. The swamp was momentarily a beautiful place, a wondrous thing. But with the heat the mosquitoes emerged; the snakes warmed and stretched and shuttled out of their secret hiding places to hunt; alligators splashed into the ponds, seeking the unwary.

Their way was clogged with hanging vines and blown-down trees, blocked by unexpected bogs. And the panther.

Shanna ducked low to clear the overhanging branch of a marsh elder. Off across the swamp she heard a loon call, and her head turned that way instinctively.

When she turned her head again she was face to face with the panther.

His eyes were sultry and mocking, his teeth white and sharp. His arms were tattooed, his glossy black hair swept back and loosely knotted.

"Yui!" Shanna breathed.

"Then you know me!" He laughed and she turned, tried to run, but he caught her arm and spun her around, still smiling. He was tall and powerful, graceful and quite frightening.

He was not alone. Five men came from behind Shanna. Two of them held Lychma's arms tightly, although she was obviously not going to attempt an escape. She moved on

64

rubbery legs toward Shanna and the Seminole war chief, her blue eyes showing quiet despair.

"Leave us alone!" Shanna said angrily, trying to shake off the man's dark, muscular hand.

"I am afraid I cannot, small one," Yui said. He still smiled, but now he released Shanna and stood back, arms folded across his bronze chest, looking at Shanna and Lychma.

"We are nothing to you. Leave us alone. Why have you set upon us?"

"You belong to a friend of mine, slave girl."

"We belong to no one! A *friend*! Potaqua, you mean. Who could be a friend of that black savage?"

Yui laughed and nodded, then replied. "You are correct in your estimate of Potaqua. Perhaps I should not have chosen the term 'friend.' Potaqua is my ally."

"He is a thug and a criminal," Shanna said hotly.

'Yes. Perhaps so. But he is Seminole. We must ally ourselves, we must fight back the whites. We must pretend friendship. We must," Yui said with white intensity, "or we will cease to exist, all of us."

"What have we to do with this?" Shanna demanded. She tossed her head, and the gesture produced a laugh from one of the other warriors, a huge man with a big belly and a bulbous nose. "What is amusing about us?" Shanna shouted. Her eyes were brimming with hot tears now, and that made her more angry than anything else.

"Nothing, small one," Yui said. "Nothing is amusing."

"I do not care to be called 'small one.' My name is Shanna."

"Yes." Yui nodded his head thoughtfully. He turned to the man with the big belly. "Pohoy, see if our prisoners would like to eat. We have venison?"

"Yes, Yui," the man called Pohoy said. "We have venison and duck."

"Then feed them if they will eat," the Seminole warrior said. He turned then and walked away, drawing his men after him as if he were a lodestone.

Shanna, glancing around, saw that only this Pohoy had been left to watch them. She thought fleetingly of making an escape, of running into the deep swamp. Pohoy smiled.

"You would get nowhere. We would run you down within

five minutes." He nodded. "Come and eat. We will roast a joint of venison for you. You look tired and hungry and thirsty."

"What will he do to us?" Shanna asked, her eyes indicating Yui, who sat crouched in the clearing, encircled by his men.

"What will he do?" Pohoy shrugged. "What he always does, what must be done for the best of his people. He will return you to Potaqua."

"Potaqua is a dog!"

"Yes," Pohoy agreed readily. "Potaqua is a dog."

He said no more. He turned and started toward the small fire which burned on the verge of the clearing. He looked back once across his thick shoulder, waiting to see if Shanna would follow.

For another long moment she debated with herself. Run or follow meekly, surrender, let all of what had gone before, the long trek, count for nothing. Shanna looked at Lychma, and she knew. There was no choice. Lychma could not run. They could not escape this panther and his sinewy men.

"Let us eat," Shanna said.

They did eat. Roasted venison and duck baked in the glowing coals. They drank deeply from the water skins of the Seminole, and then Lychma fell asleep, perhaps grateful that the effort was over. That they had no responsibility again for their lives, no need to run, to *do*.

Shanna's mind was not so settled. Lychma slept, rolled up in a clean blanket, warm and safe, her stomach full. Across the clearing the men sat in small groups talking and laughing. Yui strode among them, pausing to slap one man on the shoulder, to jibe with another.

They were all content, all pleased with themselves. Slave masters and slaves. A perfect world.

Shanna sat up, threw her blanket aside, and walked from the camp into the darkness of the everglades. No one tried to stop her. They knew this much about her: She would never leave her sister under any duress.

She stood in the darkness. A great mangrove tree loomed over her, casting dark stains against a starry sky. A warm breeze sifted through the swamps, bringing the scent of wild orchids and magnolias and the sour smells of the bogs, of decaying vegetation and still waters.

Shanna looked to the distant stars. There was peace, perhaps the only peace. For there was none on this earth, had been none for these Shawnee.

She was aware only of the shadow flitting across the mangrove tree, for he came on silent feet, a thing of no substance which pressed against her and took on strength and weight and violent intention.

"No!" She tried to twist away from him, but the panther's grip was powerful.

"Be still, girl," Yui said. His voice was more of a growl, an animal utterance, than human speech. His hands were on her breasts, her hips; his mouth sought hers.

As he kissed her, his lips pressing against hers, bruising her lips against her teeth, Shanna felt white fury building. She opened her mouth and bit down savagely through Yui's lips.

Warm, salty blood filled her mouth, and he fell back, holding his mouth.

Then he laughed and lunged again from out of the darkness, and his hands found her thighs. His fingers dug into her flesh, and he was kissing her with a bloodstained mouth, his lips crawling along her neck, his breath in her ear.

Shanna's stomach tightened. It was not fear or revulsion. It was anger. Anger that this man, her master, should come upon her like this. They had left her little dignity. This last attempt would strip her of all she retained.

She lifted her knee savagely, driving it at his groin. At the same time she smashed her skull against the bridge of his nose, hearing with satisfaction gristle crackling, hearing Yui's grunt of surprised pain as he backed away, his hand raised.

For a moment she thought he would strike her, and knowing his strength, she was afraid that the blow, if it landed, would kill her, snapping her neck, crushing her skull.

He stood like that for a long moment in the starlight, arm upraised, nose and mouth leaking blood, muscles standing taut.

Then, with another grunt, this one amused or puzzled, he turned away and strode toward the camp, wiping his hand across his battered face.

Later as she stood shuddering, leaning against the tree for support, her knees weak, her heart racing, she heard deep-throated laughter from the camp. Shanna's ears burned, and she wished that she had a musket, a knife, a war hatchet to kill the panther.

But she had nothing. She could not flee; there was Lychma to think of. Slowly, filling her lungs deeply, she walked back to the camp, past the eyes of the men who sat together watching her like a pack of sated wolves.

Lychma slept, and Shanna lay down beside her, her eyes open. The men's voices droned on, and now and then some-one laughed again. She could not hear their words, did not want to.

Now she belonged to this man. Temporarily, at least. Now Yui owned her, owned her body and her spirit, or believed he did. Do what you want with her, she is only a slave. Only a woman, only a Shawnee. Shanna's thoughts twisted her stomach into knotted nausea. She felt a fever of rage flush her skin.

He was worse than Potaqua. Potaqua might kill them, might crush them, but he did not assault the soul.

With astonishment Shanna realized that she had managed to fall asleep, and now gray light was tinting the eastern skies. It was morning, and she looked up through heavy eyelids to see the big one, Pohoy, tugging at her foot.

"Get up, little one. We must travel far this day."

"I do not like to be called 'little one,' " Shanna said, and Pohoy laughed, falling back in mock terror.

"Do not assault me too, little one. Do not batter me as you have my chieftain!"

Someone near the fire laughed in appreciation, and Shanna rose from her bed slowly as Pohoy walked away, shoulders rolling. She was happy she could not see the expression on his face.

"We are nothing. Toys, amusement, tools."

"What?" Lychma was yawning. It took her eyes a while to focus, it took a while for knowledge to creep into them, and then she frowned. "What has happened?"

"Nothing, Lychma."

"I thought I heard you speaking. I thought I heard angry words."

"Nothing has happened. Rise and eat, if they will feed us. We are traveling again. Southward."

Lychma said nothing. It felt to her as if her body had been drained of blood. Potaqua! Worse still, Tohope. What would become of them now? Her eyes asked the silent question of Shanna, and Shanna just as silently answered with a slow shake of her head.

They were fed, and as they ate Yui stood to one side, arms folded, staring woodenly at Shanna. His lower lip was purple, his nose swollen. His expression was impenetrable.

They ate and were on the trail as the sun crested the horizon and the swamp came to life. Two young Shawnee women and a band of tattooed, fierce Seminole warriors.

At noon the sun was high in a hot, clear sky. They sagged to the earth and watched as the men passed the water skin from hand to hand. Then Pohoy, the big one, brought water to Shanna and Lychma.

"Drink," he said.

"Why are you doing this?" Shanna asked.

"Giving you water? Because you must be thirsty."

"Why are you taking us back to Potaqua? Why are you delivering us to him? I understood Yui was no friend of Potaqua's."

"Did you?"

"Yes. I have been told this. I have been told that it is because Potaqua allies himself with the Spanish men and Yui trusts no one who is not Indian."

"Perhaps it is so." Pohoy shrugged.

"Then why?"

"We are Seminole." Pohoy watched as Lychma drank. He drew in the earth with his finger as he crouched, waiting for them to finish.

"Are all Seminole filthy?" Shanna asked. Lychma looked up at her sister with amazement. Pohoy tensed.

"What are you saying, woman?"

"I am saying that Potaqua is a filthy man. Is Yui no better to ally himself with such a warrior?"

"Yui is noble. Yui is courageous and honorable."

"A seducer of reluctant females."

"I know nothing of that."

"Last night you laughed about it. You know enough. Is that Yui's character?"

"I cannot speak for Yui."

"Can you speak for Pohoy? Why does Pohoy travel to deliver innocent women to Potaqua? Potaqua who will likely kill us, will certainly beat us. Potaqua who is evil and sly and does not know what honor is."

"It is Yui's command," Pohoy said, looking decidedly uncomfortable now.

"And you follow him."

"Anywhere."

"Obey him, no matter what he commands?"

"No matter what," Pohoy said.

Lychma was finished with her drink, and now Pohoy took the water skin from her and, plugging it, walked away, leaving Shanna to stare at his broad back, knowing that she would never be able to receive help from Pohoy—not if it contradicted the will of Yui.

Yui was a god to the man, a king, a giant, a figure of strength and valor.

"He is, after all only a man, a dirty brutal man," Shanna said.

"Is he?" Lychma asked, and Shanna turned toward her sister. Had she been speaking out loud?

"Of course," Shanna said. She still had not told her sister what Yui had attempted. "How can you challenge that?"

"I challenge nothing, sister. It is your own eyes which contradict the passion of your words."

"You anger me!" Shanna said. "Are you still feverish? You speak nonsense. The man is a beast."

"Yes, Shanna," Lychma said meekly.

"A beast."

"Yes, Shanna." This time a small smile crept across Lychma's lips, and Shanna rose angrily, turning away.

The afternoon continued hot. With the Seminole war party they traveled much more quickly, deftly, than they had on their northward trek. Yui seemed to know each bog, each twist of the trail.

They did not halt until darkness made rapid travel impossible. Then they started a small fire and cooked their venison, drinking as much water as they could hold as the smoked meat worked its magic on exhausted bodies.

Shanna had seen the other fires, the distant buildings, and at nightfall when the cicadas sang and the frogs grumped, when the mosquitoes on their evening rampage hummed about, she walked to the hill crest to look out across the dark land toward the glowing cones of distant fire.

"Cherokee," Yui said.

She spun around. He had crept up beside her in his silent way. He gestured with open palms, his mouth tightening.

"Be at ease. I have not come to harm you. I will harm you no more. I am a simple man," he said. "I saw you with your wide hips, with your ripe breasts and moist mouth. I thought: Here is a place to lay a child. Here is a rich and fertile field. It was the thought of a man's body, not of his mind. I will not attempt such a thing again."

Shanna looked away as if she had heard nothing. The distant settlement, the same one she had seen a week earlier, sat against the dark earth.

"Peace." Shanna looked at this tattooed panther, at this Seminole warlord. "Why can you not live in peace, Yui? Why must you run the swamps, why must you deal with men like Potaqua? There"—she nodded—"is what can be. The Cherokee at peace with the whites. The Creek farming the land."

"You would ask me to be a farmer!" Yui laughed.

"I would ask why you could not be a farmer. The soil can be tilled in peace. Your way can only lead to death."

"All ways lead to death."

"You know what I mean."

"No." Yui stepped nearer, and she could sense his body heat, smell the man-scent of his body. "I do not know what you mean. Nor do you, woman. You speak as a child. The Cherokee do not live in peace, they live in slavery."

"Slavery! What do you know of slavery, Yui, Seminole! It is I who am a slave. I who have no house of my own. I who must wonder if I will be killed by the butcher Potaqua."

"He will not harm you." Yui's voice was low and solemn and sincere. "Believe that—he will not harm you, Shanna."

Shanna did not answer—what was this savage's word worth?

He went on. "But as for the Cherokee, they are indeed

71

slaves, so too are the tame Chickamauga and the Creek. They live side by side with the white man as a dog lives with its master. They have sold their souls. Their life is a lingering death.''

"How can you say that?''

"How can I say it?'' Yui laughed bitterly. "How can I not say the truth?''

"You are another of these men who wish only for war. Any peace is a sign of softness, of cowardice, to you.''

"Yes,'' he admitted. "You are right when you say that.''

"Any death but a peaceful death.''

"Yes.''

"You will fight until there are none of you left. Like Potaqua and this Osceola.''

"Yes.''

"But why? Are you not tired of running through the swamps? Are you not weary of war? Would you not like to lay down your arms and live in quiet?''

"Yes, little one, but I cannot. I will not.''

"And why not?'' she demanded.

"The six hundred reasons,'' Yui said. Now he stood looking into the distances, his strong profile outlined by the star-spattered sky.

"The six hundred reasons?'' Shanna did not understand.

"That is the number of my people killed by white arms. That is the number—six hundred—of my tribe killed by American soldiers. Some were brothers, some family, some small ones. Some dear to me.''

"What was her name, Yui? This woman who was killed.''

"I said nothing of a woman,'' Yui answered almost with anger. He turned sharply toward Shanna in the night. "I said there are reasons why I fight. The reasons were once living. Now they live no more. Perhaps some of them wished for peace as well.''

Then he turned, nodded slightly, and was gone, leaving a bemused Shanna alone in the soft night.

They traveled southward again. The days were a blur of heat and boggy ground, swamp crossings, mosquitoes biting at exposed flesh despite the repellent coat of muskrat oil they all wore. There was the sun, high and ominous, the dark trees standing so close that boughs interlocked and shadows smothered the earth. Water moccasins and copperhead snakes watched them with jeweled, challenging eyes. There was the splash as the alligators took to the water as the party approached, and the occasional flurry of tactful withdrawal as one or another grandfather gator turned toward them.

On the fourth day, exhausted and sick with heat, dizzy with the deprivation, they reached the camp of Potaqua along the Suwannee River near the coast.

They could see the cooking fires, the new chickees, the distant glitter of the blue sea. Shanna, holding Lychma's arm, started out of the trees and into the camp, resigned to her fate.

"Wait." Yui caught her by the shoulder. His black eyes looked down into hers.

"What is it?" Shanna asked wearily.

"I had to bring you back. It is duty, and so I have done it. But I promised you that Potaqua will not hurt you. He will not—I give you my word."

"Hurt us?" Shanna snorted. "No, there is no pain in slavery, in living each day drudgelike, without dignity, in dying a little with each sunrise. He will not hurt us—*you* have hurt us. It would have cost you nothing to let us pass you by. You feel a sense of duty to this man! This Potaqua who is an animal. It reveals to me what your duty is worth."

"Take them down, Pohoy," Yui said coldly. "Give them over to the slave masters. I will speak with Potaqua if he is in the camp."

"Yes, Yui. Will we be staying?"

"I do not know. It is to be decided." He was still looking at Shanna. Now he turned his back and walked away, musket in hand, long muscular legs striding across the swampgrass-heavy ground toward the largest chickee.

"You now," Pohoy said and there seemed to be genuine regret in the giant's eyes. Regret, perhaps, but he too had his duty. Shanna looked at Pohoy in a way which seemed temporarily to shame him. Then Pohoy's eyes hardened again and he said:

"Let us go."

Lychma stood riveted for a moment, clinging to Shanna as she looked toward the Seminole camp. Then she went slack, nodded, and obediently walked forward as the dogs came out to greet them, barking and leaping.

73

The slave hut was small and close. Pohoy gave them over to two big women who guided them to the hut. The door was opened and they were prodded inside. No word was spoken. The door closed and the blue-white light of the brilliant morning was shut off.

Shanna sagged to the floor and closed her eyes. Lychma sat beside her. There was nothing to say, and Shanna could not kiss her sister and reassure her. This was the life they would lead. This was the beginning of it, and it was not so very unlike the end. To sit in darkness, to wait for the lash of a cane, to breathe in and breathe out; to work and to die.

❧ 4 ❧

"Yui! My friend!" Potaqua's voice was booming, his manner expansive, as Yui entered his chickee. His sullen, narrow wife, Tohope, sat in the corner, her adder eyes on the tall warrior who now stood before Potaqua.

"Potaqua." Yui lowered his head respectfully. Potaqua's lip turned up at the corner. Yui was a man who followed the law, who did his duty, but he was also dangerous. Where others would have prostrated themselves at Potaqua's feet, Yui lowered his chin an inch. Where others would have quivered with pleasure at having Potaqua call them friend, Yui only replied with Potaqua's unadorned name. He does not call me chief, war leader, cousin, uncle—no term of respect is used, Potaqua thought, and his sharp eyes flickered. He calls me Potaqua, as if we were of the same rank.

"What brings you to us?" Potaqua said, managing a smile despite the thudding of a pulse in his temple. "Sit down, Yui. Have food and drink. Tohope, lazy creature, fill a pipe for this guest."

"Yes, husband," Tohope said.

"I have come because you have invited me."

"Because your people have been beaten back and you lose strength with each day," Potaqua said with triumph and malevolence.

"Just so, Potaqua," Yui admitted. "They may decimate us, but we shall never surrender any more than Osceola will, any more than Potaqua will."

"I do not like Osceola. Why mention his name?"

"I consider you to be equally powerful," Yui answered. Then politically he added, "Though who knows what time might bring? Perhaps all Seminoles will come under your totem one day. That would be a mighty force."

Potaqua seemed to hear none of that. "Why don't you join Osceola then if you believe him a finer warrior, a more noble chieftain?"

Yui answered honestly. "Because he is far to the south, Potaqua, and I am ready to fight now." Potaqua, amazingly, grinned. His pointed teeth flashed.

"How many warriors have you, Yui? The truth and not the number you would give to your enemies."

"Two hundred."

"Two hundred!" Potaqua laughed out loud this time. "I had always believed you to be more powerful."

"They are two hundred who have muskets. Two hundred who have fought the Americans. Two hundred who have scars upon their bodies and scars upon their souls, Potaqua. They are two hundred who will make war as five hundred."

"Where are they camped?" Potaqua asked, leaning forward, facing Yui across the woven and dyed mat.

"East," Yui said, "awaiting my orders."

"East? That means little," Potaqua said suspiciously.

"They may have relocated."

"They may be waiting until we have spoken. They may be in the swamps. They may have slipped into my camp already."

"They are to the east," Yui answered calmly.

Potaqua had lighted the long clay pipe he held. The mingled scents of tobacco and birch bark filled the chickee. Smoke rose in lazy flat spirals. The Seminole warlord handed the pipe to Yui, who took three puffs.

"There will be much war soon," Potaqua said. "There is a man called Boggs and another called Jackson who are intent on bringing the war into the swamps."

"To do so will mean their death."

"Jackson has already met Osceola in combat. Many Seminole have died."

"Then many whites will die," Yui said simply, although he thought that Potaqua was trying to discredit the great Osceola and simultaneously convince Yui that the only safety lay in joining forces with Potaqua.

"You have not yet decided what path to follow?" Potaqua inquired. He sucked on the long stem of the pipe, black eyes slightly glazed.

"I must consider it for a time," Yui replied.

76

"Consider quickly." Potaqua leaned forward at the waist. "The war is upon us. The last war, as Osceola calls it."

"I am ashamed to have brought no gifts," Yui said quickly, changing the subject. "Yet I have done you a service."

"Yes?" Potaqua's dark eyebrows were raised.

"Yes. Two of your slaves were lost in the great storm. They were wandering helplessly, looking for your camp . . ."

"The two that ran away!" Tohope said, spinning toward them. What was that flutter of emotions behind the woman's eyes? Yui saw something in back of them. A small, leathery winged beast twisting frantically through her thoughts, a dark malevolence, a hatred. Yui frowned.

"They seemed to be lost. I came upon them and they asked me to bring them back to the camp of Potaqua. They were much afraid," Yui said to flatter Potaqua.

"Blue eyes," Tohope hissed. Potaqua glared at her. What was the matter with this silly wife?

"What you have done is a service," Potaqua told Yui. "We lost many people in the big storm. The work is suffering. What you have done is a service."

"Blue eyes," Tohope said again, and this time Potaqua half turned. His shoulder only moved, and Tohope, covering her face, fell back. The hand of Potaqua had landed many times.

Yui watched with faint curiosity. Something about Shanna's sister seemed to disturb Potaqua's wife. Potaqua himself seemed utterly indifferent to the slave girls, however. Yui shrugged these thoughts aside. They had nothing to do with him.

"May we stay for a while, my men and I?" Yui asked. "We should rest and we would like to share your bowls. We must talk again and decide what can be done about this war. For now, however, I am weary and must lie down."

Yui stood, and Potaqua rose with him. "My camp is your camp, Yui. We are brothers. We are Seminole." His broad hand rested on Yui's shoulder briefly, lying there like a cottonmouth snake.

We are Seminole, Yui thought, but we are not brothers. Not you and I, dark one.

"I have promised the girls that no harm would come to them, Potaqua. They were afraid that someone might misun-

77

derstand their absence. I have given my word that they would not be punished for something which was not their fault."

"Of course, Yui."

"My word, Potaqua. There is nothing more sacred to me than my honor. I cannot stomach a liar. I will never be one."

"You make so much over nothing, Yui." Potaqua laughed, and his hand slid away. "Nothing will happen to them. What do I care for two slaves who were lost and have now returned?"

"I wished only to make my feelings clear to you."

"And so you have made them." Potaqua turned to his wife. "Are these two not your own slaves, Tohope?"

"They are mine. You gave them to me, husband."

"Then you see!" Potaqua turned to Yui, his hands open and outstretched. "There is nothing to concern yourself about. They are my wife's people. She will not harm them."

"I thank you," Yui said. He looked at Tohope, surprised at the venom in her eyes. It was a terrible anger she nurtured, and this anger was not directed at Yui, obviously, but at . . . the girls? Yui frowned doubtfully.

"We shall speak again, Potaqua. First I must eat and sleep. Then we shall speak of war and what must be done."

"As you say, brother," Potaqua said. "Rest. Feed your men from our pots. Then we shall speak."

When Yui was gone, Potaqua turned away, his face drawing down into a deep scowl. "My brother is ambitious. My brother is a friend of Osceola, but I do not think he will accept all the plans I have devised. I do not think this Yui worships Potaqua." He smiled in an ugly way. His eyes suddenly focused on Tohope. "What are you looking at, woman?"

"Only at my warrior husband," Tohope said. "These women . . ." she dared.

"Women? What women?"

"The slaves, Potaqua."

"The Shawnee women?"

"Yes."

"What about them? You have them back. Now all will be as it was before."

"Yes, my husband. But I do not want these slaves."

"You do not want them?" Potaqua's wooden face turned toward his wife. "Why is that, woman?"

"They are not good workers. They are sly. I think one of them may have taken a necklace of mine."

She watched Potaqua's eyes as she spoke, trying to fathom any lurking secrets there. Would he let his lover go so easily? Perhaps. Knowing Potaqua, perhaps. Tohope was sure of only one thing: Blue eyes must be done away with. That was the only way her mind could ever be set at ease.

Potaqua only shrugged, giving nothing away. "Give them to your cousin Shael," he said.

"They are thieves!" Tohope said more violently than she intended. She immediately recoiled. Potaqua did not like a woman to raise her voice to him.

His brooding eyes met hers. "Then go now and kill them."

"You have promised Yui that nothing would be done to them."

"Yui? You speak as if I need fear this man."

"No, husband. I know you fear nothing. I only thought that you wished to add his warriors to your forces."

"What then do you want me to do, woman?" Now Potaqua was angry. That dark, familiar, deadly light had come into his eyes.

"Send them with the others who wait for the ship. Yui will not know. The Spanish man will give you muskets and powder for them."

Potaqua nodded thoughtfully. "It shall be done. As you like it. Go now, woman. You tire me with your yammering. Go now and count your necklaces."

Potaqua yawned and turned away. He would have been astonished if he had turned back suddenly to see the mingled hatred and triumph on the face of Tohope. Potaqua was not an intelligent man, only sly. He would not have known what caused such emotions.

Tohope left before her husband could notice anything. She walked across the camp, watching the women parch corn. She enjoyed the way they looked up at her with fear and jealousy. She enjoyed her power and the finery Potaqua had always given her.

She paused and stood over an old crone with gnarled hands, with a sun-lined, careworn face, her hair white as snow hanging into her dull eyes, and Tohope shuddered. This was what happened to women who did not fight for what they wanted. This was what could become of Tohope if Potaqua decided to cast her out or take a new wife. She turned quickly away from the old woman, who labored on, slowly grinding her corn, and Tohope felt a sudden, sharp exhilaration. It was good to be the wife of Potaqua. No one would ever displace her. Certainly not blue eyes. Tohope laughed and walked on, watching the activity all around her as she indulged herself in luxurious indolence.

Yui frowned, turning away from the beach. Pohoy was with him, and Cascala, the old one.

"More of Potaqua's friends," Pohoy said, rubbing his massive belly. "Why do we stay with this man, Yui? He is filth."

"He is Seminole. He is a strong man."

"You despise him."

"Yes." Yui smiled faintly, returning his eyes to the sea, which rolled in to the white-sand shore in constant rhythm, the breakers crackling and spuming.

"We cannot fight without muskets and gunpowder," Cascala said to Pohoy.

"We can fight with arrows and bare hands." Pohoy grew heated.

"With the guns we make a better war," the old one answered, unperturbed.

"Cascala is right," Yui said, "yet I am as troubled as Pohoy by the source of these weapons. They come with gifts, but their thoughts too are on conquest. We are an ally, but when we have driven the Americans out, why then should they remain friendly? Why then should they give us powder for our weapons?"

Yui crouched down in the shade of the swaying palms. "I do not like these men, Pohoy. I do not like them at all." He looked again at the ship lying at anchor beyond the breakers. The sea breeze toyed with the Spanish flag which flew from the mainmast. Yui rose, threw down a handful of sand, and turned, walking away from the sea.

"I do not know why we remain here," Pohoy said when Yui was gone. The older man chuckled. "Do I amuse you, Cascala?"

"Yes, Pohoy. You are a mighty warrior, a silent hunter.

You observe all when you move through the forest. Yet you do not see what is before your eyes. There is a very strong reason why Yui chooses to remain in the camp of Potaqua.''

"Guns?"

"No, Cascala. Something much more dangerous and to Yui more important. His lip is not yet healed.'' With that Cascala, still chuckling, walked off, and Pohoy was left to stand scratching his massive belly, eyes narrow in puzzlement. Slowly then it dawned on him, and with a grin of astonishment he too began making his way back toward Yui's camp. Only once did Pohoy pause and glance back toward the Spanish ship, and then his smile fell away to be replaced by a dark, concerned scowl. There would be trouble. The Spanish men had come.

❀ 5 ❀

Don Carlos Cervera y Ybarra was a tall, swarthy man with jet-black hair, striking deep-green eyes, and the contemptuous, haughty expression of an aristocrat. He was as dark as any Indian, and it had been suggested that there was more than a little Moorish blood in Ybarra's family, a suggestion which Ybarra hotly denied and which had once led to a fatal duel.

He wore silk and gold on this occasion—it was always best to impress these savages with the wealth of the Spanish Empire—and he wore his silver-hilted sword. A small poniard rode on a crossing belt at his right hip. His mustache was newly waxed, his pointed beard combed. With thirteen men in breastplates, Don Carlos Cervera y Ybarra strode up from the beach where the launch waited, through the ranks of wind-blown palms, and into the camp of Potaqua, the savage.

And he was a savage, in every sense of the word. Ybarra recognized an innate cunning, an opportunism not dissimiliar to that which motivated Ybarra. For Ybarra felt himself to be desperately in need of money. A dissolute uncle had ravaged the family fortune. Ybarra, hating the sea, had nevertheless taken to it, recognizing the opportunities for a bold man in King Philip's service.

Potaqua stood waiting, done up in feathers and paint. His massive forearms were crossed on his chest. A long feathered cape reaching to the ground stretched out behind him.

Ybarra arranged his features into what he hoped was placid dignity. He loathed this man Potaqua, but knew that it was dangerous to let even a hint of that feeling show. Potaqua could not only do King Philip's work, drive the Americans out of Florida, he could also make Ybarra a wealthy man—and that, of course, was of the first importance. Already Ybarra was tired of the life of a soldier. He found that it bored him. Already he had decided that the only way left to him was the way he had chosen—reprehensible under certain conditions, but hardly here. If his conduct had become self-centered, possibly criminal, who was there to bring charges against him? A band of ignorant savages? His men who grew wealthy themselves as Ybarra played the adventurer?

The worst of it all, Ybarra decided, was having to deal with men like Potaqua.

They shook hands and embraced each other.

"Come into my house," said Potaqua in passable Spanish.

"I would be honored, Chief Potaqua. I have gifts for you from the King of Spain, who values your friendship highly and speaks of you constantly in his letters."

Potaqua beamed momentarily at the flattery, then resumed his habitual scowling expression. "You have muskets?" he asked suspiciously.

"Of course, Chief Potaqua. I have everything you have asked for. Now, let us speak of what must be done."

Ybarra felt the fool climbing a crude ladder, sitting on the straw mats in a straw-roofed house. He forced himself to be effusively flattering. This was the man who would make him wealthy.

They smoked a pipe, which Ybarra detested. Then they ate. Dried, metallic-tasting fish, a bowl of crushed hominy and honey, some sort of pasty, bland food which Ybarra could not even identify, some passable smoked venison. Then, snapping his fingers at one of his officers, Ybarra presented a quart of brandy to his host, whose eyes immediately lighted.

"This is the greatest of your gifts," Potaqua said, leaning back with the bottle held on his chest. "I drink and I have dreams. I see the truth of the future in these dreams. The spirit of the bottle shows me the Seminole driving all their enemies from this land. I see the blood flowing like rivers to the sea, the long rain which cleanses the land. I see Potaqua as the leader of a great Seminole nation with my adversaries at my feet."

"Your vision is a true one, Potaqua. On my ship I have rum in barrels for your warriors. Perhaps they will share your vision. Perhaps it is time to strike against the American Jackson and defeat him completely."

"When it is time," Potaqua said, "I shall know. The spirits will tell me."

Ybarra's lips tightened with disgust. He placed his hand over his face, letting the emotion seep away. He had to persuade this Potaqua to do the king's work or be replaced, losing a remarkable opportunity. And the king's work at this time did not mean harrying forays; it meant an all-out attack first on Boggs, who held the fort at St. Augustine, and then on Jackson, totally destroying American strength on the Florida peninsula. But Potaqua would have his visions.

"I have brought your gifts with me, Potaqua. Shall I have them brought ashore in the morning?"

"Have the rum and muskets brought tonight," Potaqua said. He had the upper hand here. Ybarra was weak, Potaqua decided, a man easily manipulated—but not to be trusted, never to be trusted. He looked into those green eyes and smiled. "Tonight, señor."

Ybarra agreed readily. That meant that by morning Potaqua and his men would be a drunken rabble. Once the kegs of rum were opened it would be too late to discuss tactics and the king's will. Ybarra silently ground his teeth together.

"Let us speak of this war, Potaqua. Let us speak of driving out your enemies."

"Later, Ybarra. After a while. For now let us drink and smoke the pipe." Potaqua's eyes glinted with dark knowledge. "Perhaps we have other things to discuss. Perhaps I have something you want more than war."

"I do not understand you."

"I have slaves for you once more."

Ybarra leaned closer, and Potaqua was pleased to see the avarice his offer had produced on Ybarra's face. "How many?"

"Many. Let us discuss the price, Ybarra."

"Yes."

No matter the price, they were worth it. Once the native population on the Caribbean islands—tribes such as the Caribs, warlike cannibals, the Island Arawaks, the Ciboneys on Haiti and the Antilles—had been considered only a nuisance, a threat, people to be done away with or pushed into the hills. Now they were planting sugar cane for the rum trade and there were no people to work the crops. Africans were being imported, but the voyage was long, many died, the price was high. The people Potaqua could supply had a great value as plantation slaves in the Caribbean, and the old devil knew it.

"They make you wealthy, no, Ybarra? They will make me wealthy as well." Then Potaqua threw back his head and laughed, drinking the brandy even as he did so until it spilled from his mouth and ran down his neck. "We must, I think, be friends." *For now*, he added silently. *For now, Ybarra*.

"Come along."

Shanna looked up from her work. She had been weaving a large mat from corn husks. Now she found Nokatak, one of the slave overseers, standing over her.

"What is it?"

"Come along. There's new work for you."

Shanna sighed and got to her feet, wiping her brow with the back of her hand. Looking across the compound, she saw Lychma walking quickly toward them.

"You and your sister will be together," Nokatak said. Shanna found that there was something about Nokatak's smile she did not like. But the overseer would answer no questions. There was nothing to do but go along.

"Where are we going, Shanna?" Lychma asked brightly.

"I don't know."

"We're together, at least. And no Tohope." Lychma laughed. Tohope had refused to have either of them around her chickee; nothing could have pleased Lychma more.

"I saw Yui today," Lychma said more softly, bending her head toward her sister as they followed Nokatak through a shadowed glade.

"Did you?"

"He could not speak to me, but he made a sign. He is not a bad man, Shanna."

"Perhaps not. But he is a man," Shanna said. *And a Seminole*.

"If you do not wish to talk about him, say so," Lychma answered with a shrug. "Where are we going?"

They had been walking for half a mile, working gradually closer to the sea. They could see the ocean blue beyond the palms.

"Nokatak?"

"Be quiet, woman. Follow me and be still."

Lychma made her face long like Nokatak's and swung her arms out in the exaggerated manner of the overseer. Shanna laughed.

They walked another quarter of a mile, then started through a dense stand of cabbage palm, using their arms to fend off the low-hanging prickly fronds. Then they were into the clearing.

"Shanna!"

No sooner had Lychma cried out than two men took hold of their arms. Nokatak laughed. "Goodbye, Shawnee women. Goodbye."

Ahead of them was a low stockade, no more than head-high. Inside, some squatting against the earth, some pacing restlessly, were dozens of men and women. Some were Cherokee, some Creek. There were two Mococos, and as Shanna saw as they were pushed inside the crude enclosure, several men with their skin as black as obsidian. These sat together against the wall, yellow eyes glaring.

"What is this?" Lychma called out loudly. "What is happening?"

"No one knows," a Creek woman answered. "No one will answer."

"Where did you come from?"

"All over. All over. I was taken from my village when the man Potaqua raided us. Every day two or three more are brought. No one knows why."

Lychma turned around in a tight circle, angry and confused. She went to the gate, tried it, and then tried to pull herself up to look over the wall. A club landed next to her hand and a voice growled, "Get down. Stay inside."

"What is this, Shanna?"

"I don't know. We are all slaves here. Perhaps Potaqua has some special job for us."

"Perhaps he will kill us! It is because we ran away!"

"He will not kill us. Not so long as we have value."

What then? Shanna couldn't guess. Why take valuable slaves and pen them up where they could not work? And these others—there were none Shanna knew from the village. They had to have been brought here secretly by Potaqua after his raids. For what purpose?

She sagged to the hot, sandy ground, looking around at the blank, staring eyes, the expressionless faces. There was no water to drink, no food to eat. The sun hammered them into a stupor as the hours passed.

The black men spoke together in a strange tongue. The Creek woman chanted a low-voiced song. Lychma sat, arms around her knees, not blinking her eyes for minutes on end.

Shanna shook herself out of her sun-induced lethargy. They needed to know what was happening. They needed to know why. They had to decide upon a course of action. She nearly laughed out loud at her own thought.

What course of action could be taken? If you ran you would be captured; if you were captured you would be brought back to this or worse. They had run before and it had availed them nothing.

"Creek woman," Shanna hissed. "Have you heard nothing? Can you tell us nothing at all about where we shall work, what we are doing here, what shall become of us?"

But the Creek woman was lost in her chanting, and she did not even look at Shanna. The sun was sinking lower now. The shadows crept out from the western wall of the stockade, cooling them. Sundown-tinted clouds drifted past, broken and woven by the winds aloft.

Darkness fell an hour later. The moon would not rise until late. It was then, when the night was black, when the slaves were exhausted by the mere sitting, waiting beneath a blinding sun, that they came.

The gate to the enclosure was flung open, and Shanna saw the men in armor enter. At the same time she saw the black men leap. They had obviously been planning this desperate attempt, for there was no hesitation at all.

They rushed the soldiers, and a musket bellowed in the night. Red fire gushed from the muzzle of the soldier's weapon, and one of the blacks was hurled back to land on his back, writhing, holding his belly as life seeped from him.

The second black man tried to run past the soldiers. He was cut down by a sword which bit deeply behind his knees, cutting the tendons there, and he went down on his head, raising a cloud of dust. He lay still, quietly moaning. The third man had run to the back of the stockade, considered leaping the wall to make his attempted escape, and then simply given up, sagging to the ground to sit, holding his head, rocking himself from side to side.

The white man in armor shouted something which no one understood. His meaning was clear, however, and the slaves rose and filed toward the open enclosure gate, stepping past the dead man, past the wounded one who could not rise to walk.

Starlight glittered faintly on the white sands. The slaves walked through the palms to the beach, and there in groups of ten they were taken to a small boat.

The sea was black. Swelling and receding, it rumbled its constant challenge. Lychma and Shanna were placed in the boat, and six strong-smelling, competent men with growls of habitual complaint and grunts of effort placed the bow of the boat into the curl of the onrushing swells and, dragging skillfully, in practiced cadence, on their oars, put the boat through the line of surf and rowed toward the squat three-masted ship which bobbed at anchor, black against a black sea.

Lychma held Shanna's hand tightly, but they did not speak. There was no sound but the effortful breathing of the boatmen, the creak of the oarlocks, the splash of the dipping oars, and the muffled surging roar of the sea pounding the shoreline.

There was a single lantern in the aft cabin, a single lamp upon the deck. Lychma and Shanna were prodded up the webbing of a rope ladder, and there was a moment when they stood on the rolling deck watching the shoreline, dark and distant. Then, as the last of their party clambered aboard, damp with salt spray, shivering with the cold or with fear, with undefined, animal emotions, they were herded toward the stern of the musty-smelling ship and into a dark, deep hold.

They were forced downward. The hold was acrid and dank. Human beings sat hunched against the flooring. Shanna saw only the starlight gleaming on an eye, the rounded silhouettes of men and women merged into one breathing, perspiring mass.

She kept hold of Lychma's hand. Together they sat on the floor, feeling the close contact of other bodies as they were jammed together, as others were forced down into the hold after them.

The hatch was drawn shut and total darkness descended.

There was the scent of urine and dirty bodies. The sounds

88

of exhalations and low moaning. The touch of a bare shoulder against Shanna's own as someone shifted uncomfortably. The desperate squeeze of Lychma's hand.

The darkness was absolute. They might have been at the heart of the earth or in a mass grave. They were the condemned, and the eyes of Manitou could not find them; his grace was a distant promise, a myth, a lie. Shanna's head sank down.

"We are dead," Lychma said, not to Shanna but to the darkness. "We are dead. We are sunk beneath the sea."

Shanna tried to comfort her, to murmur, to pat her fears away, but Lychma could not be silenced, and her voice, speaking in the old tongue, the Shawnee tongue, rambled on, whispering and faltering, until the last of the slaves had been placed in the hold, the hatch shut for the last time, a lock placed on it.

The boat shifted, and the silent ones around them sat resigned to all of it. To death in life, to slavery, to pain, to the darkness and the power of the sea and the men who sailed it.

"Where is she?"

"I do not know. I did as you asked and walked through Potaqua's camp. I saw nothing of her, nothing of her sister."

"They are locked up in a slave hut then."

"I looked in each one, Yui," Pohoy said. "The slave overseers did not like it, but they did not dare challenge me. I saw a hundred women. I saw old ones and young, heavy women and some as thin and frail as autumn leaves. I did not see the Shawnee woman, nor did I see her sister."

"No one could tell you?" Yui asked. He rose in agitation.

"Few spoke the Seminole tongue. Those few feared to answer. No one knew." Pohoy shrugged massively.

"Something is wrong."

"Perhaps they have gone to a rice field, to pick berries, to pick corn, Yui. We know nothing about this camp. Many things are possible. Ask Potaqua."

"No," the Seminole war leader answered, turning around, "that is one thing I will not do. But you know as well as I, Pohoy, that it is too late for them to be working at anything you have suggested."

"I have seen rice cropped by torchlight."

"Yes, so have I. But there is no torchlight."

"Then what?"

"Then what indeed? I have asked Potaqua to do nothing against those Shawnee women, but what is Potaqua's word ever worth?" Yui frowned and looked around his small camp, at his men who were sleeping or playing at sticks or speaking in low voices.

"Do you wish us to search?" Pohoy asked, and now he was smiling.

"Yes." Yui rubbed his arm. "There is nothing amusing about this, Pohoy."

"No," the big warrior agreed quickly. "I do not smile because the situation is amusing. I smile because my war leader is so concerned about a woman who—forgive me—cannot stand the sight of Yui's face."

"It requires little to amuse you," Yui grumbled.

"What will you have us do then, Yui?"

"Search!" He waved his hands in a wide arc. "Look for the women. Something is wrong."

"Yes, Yui." Pohoy started to smile again, but there was an urgency in Yui's voice. The spirits had fluttered down to whisper in his ear. He knew something his senses had not told him.

Pohoy rousted Yui's warriors. Dividing them into four teams, he sent them out. Then he returned to Yui.

"Which way for us?"

"I don't know." All the same Yui was up, walking toward the sea. Pohoy, musket in hand, war ax at his waist, trailed after his leader.

"The Spanish man," Pohoy said suddenly, sharply. He stopped, and Yui turned toward him.

"What did you say?"

"The Spanish man, Yui. Can he have anything to do with this?"

"Anything is possible. Let us look at their ship."

"How?" Pohoy laughed in astonishment. "It is far at sea."

"Can we not swim?"

Yui turned and hurried on. The moon was slowly rising now, a pale sentinel above the dark forest. Strong shadows appeared beneath the trees.

"We will not have to swim," Yui said. He crouched down, looking at the moon-bright beach. There sat the Spanish launch with two sailors.

"They are Potaqua's friends," Pohoy said cautiously. "There may be trouble."

"Yes."

Yui walked parallel with the beach, staying just within the forest. He stopped and crouched, holding up a hand. Pohoy went to him.

The moon showed them clearly. Many tracks. Fifty people or more had come this way, walked down to the beach and vanished into the sea. Some of the tracks were those of boots. The type worn by the Spanish men.

"Potaqua has . . ."

Yui shushed his lieutenant. Creeping to the verge of the trees, he got to his belly, studying the sailors and the waiting launch, lifting his eyes to the sailing ship at anchor beyond the surf.

"What do you want me to do?" Pohoy asked, and Yui told him.

The big man waited while Yui slipped away to the north, then he retraced his own tracks southward. Placing his musket aside, Pohoy walked onto the beach, gesturing to the sailors.

"Hey you men. Come here. Let's have rum and dance!"

Pohoy's Spanish was atrocious. He heard the sailors laugh. "Sounds like this one's already had enough of that stinking rum."

"Go away, Seminole!"

"Come here! Let's have rum together like friends!" Pohoy shouted again. The sailors' eyes were on Pohoy. They did not see the darting shadow cross the beach to the north and slip into the sea like an otter.

Pohoy, staggering to fit his role, started toward the sailors, his hands spread wide. "Come on, Spanish. Our chiefs drink rum together. Let us also."

"Go away, Indian. You will get us in trouble," the sailor shouted back.

Before the last word was out of his mouth, Yui had emerged from the dark sea. Leaping across the boat, he took the first man before he had turned around. The second turned and

91

started to run, but Yui dragged him down by his heels and clubbed him.

"Now. Let us see if our people should have been sailors," Yui said.

Pohoy shoved off, running into the surf with the boat as Yui rowed. The first wave nearly swamped them, but they made it through the surf line, both men pulling strongly on the oars as the coming moon painted a golden band across the dark sea.

There was no sound. Even the working of the oars, the small splash as they dipped into the sea, the squeal of the oarlocks, was covered by the hammering of the distant surf.

There were only the two silent men, the dark bulk of the sailing ship against the western sky, the rising moon. Yui rowed well past the ship, keeping far away from it to turn and come up on the seaward side where no intruder would be expected.

Pohoy leaned out to hold the boat away from the ship. The sound of the boat knocking against the hull would be clearly audible inside the Spanish ship.

Yui nodded, looked up, and found purchase. He climbed like a dark cat and then was up and over the rail, lying panting in the darkness.

Ahead he heard the slow pacing of a sentry, above him the creak of rigging. The sea slapped against the hull of the ship. Otherwise there were no sounds.

Yui lifted his head, looking around. He had never been on a ship before. Where would they keep a slave? Obviously the belly of the ship was larger than its head. Below the decks, then. There must be a door of some kind. Since there were no guards on the deck but the one forward, the door was one which could be closed and latched from the outside.

These thoughts ran through his mind in a fraction of a minute. He crept toward the mainmast, eyes searching the deck. He did not see the hatch at first. It wasn't what he had expected, but crouching down, he found the latch, and putting his ear to the hatch, he made out low murmuring, quiet sounds of despair.

Sucking in his breath, Yui rose and made his silent way across the deck. The lookout must be done away with.

He slipped through the shadows and stood beside the high

deckhouse, where he had seen the lookout pass twice before. Pressing himself against the salt-smelling wood, Yui waited.

He counted the steps of the lookout, holding himself perfectly still, and as his head came around the corner of the cabin Yui smashed down with his closed hand, landing a solid blow at the base of the sailor's skull.

Then he recrossed the deck, searching for and finding a prybar to break the latch free. Yui crouched to his work, eyes shuttling about the deck of the Spanish slaver, knowing that there must be other sailors aboard, perhaps many of them.

He forced the prybar into the hasp and tugged twice before metal snapped and the latch flew free, landing on the deck with a clattering metallic sound. Yui placed the bar aside and slowly lifted the edge of the hatch, recoiling in disgust at the fetid odors which wafted up from the crowded hold.

Shanna looked up, certain she had seen cold starlight seeping into the hold. Her hand tightened over Lychma's and her head came up.

"What is it?"

"Sh!"

"Someone is up there. Now they're going to kill us," Lychma said positively. "It's over and we're dead."

"Be quiet," Shanna hissed. The hatch had been lifted higher, and now a murmur ran through the hold. People stood and started waving their arms.

"Be quiet," Shanna told them. But they would not be silent. They were desperate people, and this was a desperate chance. They surged forward toward the ladder which led to the open hatch, toward clean air, freedom.

Shanna herself looked up, seeing the dark silhouette of their rescuer against the star-strewn sky. There was something familiar about the man.

"Shanna?" he called, bending down. Already people were scrambling up the ladder, jostling each other, knocking each other aside.

"Yui!" Shanna's exclamation was a gasp. She grabbed at Lychma's hand. "Come on. Quickly."

Lychma followed docilely, but the situation was hopeless. The slaves were storming the ladder, their voices raised in pathetic cries, and although Yui was begging them to be silent they continued hysterically.

"Shanna?" Yui had to fight off the upward-rushing slaves. Shoulders slammed into him. Those below clawed at his ankles. "Shanna!"

"Here, Yui!" she called. Her hand was clamped around Lychma's wrist. She could see Yui above her, peering down into the black pit of the hold, trying to find her as he fended off the mob. Then he saw her.

"Wait there. Wait there!"

He turned and was gone, and Lychma moaned. "Now they will kill us."

Shanna turned her sister's face toward her. She shook her shoulders. "Lychma!"

"It is over. Small ones whisper death."

"Lychma!"

Shanna felt the tears sting her eyes. Lychma was aware of nothing. She was lost in an underworld peopled by mad things. She shook her again, but Lychma's head only snapped back and forth on her neck. Her eyes glistened in the starlight. She looked directly at Shanna and asked: "Who are you, woman? Am I always to be your slave?"

Above decks, Yui hastily snatched up the coil of rope he had found. He looked around in dismay. The slaves were running to the rails, leaping into the dark waters. Others shouted and yelled. Some were trampled to the deck.

The lantern flooded the deck suddenly, and from a cabin door burst a dozen Spanish men in night dress, muskets in their hands.

No sooner had Yui seen them than the guns opened fire. The roar of the guns was deafening in the night. Flame spewed from the muzzles of the muskets, and the slaves screamed.

A man beside Yui went down, holding his bloody face. Yui ducked low and rushed back to the open hatch, where the slaves were in vast confusion, those below pressing upward, those above who were caught in the murderous assault trying for the safety of the hold.

He heard a savage cry behind him and by lanternlight saw the sailors wading into the mob of slaves, cutting right and left with sabers.

Yui called down again: "Shanna!"

"Here!" Her voice was barely audible above the roar.

Yui uncoiled his rope and tossed the end down. "Take it," he cried.

"Lychma!"

"She will be next." A musket ball flew past Yui's head and buried itself in the mast behind him. "Hurry, Shanna! Lychma will be next. Take the rope!"

He felt her weight on the line, and, standing, bracing his foot against the hatch frame, he began to haul her upward, his great shoulder muscles working desperately until her face appeared above the hatch frame. He reached down, yanking her up onto the deck.

"Stay down!" he shouted. With dismay Shanna surveyed the slaughter on the deck. The slaves were dying before her eyes. Others leaped wildly into the sea. The sailors advanced with muskets and sabers, cutting down those few who tried to fight.

Yui was lowering his line again, and Shanna crept to the open hatch.

"Lychma! Lychma!"

She saw her sister's face turn up to her, saw the blank expression, the limp posture, the vacant eyes.

"Lychma, take the rope!"

"I will not be your slave!"

Yui spun. A sailor, saber raised, was upon him. The Seminole ducked low, came up with his knee lifted high, driving it into the sailor's belly, and slammed his clenched fist down on the back of the man's neck.

Shanna had caught the rope, and now with dismay she felt it being torn from her grasp. Looking down, she saw a dozen hands grabbing for the line. Frantic, upturned faces looked toward her. Lychma was among them.

"Lychma!"

"Lash the line to the mast!" Yui shouted.

The rope was being torn from her grip. Shanna's hands were burning. The flesh was being torn from them as five slaves tried to climb the rope which she held in her hands. Lychma stood alone, laughing madly. Yui turned to meet a second sailor, their bodies colliding with a loud slap as Yui tried to tear the saber from the Spanish man's hands.

"Yui!"

He could do nothing. He fought desperately with the sailor.

95

Across the deck the muskets opened fire again, and again slaves fell, the reek of gunpowder drifting across the deck.

"Lychma!"

She could hold it no longer; the rope was torn from Shanna's hands, and she fell to the deck.

The strong hands were around her waist, and she was snatched up and thrown across Yui's shoulder.

"My sister!"

Yui did not answer, or perhaps he did. The din on the tumultuous deck was deafening.

"My sister!"

More sailors had appeared on the deck, and they continued to fire muskets at close range, to hack out in frenzied panic at the confused slaves. Perhaps the sailors, awakened in the dead of night, believed themselves to be under attack.

Yui looked again at the hatch, where screams still sounded, at the deck, washed with lanternlight and blood. There was no returning for Lychma. To try it would mean death for Shanna and himself.

Moving swiftly through the dense cloud of powder smoke, Yui reached the railing. Shanna struggled desperately in his arms, but he held her tightly. Then, stepping over the rail with Shanna on his shoulder still, he leaped into the black water.

They bobbed up from out of the temporary liquid silence of the sea, and Pohoy's hands reached out for them. Shanna was dragged aboard the launch, and Yui slithered up to sit in the bow, his hands already working the oars.

They rowed seaward, still watching the deadly pantomime on the ship's deck. Shadows writhing in the lanternlight, leaping men. People falling silently. Dying.

Shanna could only stare. She was soaking wet, her hair across her face. Yui and Pohoy rowed silently. The gentle swell of the dark sea lifted them. And on the black three-master people were dying. Shots echoed dully across the water.

In the hold Lychma, half mad, was watching, listening to the sounds of death. And she was alone. Shanna turned her eyes toward Yui, despising him at that moment. It was because of his interference that Lychma was enduring that; it was because of Yui that the slaves had died.

"What did you bring me out for?" she asked.

"Shanna."

"What did you bring me out for? Have you decided I will be useful to you? Have you decided to take me for your slave?"

"I have freed you."

"You have torn my heart out! To be separated from my sister is worse than slavery."

Yui clamped his jaw tightly and bent his back to his work, and Shanna sagged back against the thwart to stare at the dark and empty sea.

They beached the launch a mile south and made their way back toward Yui's temporary camp. Shanna knew what was happening, but she seemed not to be taking part in it. They had told her to step from the boat, and she had. Now they were jogging through the palm trees, the sand soft underfoot. She was another person in her own body. Her soul, her mind, floated on the sea. Each man had taken an arm, and they rushed her forward.

"Run, Shanna," Pohoy encouraged her, and she tried. But she did not care. What was the good of running? Where were they running? Why?

All of her life had been an escape, given meaning only as long as there was Lychma to be taken care of, and now there was no Lychma. Only two Seminole men she cared nothing for.

"Look!" Pohoy lifted a hand, and Shanna's eyes shifted toward the sea and the Spanish ship. Sail was being run up. Men clambered in the rigging.

They stood soundlessly watching. Wind filled the sails and the dark ship creaked into motion. Then it was away, sailing southward toward distant lands, leaving behind its human flotsam, carrying in its hold misery and madness. Shanna felt her knees buckle, and she fell. They did not try to hold her up; no one spoke.

After a long while, when the ship was only a small indistinct dot against the moon-glossed sea, Yui touched her on the shoulder, and she rose, turning toward him.

"We must travel on. Potaqua will already know of this. He will see it as a betrayal."

97

"Yes," Shanna agreed, although she was indifferent to Potaqua's vengeance.

"Shanna, I do not want you to be afraid. I do not want you to worry. I can do nothing to bring Lychma back, but I promise you that I will take care of you. You will never again be a slave. Listen to me! Perhaps now you do not care in your grief, but I want you to understand that I will let nothing harm you again."

"It is time, Yui," Pohoy said.

"Yes. It is time." Yui turned away briefly, and Shanna saw his shoulders lift as he took a slow deep breath into his lungs. "Let us go, Shanna. We have done what we could do."

She nodded, and they started on again, into the swamps, turning their backs on the vast and mocking sea.

They traveled eastward through the week, making their way along the hidden trails. At the end of the week they came finally to Yui's camp along the Saskatch River. There were a hundred chickees scattered along the river's edge, extending back into the bay cedars which dominated this area.

Smoke rose from cooking fires, dogs yapped, children came running, and men emerged from their houses to greet the returning warlord.

They crowded around Yui, calling to him, slapping his back, shouting questions he could not hear.

Shanna stood aside, ignored, weary. Yui drew the eyes of all of his people. He was the focus of their attention. With one exception.

The woman was young and sleek, haughty and quite beautiful. She wore silver bracelets of white manufacture. She alone stood, arms crossed, staring at Shanna. Shanna was too exhausted, too empty, to care. Perhaps this woman would be her new mistress.

Then, with a toss of her head, the Seminole woman pushed through the assembled crowd and walked to Yui, putting her hands on his chest, and Shanna understood the veiled hostility she had seen in the other's eyes.

You need not concern yourself, Shanna thought. I do not need a man; I do not want one. If I did it would not be this savage of yours.

"Shanna?" A hand touched her shoulder, and she twisted around to find Pohoy standing there.

"Did I startle you?" he asked.

"Of course not."

"Let us eat. Then I will find you a house to stay in."

Docilely Shanna went with Pohoy, feeling the gaze of the other woman on her back.

"Teska sees you as a rival," Pohoy said.

"Is that her name?"

"Yes, Teska."

"You will tell her that this poor slave girl cares nothing for her man."

"If you wish it, Shanna."

"And," she added, "you may say the same thing to Yui."

"If you wish it, Shanna."

They had come to a communal pot which simmered away in the shade of a thatched lean-to. There two older women chatted away, stirring the pot, which contained fish chowder strengthened with maize and wild onions.

Pohoy greeted them both, hugged one, and allowed them to fill a bowl for him. "This is Shanna," he said around his mouthful of steaming food. "A woman of the Shawnee nation who has come to stay with us. She will need a bed and work to do."

"Yes, Pohoy."

He waved a finger. "But no work for a while. The woman is tired. Her journey has been a long one."

"Can she speak our language, Pohoy?"

Pohoy looked at Shanna and smiled wryly. "When she wishes it, Mother Holotok."

"I see." The Seminole woman nodded. "I only asked so that I would know where to put her. How can she work with people who cannot speak to her? If she could not speak our tongue then I would have her live with the strangers." She put her hands on her massive hips and peered at Shanna. "Eat, child," she said. "Eat and then we will bathe you and give you new moccasins. I am Mother Holotok. Mother to all of the people. Eat now and do not worry—Mother Holotok will take care of everything."

The woman's words were kind. She was gentle and generous, but Shanna could not respond to that generosity. She took a bowl and ate silently while Pohoy regaled the women with war tales and bold, funny lies.

Finally Pohoy rose and stretched. "I must see my wife. I must bathe. I must sleep. Go with Mother, Shanna. She will give you what you need."

"Yes, Pohoy."

The girl was listless. There was no gleam in her eyes. Pohoy looked at Mother Holotok and lifted a shoulder in a slight shrug. Then, picking up his musket and war bag, Pohoy turned and strode across the camp toward the crowd which was still gathered around Yui.

Shanna put her bowl aside, the chowder half eaten. Then she too rose. "I am ready, Holotok."

"You must call me Mother Holotok."

Shanna nodded absently. She felt the Seminole woman's hands on her shoulders, and she looked up.

"Shawnee girl, we all have misfortune. It is the way of this life. I see that you carry a burden of sorrow. So do we all. I will not tell you to forget the grief you feel, but do not let it cripple you, Shanna."

"I am ready to be shown my bed," Shanna said. Mother Holotok nodded, her hands falling away from Shanna's shoulders.

"All right. I will show you where you will live and then you may bathe in the river. I have salve for your feet. You have come far; they must be sore. If you wish to sleep, do so. If you grow hungry again, come back. Our pot is always on the fire. We never know when the hunters will return, and they are ready to eat at all times."

"Yes, Holotok."

The woman shook her head, told the other woman she would return shortly, and led Shanna off toward the bay cedars which grew in profusion to the south of the river. There were dozens of chickees scattered among the trees. Small children looked up from their play to greet "Mother" Holotok and gape at Shanna. A few followed along behind as Shanna was taken to a hut far back in the trees.

Sunlight twinkled through the foliage. The air was still. Somewhere far away a loon cried.

"This girl is called Pamda. It is not her real name, but that is what she chooses to be called. She is a gentle creature, Shanna. Small. I wonder at times how she came to be upon this earth. She will make a good friend, but she will not understand harsh words. Do I make myself clear?"

"I will be kind to her, Holotok."

"Yes, I believe you will." She lifted her chin. "Come along then, let us go up into Pamda's house."

Shanna climbed the ladder behind Holotok, whose massive frame caused the ladder to tremble. Soon they were up into the chickee and Shanna got her first look at her housemate.

"Small, gentle" did not describe Pamda.

The girl cowered in the corner. She was dirty and frail, with huge round eyes, a small nose, and a wide mouth. Her lip was trembling.

"It is I, Pamda, only I, Mother Holotok."

"I did not know you," a small, distant voice answered, a voice which might have come from anywhere but which apparently had come from the tiny cringing woman in the corner of the chickee. Pamda lifted a trembling finger, pointed at Shanna, gargled something, and turned away, burying her face in her arms.

"It is all right, Pamda," Mother Holotok said, sitting on the mat beside the girl. She did not touch her, however. "This is Shanna. She has come to live with you and be your sister."

Slowly the head came around and a wan, fleeting smile passed over the girl's lips.

"She will be all right now," Mother Holotok said, slowly raising herself to her feet. "Pamda, you take care of Shanna now. Give her a blanket and whatever else she requires."

"Yes, Mother," Pamda replied.

Then with a small nod Mother Holotok was gone, and Shanna stood wondering what she had gotten herself into now. Pamda, if not insane, was on the edge of sanity. Her eyes glittered and failed to focus properly as she moved about the room, looking for a blanket.

She opened a cane trunk, and Shanna saw a number of burned and broken objects: a straw doll with no head, a rabbit-skin cape scorched and mutilated, a comb which had been snapped in half.

Shanna was too tired to wonder much about those objects. She wanted to sleep for days. To bathe first and then to crawl beneath a blanket when the evening came in on cooling wings.

Pamda had found a blanket. She placed it on the floor between them, watching Shanna with doe eyes. Shanna thanked her.

She selected an empty corner and put the blanket there. "I must go to the river to wash, Pamda," she told the young woman. There was no answer. Pamda put her hands to her hair and lifted it high above her head, grinning madly for a moment.

Shanna sighed and went out.

She walked deeper into the forest, avoiding the camp. The cedar trees were tall, stately, and comforting as they closed around her. She passed an ancient black mangrove hung with greenbriar vines and Spanish moss. A scarlet cardinal bounced from bough to bough, following her for a way.

She reached the riverbank at a point half a mile or so upriver from Yui's camp. There the Saskatch looped around in a lazy bend. There the water was clear and free of the pests born of stagnation.

"Shanna."

She spun around angrily. It was Yui, emerging from behind a towering magnolia tree, his hair freshly combed, his body freshly washed.

"Why are you following me?"

"I wanted to talk to you."

"Go away, Yui, master, warlord."

"Shanna . . ."

"Yui," she said, "I am weary. I cannot listen to you."

"You are still angry."

"Angry?" She was thoughtful for a moment. "Yes, I am angry. I cannot forget, Yui, that if it had not been for you my sister and I would be traveling northward still, perhaps nearing our home."

"You do not understand." Yui took a few steps forward. The shadows cast by the silent tree played across his chest and arms. "It was something I had to do."

"You had to do it!" Shanna's laughter was harsh, mocking. "You had to take two women and deliver them into slavery."

Yui was angry now. When he spoke the muscles of his jaw twitched. His eyes were cold. "I had to maintain a good relationship with Potaqua. There is a war moving across the land, Shanna. We are a small tribe and we are alone. With Potaqua we would have had strength. I did it for my people. A small gift, a small gesture."

"Two small lives!"

"I did not know you then."

"Would that have made a difference?"

"It did, did it not—later? I threw away an alliance I sorely needed to bring you off the Spanish slaver."

"Should I be grateful? Grateful that you destroyed my only chance for happiness. Grateful because belatedly you did what was right, causing more deaths."

"I had hoped you would understand, Shanna. Understand that I meant to do what was right for my people, for the hundreds who trust me for their protection. And I did hope for your gratitude. I hoped that you would understand what it cost me to insult Potaqua by trying to free you and Lychma. I see now that you cannot understand. Will not. You do not think of the hundreds who are now in danger because of my act."

"I wish to bathe." Shanna turned her back. Her heart was thumping annoyingly. "Please go away now, Yui. Go back to Teska, who must understand more than this poor Shawnee woman can."

She stood waiting for his retort, preparing another sally of her own. But there was no sound except the whispering of the wind, the far-off cry of a mockingbird. She turned to find Yui gone.

"Good," she thought, removing her skirt and linen shirt angrily. Her eyes, however, went to the forest, and her heart continued its incessant thumping. She spun around and walked into the river, ducking under to rise and wipe back her hair, letting the river current swirl around her as she stood looking toward the shore, feeling suddenly foolish and small and quite lonely.

The clouds beyond the trees were pink and swirled when Shanna stepped from the river and trudged back toward the village of the Seminole, Yui. She was no longer tired, and she found that difficult to explain to herself. Nothing had changed and yet she felt that much had.

"You are free now," she told herself. "Take new moccasins and food and walk northward. Perhaps you could not go to the land of the Shawnee. But there is a world to the north and east where people live in peace. Where Cherokee and Creek and white men live side by side."

And he would let me go, she thought. Oddly, that thought

irritated her too. Where was he now? In the forest with the woman Teska? Lying beside her, speaking softly. Perhaps they laughed together at the foolish Shawnee woman. . . .

She had reached Pamda's house. Beside the ladder stood Mother Holotok. She smiled as she looked up.

"I was hoping you would be back."

"Did you think I would not?"

Mother Holotok only shrugged. "It is for Pamda that I wondered. She finds it difficult to sleep if no one is with her. Before I always sat with her until she fell off to sleep. Then she is all right; she sleeps heavily. I wondered if you would come back or if I should sit with her, that is all."

"Pamda is not well," Shanna said. She leaned against the ladder, placing her foot on a cane rung, looking at Mother Holotok, whose silhouette was backlighted by the flaming sundown.

"She is not well."

"What happened to her, Holotok? Or has she always been like this? Where are her parents, her family?"

"I am her mother as I am mother to all the tribe," Holotok answered.

"But her real mother."

"She who cares is the real mother of a child."

Shanna decided that Holotok was not going to answer the questions she had put to her. But the Seminole woman surprised her. She began to speak, and when she did it was as if the sea had been turned loose to flood the shores. Her words followed one upon the heels of the other.

At first she said only: "Pamda is the six hundredth."

Shanna did not think she had heard right, although the number was immediately familiar. Perhaps her knowledge of the Seminole language was not so good as she had thought.

"The six hundredth?"

"Yes."

"I do not understand you, Holotok."

"It is this way—Walk a little way through the forest with me, Shanna. . . . When the war was only a distant rumor we lived along the Suwanee. White men came to our camp to speak to the war chief of our people, Kamdawotekee, who was the father to the man Yui."

They moved through the darkened forest now, Mother

105

Holotok leading the way. "These white men called themselves Americans. Their leader was the war chief Boggs. He had come to tell Kamdawotekee that he must join with the Americans and fight back the Spanish men.

"Kamdawotekee said he had no wish to war. He was a peaceful man who fought when aroused, but the Spanish men had done him no harm. If they did do his people harm, then Kamdawotekee would make his own war. He did not want an alliance with the strangers.

"But Boggs warned him that he must fight with the Americans or against them. He grew very angry, and then Kamdawotekee, who was a composed man, grew angry as well.

"A man does not come into your home and make demands, threaten, insult his host. Kamdawotekee threw the man out and told Boggs never to return.

"But he did. He returned in a horrible fashion."

Mother Holotok had stopped, and she lowered her great bulk onto the twisted, arched root of a mangrove tree. Beyond Holotok the land was dark, but Shanna could hear moving water splashing merrily into a pool beyond the trees.

"What happened?" Shanna asked.

"Who knows?" Holotok sighed heavily. "Perhaps the man Boggs is vengeful. Perhaps he feared that Kamdawotekee was allied with the Spanish men."

"He returned."

"He returned with fire and death and terror. In the dead of night we fled our chickees, but it was too late. They were among us and they struck us down. Men were shot in their beds, women were butchered, children put to the sword. We ran into the swamps and we watched, we listened to the horror of it. We heard our own husbands dying, we heard our own children screaming, women crying for mercy . . . and then they were all gone. The flames were long in dying.

"My children. I found them dead. Five children. Dead in their father's arms. I had no one. I was mother to no one.

"We counted them," Holotok said. Her voice was still passionless, but her hands tore at her thighs. Her mouth was pulled down with grief. "Five hundred and ninety-nine of our people were dead. Five children, one husband. Five hundred and ninety-three friends. And the last one."

"Pamda."

"Yes, Pamda," Holotok said. "She was a child. She had seen her family murdered. I found her wandering the camp. Her hair was smoldering, her hands were burned. She was carrying a small box with her little toys in it. The box had been ravaged by fire.

"I took her to me. I took her for my daughter. I took all of them. All who had lost their mothers to be my own. My children . . . were gone."

"And Kamdawotekee? What did he do?"

"Kamdawotekee? What could he do? He was dead as well. He had been the first man to be killed. His body was humiliated. They tore him apart as wolves will savage a fox. He was dead, our leader. He was dead and he too had left an orphan. But the orphan of Kamdawotekee was not one to sit stunned and crying, to wail to Manitou, to weep against the ashes. He was a strong boy, this one, and as the fires still burned Yui stood among the men and said: 'I am now war leader. Let us follow Boggs. Let us avenge this cowardly attack.'

"The older warriors, of course, argued against it. It was folly to pursue Boggs, who had come with a thousand men and a dozen cannon. Yet they recognized the courage in the youth and applauded it. When it was time for Yui to be confirmed as war leader they voted enthusiastically for him.

"He was war leader. The youngest ever to rise from our ranks. He spoke to all of us on that night. His voice was intense, his eyes hard and slashing. He made the promise to us."

"The promise?"

"The promise, which is all we ever call it. He promised that such a tragedy would never happen again. He promised that no white man would set foot in our camp. He promised that he would do what needed to be done to avenge the massacre. He promised that he would make strong alliances which would prevent the whites from returning."

With Potaqua, Shanna thought. With Potaqua and with any other who would make Yui's people strong enough so that they did not have to fear a repetition of that night's slaughter.

That was how much an alliance with Potaqua meant: a sacred vow, a promise made to his people. The six hundred. How could he have acted other than he had when he had found Shanna and Lychma wandering the swamps, knowing that they were Potaqua's property? And how much had it cost him, she wondered, to free her from the slavers, knowing Potaqua would turn his back on Yui's people, knowing that without allies these people were subject to another brutal attack?

"Your thoughts are far distant," Holotok said. "I only spoke so that you would understand us. So that you would understand Pamda, who is the six hundredth. You see, Shawnee woman, Pamda died that night. Her soul was taken. She is only a husk, a wandering child in a woman's body. Slight, frightened, helpless."

"I will be a friend to her," Shanna said. She was moved by Mother Holotok's tale, yet she couldn't help wondering if there wasn't another reason besides explaining Pamda's behavior for having been told it.

They parted in the forest. Shanna picked her way back to the camp and climbed the ladder to the chickee. Pamda sat up abruptly, staring at Shanna in the same wide-eyed desolate way.

"Go to sleep, Pamda. It is only Shanna."

"They come at night. They come and do terrible things. They come with fire and thunder. They come and in their rage do evil things."

"But not tonight. I shall watch for them."

"They can fly. They fly and then they swoop and one sees only their shadows. Then there is nothing at all because one is dead. It is odd being dead," Pamda said. She sat perfectly still, her head cocked to one side. Then, somehow satisfied, she lay down and slept while Shanna sat in the entranceway of the chickee, a blanket around her shoulders, watching the fires from the Seminole camp dance on the river, watching the distant beaming stars, wondering where Lychma was on this night, thinking about distant wars and the man Yui.

"Twenty-two men, one child, three women, sir."

"The bastard." General George Boggs drummed against his desk top with his stubby fingers. His other hand held a cigar. His pale-green eyes searched the young officers' faces, peering out of a fleshy, florid face decorated with white muttonchop whiskers.

The younger of the two junior officers, Captain James

Dawes, thought that the general's eyes reflected little compassion for the twenty-six Cherokee Indians killed by raiding Seminoles.

The general put them at ease, and they took seats across Boggs's desk, accepting an offer of brandy. In the meantime Boggs paced the room, his office in the headquarters building of the rough stockaded fort named for President Madison.

Fort Madison, on the St. Johns River, was squarely in the middle of the agricultural preserve allotted to the southern Cherokee. The garrison was composed of five companies of infantry, one of artillery. The Seminole Potaqua had boldly attacked a Cherokee camp not three miles from this military post, the symbol of American strength along the St. Johns which had been built as a warning to Spanish forces and as reassurance to the "civilized" tribes of northern Florida and southern Georgia.

True, it was secretly intended as a device of intimidation. The Cherokee and Creek, many of the Choctaw, had laid down their arms and taken up white agriculture. They were told that they needed no arms. Fort Madison was at once a reinforcement of treaty terms and a promise to the Cherokee that America would henceforward be their protector.

"Damn him," Boggs said with no more anger than before. It was a mathematical problem to Boggs, not a matter of life and death. He was a great tactician, but cold as ice.

"What will be our course of action, sir?" Major Thomas Harkness asked. Harkness was a confident, self-important, red-haired man. He drank too much. He despised all Indians.

"Counterattack. You know me that well, Tom." Boggs managed a dry laugh.

"He's had time to reach the swamps again, sir," James Dawes said. "We haven't had much luck following Potaqua into his refuge."

"I have no intention of pursuing Potaqua, Captain Dawes."

James Dawes lifted an eyebrow. Thomas Harkness, who somehow found this amusing, smiled at his surprise.

"Excuse me, sir. I assumed we would pursue and punish."

"And lose another company of men out in those swamps? Not likely, sir."

"Captain Dawes was not with us on that expedition, sir," Harkness reminded the general.

"No." Boggs cleared his throat and spat in the corner. "Well, he drew us in after him, the old fox Potaqua. Drew us in and bogged us down. The caissons went first. Sank into quicksand out there. Three cases of snakebite. Two fatal. Yellow fever killed thirteen men and made a dozen others unfit for combat.

"We trudged on, wanting by this time to meet the devil and inflict some casualties of our own. But the Seminoles are ghosts in the swamp. They flanked us and sniped at us—used poisoned arrows too, the savages." Boggs furrowed his brow. Poisoned arrows seemed to strike him as barbaric compared to a clean musket ball.

"I couldn't swear we took a single Seminole warrior in combat, Dawes."

"The official report was thirteen dead," Harkness interjected. He still smiled. Thomas Harkness appeared to have an odd sense of humor.

"Thirteen by guess and by damn. I saw only two corpses, and one I suspect was dead of the same fever we had got, the other I am not sure was Seminole—the alligators made identification difficult."

"What then is your plan, sir, if I may ask?"

"We will retaliate, Captain Dawes, have no doubt about that. I assure you we will retaliate. The Seminole must be taught that they cannot act with impunity against America or her subjects."

"The Saskatch Seminoles?" Harkness asked.

"Precisely. You understand my methods well, Major Harkness." Boggs seated himself in his leather chair and leaned back in deep satisfaction. He toyed with his sideburns. "You will therefore organize an expeditionary force to that end, major."

"I beg your pardon, sir," Dawes said. "It seems that you and the major have a perfect understanding of this strategy. I must admit, however, that I am a bit confused by this. Perhaps I do not see your objective clearly."

"I don't see what in hell is the least bit confusing, Captain Dawes."

"You mean to attack the Saskatch Seminoles. That is—a people who had no part in this battle."

"Who is to say they did not?"

"I thought I heard the general say that it was certainly Potaqua who was responsible."

"Only Potaqua? Did I say that, Major Harkness?"

"No, sir, you did not," Harkness answered.

"No, I did not. The fact is that warriors from many Seminole subtribes could have been involved, Captain Dawes."

"But, sir, if you are positive it was Potaqua and unsure about any responsibility on the part of the Saskatch Seminoles . . ."

"Captain, I hardly expected criticism from my junior officers." Boggs's red face deepened to a red-violet. "You are recently arrived here from Jackson's force. Perhaps Andrew Jackson fights a different sort of war than I have been forced to fight. Perhaps he can afford to be merciful and meek."

"I am not sure either adjective applies to Jackson, sir. However . . ."

"There is no however, captain. I was wondering how it came about that Jackson made available a man of your record. Perhaps I am beginning to understand." Boggs went on, "The Seminoles came onto the reservation and killed twenty-six of my charges. They have thrown their challenge into my face, captain. I cannot let this pass unavenged, not if I do not expect a repetition of this event. I will therefore punish the Seminoles. If one tribe of Seminoles cannot be found, then another will have to do. I know the leader of these Saskatch Seminoles anyway. A man named Yui. He has given me trouble in the past. His father gave me trouble. They are a recalcitrant lot. It can do no harm to give them a taste of powder and lead. That is what I intend to do. That is what will be done.

"Now," Boggs said, leaning back, "I think I've gone quite far enough out of my way to explain a simple matter to a junior officer who seems not to understand what this Florida war is all about. You are dismissed, sir."

"Yes, sir." Dawes stood and saluted, his face expressionless, his eyes staring at a distant point beyond General George Boggs's head, beyond the wall of the fort.

"By the way, captain," Boggs said after Dawes had already turned away and started toward the door, "what is your real name?"

"Sir?" Dawes felt his back go rigid. He continued to face the door, not turning back toward the general. Harkness was smirking insufferably. *He knows*, Dawes thought.

"Your true name, captain?"

"My legal and true name is James Dawes, sir."

"And your father's name?"

"Sir?" Dawes' mouth was dry and cottony. His throat was constricted.

"Your father's name, Dawes. Is that too difficult a question, or do you not know your father's name?"

Harkness—damn him—laughed again.

"My father's name was William Van der Veghe," Dawes said. He still had not moved. "Will that be all, sir?"

"That is all, Dawes," the general said, his voice reflecting amusement and triumph.

"Very good." With that Dawes walked out the door, strode through the orderly room, and walked out onto the plankwalk before the headquarters offices.

He swore beneath his breath and looked to the skies, which were an incredible blue flecked here and there with puffball clouds scudding seaward, riding the winds aloft. Dawes pulled on his chin strap and looked toward the officers' quarters across the parade ground, automatically seeking Julia's window. He felt the plankwalk move beneath his boots and turned to find Major Thomas Harkness, the general's fair-haired boy, the young and arrogant and haughty Thomas Harkness, standing behind him.

"Don't pay any attention to all of George's blustering," Harkness said. "He is a man who is watching his career be eroded. He wishes to rival Jackson and knows he cannot. Overall our general's campaigns have been inept and ineffective, you see. He has to show some result, doesn't he? When you challenged his tactics, you were scratching at old wounds, James."

"I suppose so." They had started walking toward the officers' quarters, listening and watching as a noncommissioned officer put an infantry platoon through its drill. "Dammit, though, Harkness, this striking out angrily in all directions at any target is going to stir up more resentment than anything else. Potaqua is guilty, but the camp of Yui is more accessible; therefore Yui is attacked."

112

"Absurd, is it not?" Harkness yawned. "He will be found out, our General Boggs, and he must know it. He has been peculiarly ineffective for such a tactical genius. But then the Florida swamps are hardly Yorktown."

"How did he find out?" Dawes asked.

"Find out what, James?" They had halted before the officers' quarters. The foot soldiers still drilled on the parade ground. Beyond them the trading post was bustling with activity as the Cherokee unpacked bundles of furs, otter for the most part, and muskrat and skunk along with varieties of snake skins, coral, shells, feathers, and an assortment of gathered oddities.

"Find out about me, my name?"

"Is that why you left Andy Jackson?"

Dawes hesitated. He removed his cap and wiped back his pale hair. "Yes," he said finally.

"I thought as much."

It was at that moment that the door to the dependents' quarters opened and Julia Trevor emerged. Her green eyes were bright. Her full lips parted in a smile.

"James," she said, nearly breathlessly. Then she saw Thomas Harkness standing in the shadow cast by the roof and her manner became more formal. "Good morning, Captain Dawes, Major Harkness."

Harkness removed his cap. "Good morning, Miss Trevor."

"Lovely day," she said, and then she stepped from the plankwalk and made her way toward the sutler's store, her chestnut hair catching the sunlight, her back straight and proud, shoulders set, hips swaying slightly. Only once did she glance back across her shoulder at James Dawes.

"What would she think, I wonder, if she knew?" Harkness said.

"If she knew what?" Dawes felt his blood going cold. Harkness smiled, and it was not a warm expression.

"All about you, James. If she knew that you were born James Van der Veghe. If she knew that your mother changed your name to her own because your father, who was a soldier, turned renegade and fought with the Shawnee against us. If she knew that you are part Indian yourself!"

"It would not matter to Julia. Besides, Thomas," he said, turning toward the major, "how would she find out?"

113

"You know how these matters become common knowledge." He shrugged. "Isn't that what happened with Jackson? Wasn't it suspected that your sympathies lay with the Indians? Isn't that what Boggs suspects right now? As for her not caring, James—you can't have forgotten already that the Seminoles killed Julia's father." He smiled again, his eyes cold and arrogant. "Good day, James. I have to see about preparing the expeditionary force. Give my best to Julia if you should run into her again."

You cold-blooded bastard, Dawes thought. He watched Harkness stroll away, knowing that before nightfall Julia would somehow be let in on the "common gossip."

He walked into his quarters and slammed the door behind him. Taylor and Murchison, the two young officers who shared the apartment, were both out. The room was empty and slightly sour. Dawes flung himself down on the bed, which was of barked logs and leather straps, a tick mattress covered with a blue army-issue blanket.

"I'd better start thinking of a new line of work," he muttered. It had happened twice now and it would happen again. The early career of James Dawes had been a brilliant one. He had risen through the enlisted ranks, received a battlefield commission, and made captain on the first eligibility list. Then it had ended.

Four years a captain. The other officers began to avoid him. At last it came out. The young lieutenant who had taken Jessup's place under General Jackson had been an Ohio man and he knew the story of the Van der Veghe family very well.

The first Van der Veghe on this continent had been a naturalist who had married an Oneida headwoman. There had been some trouble with the British and with the French. The war had broken out in the Northeast, that war they were now calling the French and Indian war, and Van der Veghe had moved west. There one of the Van der Veghe children, the daughter, had married into the Shawnee nation. The son of Van der Veghe, this adopted Shawnee's brother, had been James Dawes's father.

When war broke out in the Ohio Valley, Dawes's father had fought with the Americans. He had a grudge against the Shawnee chief, Ousa, of some kind. He also was a skilled tracker, a brave soldier.

Something had happened, what James was never sure, but his father had turned traitor and joined the Shawnee himself. "His Indian blood just came out" was what they said.

James's mother had said nothing about the man who was his father. Ever. James's name was changed to Dawes—his mother's maiden name—and he was forbidden to ask about his father or even mention his name.

All long ago, far away, half forgotten.

Perhaps, thinking about it now, that was what had encouraged James Dawes to become a soldier himself. Some sort of search for absolution. Maybe he had set out to prove that the bad blood of the Van der Veghe men did not run in his veins.

A futile quest, and a childish one, but Dawes had come to love the life of a soldier.

It seemed now that he would not be one much longer. The promotions would never come. He would not be given the assignments which required trust. His fellow officers' conversation would break off as he came into the room—as it had with Jackson.

"Julia . . ." He rolled over on his bunk, feeling immense frustration. He loved her and knew that she loved him. Julia's father, as Harkness had so thoughtfully reminded him, had been killed by the Seminoles. She detested Indians. It was a vindictiveness which bordered on madness. She had loved her father deeply.

Julia could not bear to go out among the Cherokee whose farms spread around the fort. She swore she could not look a red man in the face. It was extreme, this malice, this heartache, and Dawes knew it. He hoped that she would grow gradually better, for it was the only flaw in her lively personality, the only subject which could cloud those blue eyes.

"By the way, Julia," Harkness would soon be saying, "you did know that Dawes has Indian blood in him."

Dawes pounded his fists against his skull in anguish. There was only one thing to do, of course. Tell her himself before the word could reach her in that way. A hundred times he had started to tell her, but each time he coaxed the conversation around toward that subject, Julia began to revile the Indian and the God who had been mad enough to create a red man.

She lived on in the fort with her mother by the army's generosity. The family had a home in Maryland, but Julia could not be transported back there. She refused. She would stay until her father's murderer was caught. Until she had seen this man Yui hung on the stockade gibbet.

Harkness, no doubt, had already informed Julia that this morning at commander's call James Dawes had spoken up in defense of Yui.

Bad blood. Dawes rolled from his bunk and walked to the window. There was nothing to be done this sultry morning. The punitive expedition could not be mounted until Taylor and Murchison returned with their patrols. Otherwise the fort itself would be undermanned, an invitation to disaster. It might be days or weeks before Boggs counterattacked; but when he did he would throw the full force of his command against Yui, and the man would be crushed.

In the meantime there was nothing to do. Later he would take a tour of the enlisted barracks on general principles. Then, after midnight, he had officer-of-the-day duty. Until then Dawes could only sit and fret, wondering how in God's name he could tell Julia. He imagined her horrified face; he knew that the marriage would be off. Julia bearing children with Indian blood! No—his desolation was complete. His father's sins had been visited upon him. Life, for twenty-four-year-old James Dawes, Captain, United States Infantry, seemed to be suddenly at an end.

"Damn you, William Van der Veghe! Damn you for being my father. Damn you to flaming, everlasting hell. Your shadow has been cast across my life. I am not free, not while your blood runs through my veins." *Bad blood*, Indian blood. A traitor's blood.

Oddly, at that moment, another oblique thought crossed his mind. He had three cousins among the Shawnee far to the north. He even knew their names: Kokii, Shanna, and Lychma. How had it gone for them? For those who lived among the Indians and had white blood? Perhaps he would find out one day. One day he might return to the Ohio Valley, and perhaps it would be soon. All depended on Julia. She must not despise him.

Dawes smiled. He thought of her face, her laughing eyes, of the intimate conversations they had had walking along the riverbank as the sun sank low in the west, as the dove sang in the great white oaks.

116

"I am doing her an injustice," he said to no one. "Surely I am doing Julia an injustice. Nothing could shatter our love. Nothing!"

Save bad blood.

He flung open the door of the base officers' quarters and stood there, staring at the pale and empty sky. When the sky had begun to darken, to take on a rose-colored tint, when the shadows began to creep out from their secret hiding places and darken the fort, he turned, slammed the door, and threw himself onto his bunk again, trying to sleep, trying to think of nothing—for if he thought, he began to brood, and in those moments he knew. He knew that it was already over and there was nothing in the world left to live for. And in those moments he could not decide which of the two men he despised most—William Van der Veghe for fathering him or the Seminole, Yui, who had destroyed the woman who could have loved him.

❀ 7 ❀

In the quiet of the glade where the deep shadows fell and the soft wind whispered through the forest carrying the fragile scents of orchids, of cedar and magnolia, the woman Shanna, the stranger, slipped from her skirt and cast her shirt aside.

From a small cleft high on the rocky ledge above her a thin waterfall trickled downward. Splashing into the pool at the base of the stone ledge, it swirled and stammered its way down an uneven rocky chute which led to the river beyond the trees.

There were the trees, black and comforting, the whispering of the water spirits, the silky embrace of the water, the accompanying sense of weightlessness, the deep violet of the sundown sky, the peaceful cooing of mourning dove, the faraway rush of sounds which was like leaves rustling in the wind and which was the sound of Yui's village preparing for the night, of voices raised in calling children to their meals, of men exchanging jokes, of women laughing, dogs barking, babies crying, all muffled and conjoined by the distance, by the screen of lushly foliaged trees.

Shanna floated on her back, watching the late sky, seeing the first star blink on, its silver light pale, distant, mysterious.

"Shanna?"

Her head spun around in agitation. She felt her mouth tighten, felt the utter relaxation of moments ago bleed away. It was Yui, crouched along the shore, and he was watching her with eyes as mysterious as those of the single star.

"Yes, Yui." Her voice was dry and annoyed. Shanna stood now, only her head showing above the water.

"I see. You are still angry with me."

"I am not angry with you, Yui."

"No?" He filled his hand with the fern which grew all

118

around the spot where he crouched and he tore it away. "You know, Shanna," he said, looking at the ground and not at her, "I am a powerful man and a proud one. I make a fool of myself apologizing to you when I have done nothing but help you. I make a weakling of myself when I am strong."

"Why then do you do it? Why do you not go away and leave me alone?"

"Why?" He shook his head. "Why indeed? I have my people to think of. The hunt, the illness which has come to some of us. I have the threat of war hanging over me. I have broken alliances and must cement new ones—and yet I come to you here and I lower myself to you. And yet at night I do not sleep quietly as I once did, but I think of Shanna with the mocking eyes. Why indeed!

"Why do I bother?"

Then again he was gone, and Shanna realized that she did not even know why he had come. Her question had chased him away, her harshness. Well and good. What was he, this tattooed man, but a block of bone and muscle, tied together with sinews, sheathed in copper flesh? What was he but another warlord, another who did not seem to know the meaning of peace?

Why then did she feel this way? Warm when the water was cool, excited when he was near, lonely when he was away?

There were words for such sensations, such emotions, but she would not speak them. She only turned and swam across the pond, dressing quickly, cursing the nature which had given her femininity to respond to what was Yui, the warlord, the man.

In the chickee the shadows were deep. The young one rested on her knees in the corner of the hut. Outside the crickets chimed a raucous chorus. Across the river a hunting owl swooped low, and the stars blinked on one by one, illuminating the hut with pale-blue light.

The small one, the six hundredth, was silent, and now, Shanna saw, she was naked. She kneeled in the corner, watching Shanna with eyes which seemed to know nothing, but saw everything. Wide, starlit eyes which held madness and secret knowledge, which saw nothing in the darkness, and all beyond the chickee.

"And so," the small one said, "he has come to you with his manhood and you shy away from him. He has come and you see the blood of man in his veins. You see the roots of war, this pride and strength, this loin-born will to defend what is his, to claim boundaries and fight those who would take the food from his mouth, the women from his house, the land of his fathers."

"Pamda!" Shanna staggered against the corner pole of the chickee. Someone had taken her soul from her body and spread it before these dark and shining eyes.

Slowly eyelids drooped across those eyes, and when they opened again the expression was of dull surprise. "Shanna?"

"It is I. Are you all right? What was that you were saying to me? Who told you all of that?"

"It is dark," Pamda said with her old slurred voice. "It is dark and I am tired. I wanted to fall asleep, but there was no one here to watch me. I wondered where you were, Shanna."

"I am here now." Shanna, still puzzled, went to where the small one knelt. "Put a blanket over you. By morning you will be cold. Lie down and sleep and I will keep watch over you."

"Yes, Shanna." Pamda obeyed as a child would. She lay back, stretched and yawned. "Sing the song you used to sing to Lychma," she said sleepily, and Shanna felt a prickly sensation creeping up her spine. A warm, eerie sensation like a gap in time, a fissure in reality.

"What did you say?" she demanded. "Who told you my sister's name? Who told you I used to sing to her when she could not sleep?"

"Sing to me, Shanna," Pamda said from beneath her blanket. "Sing me the little song."

Shanna sat back, her feet beneath her. Her hand was on Pamda's shoulder, and now it fell away. She shook her head heavily and then, obeying a compulsion she did not understand, she began to sing:

"Father is in the forest hunting winter bear
 Mother is by the fire sewing you dresses to wear
 Weenk is coming from his home in the skies
 To bring golden dreams, now just close your eyes."

Pamda slept. Shanna rose and walked to the entranceway of the chickee, staring out at the long rambling river, at the endless forest, at the far-running skies.

"Does she sleep?"

Shanna looked down to see Mother Holotok standing there, face lifted, arms folded, her weight resting on one foot.

"She is asleep."

"I heard you singing to her. She likes that, does our Pamda. Her mother would sing to them all at night as she made their beds for them. . . ." Holotok's voice fell away. Pamda's mother was dead. All of the children were dead except Pamda.

"Is she truly mad?" Shanna asked.

"Mad?" Mother Holotok frowned. "Did I ever say that our six hundredth one was mad, Shawnee woman?"

"May I speak to you?" Shanna asked, and when Holotok nodded she clambered down the ladder. She sat on the lowest rung and looked up at the Seminole woman, this mother of them all, Holotok.

"When I came back to the chickee, Pamda was up. She was *up*, I say, but I do not know if she was awake."

"Did she speak to you?"

"Yes. She spoke to me, Holotok, but the voice which came from her throat was not the voice of Pamda. It was stronger, more self-assured. A voice like that of—"

"Of the spirits, of course," Holotok said, nodding.

"*Yes*. Of the spirits. Eyes had seen into my heart. Ghosts had carried my secrets to Pamda. Then all of my thoughts were spoken back to me."

"Yes," Holotok said solemnly, "that is our Pamda. I have told you that Pamda is not her real name, but the one which she says she must be called. Pamda means 'the spirit friend,' Shanna. And the name which our young one has chosen for herself suits her well."

"I see. She is a holy one, then."

"She has been chosen. Pamda has no life of her own. Pamda is the name of the voice which speaks to us. The other has no name. The six hundredth is dead, killed the night Boggs came among us."

They walked a little way toward the village. Shanna was thoughtfully silent for a long while. Then she asked, "These things she says, is she always correct? Does she see the future as well as the now and the past?"

"What is always so?" Holotok replied. "What would become of us all if we knew the future, Shanna? We should fall to our knees and moan, tearing our hair from our heads. Do we not already know the past? It is only the present which the spirits illuminate for us. It is only the present which we see and yet do not know. We have veils before our eyes. We see with our hearts. We pretend, all of us, that what is is not so. This is the true gift of Pamda. The true gift of the spirits."

Shanna wanted to ask more, to speak of Pamda's gift, but Holotok touched her shoulder and said, "I must go into the village now. My children will be wondering where Mother is. Who will sing the others to sleep on this night if not Mother Holotok? Goodbye, Shanna. Watch over our daughter, Pamda, and perhaps her spirit friends will also watch over you."

With that she was gone, and Shanna stood hesitantly on the perimeter of the village clearing.

What was it she did want to know? If she could speak to Pamda's spirits, what would she ask? Nothing about the past, certainly. Nor was she sure she wished to know the future. Perhaps it was as Holotok said—it was the present, the here and now, which most confuses us. We see what we will and the rest is banished to mystery. Perhaps it is the way we protect ourselves.

Shanna looked again toward the camp and then turned and walked slowly homeward.

Across the camp where the river formed an oxbow, where lay the great oak which had been blown down in the hurricane in the year of the many foxes, the war council sat around the small fire, smoking their pipes, their faces glossed by firelight, drawn by worry.

"Then it was Potaqua?" Yui asked again.

"Yes, Yui," the runner who had brought the word from the green river assured him again. "It was Potaqua returning from the Cherokee camp, and he carried the heads of the slain with him."

"There was no white pursuit?" Chamtha asked. He was the oldest of the war chiefs, a solemn man with tattoos of valor scrolled around his arms to the shoulders, around his legs from ankles to thigh, across his chest. Chamtha had few teeth left, but his body was sinews and tortoise shells wrapped around with tanned leather. He still could run many a younger man into the ground. He had been a lieutenant of Kamdawotekee, Yui's father. Now he was Yui's lieutenant.

"There was no pursuit, Father," the runner said.

Chamtha shook his head and sucked at the stem of the long red pipe he held. "I like none of this, Yui," Chamtha said. "Why would Potaqua choose this time to attack, knowing our camp is so near to Madison?"

"Why did he not council with us?"

This voice belonged to Krawsatch, known as the Raven. He was young and ambitious and, Yui thought, insincere. Yui turned his head toward Krawsatch.

"Why would he council, Raven? Potaqua is his own councilor. He does what he chooses."

"We are on his line of march. Why did he not advise us of his intentions?"

"Yui has already answered you, Krawsatch," Pohoy said quietly. The giant was leaning on one elbow against the earth, and Krawsatch, turning that way sharply, started to say something, thought better of it, and fell silent.

"I do not think Krawsatch's questions impertinent," old Chamtha said. "Why has this happened? Potaqua has put us in danger. He must know this. Therefore either Potaqua is reckless or he has done this thing on purpose."

"On purpose?" This was Ockawa, another of the old chiefs who had appeared to be dozing before the fire. Now his eyes opened wide and he hunched forward. "Why would Potaqua do such a thing? Is he not our cousin?"

"I did not say he did such a thing," Chamtha replied. "I only said it was possible."

"It cannot be possible." Ockawa leaned back against the fallen oak, waving a disparaging hand.

"With Potaqua," Chamtha said, "all things are possible."

"Our leader, Yui, went to the camp of Potaqua to make a pact. Our leader, Yui, returned without a pact," the Raven said coldly. "Why was that? What happened in Potaqua's camp that we have not been told? Is there a reason why Potaqua would wish to harm us, Yui?"

"Potaqua was making a pact with the Spanish men,"

Pohoy put in before Yui could answer the Raven. "We did not wish to ally ourselves with these men."

"The Spanish men say: 'Go here, go there, kill these people, do what we wish and we shall give you powder and rum,' " Chamtha commented bitterly.

"Potaqua at least *has* powder," Krawsatch said sourly. "What is wrong about taking from the Spanish? They are strong. They have ships with big guns. With these they could fire upon the American forts."

"If they had the nerve for it," Pohoy said.

"And what courage have we shown?" the Raven said, throwing a short stick into the fire. "We no longer make our war."

"There are many more Americans here than there were a year ago," Yui said. He could read the contempt, and what might have been jealousy, in the Raven's eyes.

"Then we should have strong allies!" the Raven said with a laugh.

"Perhaps what Krawsatch says is the truth," Ockawa suggested.

"That was what we decided when Yui went to speak with Potaqua, was it not?" The Raven stood and spread his hands. "We are weak and so we need allies. But the allies do not suit the war leader, Yui. So we have no allies. So we are as weak as before."

"You forget yourself, Raven," Yui said in a brittle voice. His eyes were reflecting the firelight.

"Can a sachem no longer speak his mind at the war council?"

"You have spoken," Pohoy said.

"But I have not said all I meant to." Now Krawsatch's anger and his desire to make a strong impression upon the other war leaders pushed him to ask the question he had been hesitant to put forward:

"I ask you, Yui, have we been told all of the truth? Someone who was with you at Potaqua's camp has told me that we have no pact with our cousin because of this Shawnee woman."

"What?" Ockawa's eyes opened again.

"Is it true, Yui?" The Raven paced back and forth in the firelight, which flowed like liquid around his muscular legs.

"Is it true that we have no pact with our cousin Potaqua because of this Shawnee woman? Is it true that Potaqua is angry with us because you took his property away from him, because you cost him much money, powder, and rum? Is it true that you stole this woman Shanna from Potaqua's allies, the Spanish?"

"Yui?" Chamtha was watching the young warlord's face anxiously. Had Yui acted so recklessly? Had his mind been only on this young Shawnee woman and not on what was best for his nation?

A sympathetic look passed from Pohoy to Yui. The giant shook his head and looked away.

"You must answer, Yui," Ockawa said, lifting a gnarled finger in an indefinite gesture. "This is a serious charge. You must know as well as any of us how serious this accusation is."

"It cannot be true," Chamtha said. He smiled and looked to Yui for confirmation; but studying that dark, handsome face, he knew, and his smile fell away.

"Yui?"

"It is true," the Seminole war leader said. Pohoy groaned. Krawsatch threw an arm out in a gesture of triumph.

"But Yui . . . at this time when we need allies . . ." Old Chamtha was stunned. He could not piece his thoughts together. He had taken Yui as his own son after the death of Kamdawotekee. He had nominated Yui for his position.

"This is indeed grave," said Ockawa.

"What were you thinking of, Yui?" Chamtha asked, his disappointment evident. He placed his hand on top of his head and pressed down with all the strength of his arm in a gesture of frustration. "To throw away our alliance, to leave the people weaker, to enrage Potaqua, to alienate the Spanish men—all for the sake of a *woman*!"

"I had believed you a man of better judgment," Ockawa muttered without looking up.

Krawsatch beamed with pleasure. Pohoy shot the Raven a withering glance.

Yui tried to explain. "It was not a moment's decision. It was not done because I was hungry for a Shawnee slave girl."

"What other reason could there be?" Chamtha asked sternly. He shook his head heavily.

"It is done," Yui said. "I cannot defend my action to you. It is done. Now let us discuss what we must do to protect the tribe. Potaqua has attacked Madison. Perhaps he has done this with the dual idea of winning a victory and striking back at Yui. Perhaps the Spanish men told him to do this. But it is done! Now what must we do?

"We cannot fight," Yui said. "Not at this time. Our village must be well known. Boggs has his scouts."

"Boggs will come," Chamtha said. "I know the man." His old face still reflected disappointment. "All we can do is return to the swamps."

"We cannot run forever," Ockawa said. It galled him even to consider fleeing, but the memories of Boggs, of the shelling, of the dead forced themselves upon him, and his words carried little conviction.

"We will not run," Yui said strongly, rising to his feet now. "We will withdraw. If he comes, and I too believe he will, we shall strike at him from hiding. We shall fight him and then vanish into the swamps. We shall be at his back and on his flanks. We shall force him to withdraw again. We shall teach this man Boggs that he cannot afford to come against the Seminole in their homeland; in that way it will always be our homeland. I have no wish to attack his fort, his Cherokee dogs. I have no Spanish men urging me on, asking me to destroy all Americans. I want only my land for my people. This is the war we shall fight—we shall run but never surrender. We shall strike but not expose ourselves or our women and children. We shall lead him into the swamps, and there we shall destroy him a piece at a time."

"That is not victory," the Raven said.

"It is survival," Yui said hotly. "What would you have us do? Storm their fort, rush their cannon?"

"It is not for me to say what we should do," Raven said. He picked up his blanket and slung it around his shoulders. "Not now. But I ask the elders this: Who should lead us now? A man who has proved his judgment is faulty? A man who would throw away his people's lives, their contentment, for the sake of a foreign woman?" Raven shook his head. "I ask this. I ask that you consider it, elders."

Then Krawsatch was gone, leaving Yui to stare after him as Pohoy grumbled a profuse curse. The two men spoke together later as the fire burned low, painting flickering shadows on the great fallen oak, as the river murmured past and a low fog began to creep through the forest.

"Raven wishes to succeed you, Yui. He has long been jealous of you; now he sees the opportunity to assume your position."

"Never! The elders cannot be deceived by Raven's machinations. They cannot believe that he would make a better war leader than I, Pohoy."

"I do not know what they believe, Yui, I only know that Raven has planted seeds of doubt in their minds. And if the truth is to be told, his argument is a strong one. Potaqua is ever our enemy now instead of our ally. Perhaps they may decide that the only way to bring Potaqua to our side again is to dishonor you."

"You joke! These men are my friends. Chamtha is a father to me. They have seen me in war and in peace. They know that I think only of the people. Always."

"I only pointed out what they might believe. With Raven's prodding, with his whispers in their ears. You could help yourself, Yui."

"I do not understand you."

Pohoy was staring at the glowing embers. Now his broad face lifted. "You could defeat Raven's implication that the woman means more to you than the tribe. You could convince the elders that she meant nothing to you, that you acted as you did because Potaqua is an evil man, an untrustworthy one, one under the thumb of the Spanish men. You could do this, Yui, by sending the woman away."

"Never!" he said before he had even thought it out.

Pohoy grinned. "Then perhaps it is true. Perhaps she does mean more to you than anything else."

"It is not that, Pohoy. But I cannot send her away. I will not."

"I do not think she would go unwillingly," Pohoy said.

"Perhaps not." Yui stood and stretched. The silent fog had crept upon them and he stood weirdly illuminated by the golden embers, wrapped in a mantle of twisting fog. "I cannot speak of Shanna, Pohoy. Understand that. Not on this night. I will hear no more of this proposal."

"Then you will not have to hear it, Yui. Not from my lips. But a time will come when you will hear more of this. The Raven will not let it lie."

"Perhaps not." Yui stared thoughtfully into the distances for a long minute. "For now," he said, his forcefulness returning, "I and only I am war leader! I want you to send out runners. We must have eyes in the forest. I want to know immediately if Boggs appears to be making preparations for war. I want to know it the moment he emerges from his fort.

"The people must be told to have their belongings ready to move at a moment's notice. The warriors must prepare their weapons."

"I will see to it, Yui," Pohoy said. He rested a hand on his friend and leader's shoulder for a moment, and then, wrapping his blanket more tightly around his shoulders against the chill of the fog, he strode toward the sleeping camp.

Yui walked to the river's edge and stared gloomily down at the rippling water. She stole up behind him and her slender arms were around his waist, her hands flat against his chest, before he knew she was there.

Yui turned to her and gathered her in his arms, running his hand down the silk of her dark hair, bending his mouth to hers. Then, in confusion, he stopped, becoming rigid and distant. He recovered quickly and kissed Teska with feigned enthusiasm.

But the moment did not go unnoticed by the Seminole woman. She looked up into Yui's eyes, seeing the distant expression, feeling the absent movement of his hand across her slender bare back.

"And who did you think it was, my Yui?" Teska asked. "Your Shawnee woman?"

"There is nothing between myself and the Shawnee woman, Teska," Yui said too quickly, and Teska smiled.

Her voice was pleading, demanding, harsh. "Then kiss me again, Yui. Lie down with me. Beat me, curse me, pin me to the earth! Do something, I do not care what! You have hardly spoken to me since you arrived from Potaqua's camp bringing with you a young and beautiful woman who means nothing to you."

"I have said there is nothing between us," Yui said. They had not moved. Teska's arms were still around his neck, but they felt heavy and cold. Her breath was on his chest, warm and misty. The fog encircled them.

"So you say. Yet I do not believe you. How could I?" Teska's arms fell away. She laughed harshly. "She means nothing to you, yet if the stories I have heard are true, you have thrown away everything for her sake!"

"What stories have you heard, woman? Who whispers lies into your ears?"

"Are they lies, Yui? They say that we must run because we are too weak to protect ourselves. They say that Potaqua is angry. They say that perhaps Yui is not a fit war leader."

"Raven," Yui said. Who else could have told Teska all of this?

"Listen to me, Yui." Teska hooked her fingers into the band of Yui's loincloth. Her eyes searched his intently. "When you left we were lovers, bound to be married. You were the mightiest of the Seminole war leaders, respected by all. We were secure in our camp. All was well.

"Now you have returned, bringing this Shawnee woman, and everything has changed! You avert your eyes. You do not want to touch me or hold me. We have new enemies and there are those who wish to take your power and very well may succeed. All because of this Shawnee girl! And yet you can stand there and tell me she means nothing to you!"

"There is nothing between us."

"Then send her away!"

"No."

"Why, Yui? Why?"

"She has done nothing. I promised her my protection."

"And you love her."

Yui said nothing.

"And you love her more than Teska!"

"Does a woman's mind always turn to such thoughts?" Yui said, pushing her away. "Must you see rivals everywhere?"

"I do not see them everywhere, Yui," Teska said, and her voice was as cool as the fog which drifted eerily through the trees. "But I see a rival in this Shanna. I see danger in her presence. If you are wise, Yui, you will send her away before

129

there is much trouble." Teska turned away. She took three steps and halted, her back still toward Yui. "If you are wise, Yui, you will send this woman away before there is tragedy."

"Teska. What do you mean, Teska?"

Yui took a step toward her, but she hurried away, running through the fog, which swallowed her up but did nothing to erase the memory of her words, words which implied a threat, which promised tragedy.

I am a fool, he thought. They are right. I have endangered us all. I am a fool! This small big-eyed woman, what do I mean to her? Nothing. She has told me as much. Perhaps something of this could be salvaged by asking her to leave the Seminole camp. And how would she react? She would simply rise, pack her sack, and walk away, not even looking back. Yet for her you have risked all. You are a fool, Yui.

How could it be that I care for her so strongly? Although she will not rest her hand on my arm or look into my eyes save with blank curiosity, although she blames me for the loss of her sister, although I find that her expression tightens when she finds me looking at her. She recoils from my touch. How can it be that I love her?

Yui pounded his fists against his forehead. He felt like screaming at himself, cursing himself for the fool he was, but he did not. He was silent. The river was silent. The fog shrouded the land.

He stood breathing in and out slowly. He had not eaten all day and yet he was not hungry. The camp slept and yet he was not tired. Boggs was preparing for war and yet he did not discuss and devise battle plans. Teska came to him as an offering and yet he did not take her comfort.

He loved Shanna. It was simple, inexplicable. He did not know why he loved her. There was a bond between them which could not be felt or named. There was a bond. One soul which knew another, which cried out for the unity which two could devise with love.

He loved her and he was a fool and the mad and rambling river flowed away to the sea.

Pamda watched over her. She was kneeling beside Shanna's bed, looking down upon her with the loving eyes of a faithful pet. Shanna's eyes slowly focused. The sunlight was streaming through the trees surrounding their chickee. Small coin-sized golden spots of sunlight brightened the floor. Far away a loon called. Above the forest migrating herons flew southward, their flight graceful, slow, incredible.

"Good morning, Pamda."

The girl was smiling so happily that Shanna could not help but ask, "What is it? What makes you smile, Pamda?"

"It is morning," she answered brightly.

"It is hot already."

"Yes. But it is morning, you see, and nothing has happened."

She went away then, singing to herself the song which Shanna had crooned her to sleep with, and Shanna watched until Pamda was down the ladder and away dancing across the clearing toward the pot.

That was all it needed for Pamda to be happy. To pass a night in which nothing happened, in which no frightening spirits loomed up out of her dreams, a night in which the women did not cry out, the children wail, the cannon boom.

She had passed the night; she was happy.

Shanna dressed slowly. The morning sun seemed overbright, too hot. She too had passed the night, and yet there was no simple joy in it.

Why am I here? she asked herself angrily. Why do I stay? She threw up exasperated hands. Taking resolution, she snatched up her sack and stuffed her extra shirt into it. She would have Mother Holotok give her food. She would cross the river and walk toward the distant Cherokee settlement. Perhaps she would remain among the Cherokee; perhaps there would be word of the war in the north; perhaps she would return to the land of the Shawnee. But she would not stay here!

"Shanna?"

His shadow crossed the floor of the chickee, and she turned to find Yui standing before the red rising sun. He said nothing more. Only her name, and she rushed to him, feeling the warmth of his body, the strength of his arms.

She kissed his chest, felt his lips against her forehead. She closed her eyes, but the hot tears seeped through and ran across her cheeks, and she was laughing.

"I am afraid I love you, Seminole."

131

"I am much afraid that I love you as dearly, Shanna, my Shawnee woman."

He was still, and she knew his emotions ran deep. His hands were intimate, gentle across her shoulders and back. His heart thudded beneath her ear. They did not move or speak as the rising sun pulled itself free of the dark horizon and glittered across the land. They neither spoke nor moved, and the morning was beautiful, good, brilliant. She had passed the night.

❀ 8 ❀

The sunlight tumbled like molten gold through the gaps in the great cedars, dappling the fern with moving shadows. It danced on the mist cast up by the sheer waterfall and painted tiny, brilliant rainbows in the air.

There had never been a place so lovely, never such contentment. She lay beside him, his arm across her abdomen, his eyes upon her face, his voice low and comforting as they spoke.

"The more you tell me, Yui, the more I wonder. Would it not be best after all if I just left your camp?"

He lifted his head with astonishment. He blinked and then smiled.

"Could you go? Now?"

"No," Shanna said. "I do not think I could." She lay her cheek against his sun-warmed chest and traced small patterns across his muscular stomach. Shanna sat up. "But I wish to do you no harm, Yui. I do not wish to see you dragged down because of me."

"Raven!" Yui laughed harshly. "He has been trying to drag me down for years. He has not the strength. The elders are too wise to be influenced by such a man as our Raven."

Shanna found herself doubting that Yui felt the confidence he projected. Perhaps she was wrong. This was a strong man and a bold one. She did not know the elders as he did. She bent her lips to his chest, kissed him again, and lay down in his arms. The mist from the waterfall drifted over them, cooling their bodies.

"What of Teska?" she finally asked.

"Teska?"

Shanna turned her head to see the frown on Yui's dark face. His eyebrows drew together. "She must understand, that is all. I do not wish to hurt Teska, but she is a beautiful woman. Young, with much to offer. She will have no trouble finding another man.''

"Another man is not the same as having the one man you have chosen,'' Shanna said.

"Perhaps she may live with us then,'' Yui said, tickling Shanna as he said it. ''She will be my second wife.''

"I do not think that is the best solution,'' Shanna said, and she was not smiling.

"No. I was trying to make light of it, Shanna, because I know Teska very well. What you say is true—she will not quickly take another man to be her own. The reason is not simply that she loves Yui so much that she cannot bear to let him go. No, Teska is more devious than that. She craves power. She will have it. She came to me because I was war leader. I know that. We were children together, and she thought nothing of me. Then after my father was buried, she began to bring my food, to build my fire on cool nights, to laugh too loud at my jokes. I knew then what she wanted, but I was indifferent to it. It amused me at times.

"Teska will not miss her Yui so much as she will miss her chance to become the wife of a Seminole war leader, a woman like this creature Tohope who married Potaqua.''

"How will you tell her?'' Shanna asked.

"As I have told you. You are my woman. You will be my wife. Teska must understand. Now let us speak no more of Teska, my Shanna.''

Rainbows shimmered in the falling mist. Yui was against her, strong and lean and hard. Shanna watched him through half-closed eyelids, seeing the slack expression of his face, the deep distant gleam in his black eyes.

His chest was against her bare breasts, and her breath caught. Her back arched inadvertently. The length of his thighs was against her own legs. Her hands were around his shoulders, across his back, feeling the flat firm web of muscle beneath his copper skin. His mouth met hers and her head lolled back, her lips parting, her breath coming in soft, rapid cadence.

"Shanna.'' He said her name and said it again. His hands caressed her, running across the pickets of her ribs to her breasts, lingering there as he kissed her again, as her body slackened and grew heavy. She heard the whisper of his callused palm against her flesh, heard his breathing, which was like controlled desperation.

She paused, looking through her eyelashes to the canopy of dark trees overhead where the sunlight glittered and sparkled, then she drew his head down to her, her mouth agape, hungry.

He was warm and hard against her. His head rolled from side to side, kissing her eyes, her ears, her mouth, the pulse of her throat, punishing her exquisitely. The day whispered by. Her heart pounded against his, beating with the same hectic rhythm; they were separated only by the sheath of flesh around them. One heart and one body which groped and demanded and tortured itself.

He was against her, and Shanna felt herself soften, felt her head go light. Her hands moved crablike across his back. Her thighs were clamped against his. He was whispering, but she did not know what he said; she knew only what it meant, and she paused again, feeling a quivering hesitation.

He shifted only slightly and then he was her master. He was her warlord, her Seminole, her conqueror, and Shanna surrendered to his skill at arms. She breathed heavily through her mouth. Her eyes were unfocused. She was aware only of the closeness of Yui, of the richness of her own body, of the deepening rhythm, the sudden, astounding, luxuriant completion.

She sagged into sleep, feeling the weight of his slack body, feeling the gentle residual claspings of her own flesh, the lost and triumphant emotions mingling within her, the pride and sense of prowess her body had presented her with; she hugged him tightly and lay back, stroking his dark head.

"Well?" Krawsatch, the Raven, sat cross-legged on the floor of his chickee, hunched over a half-eaten bowl of food. Now he looked up expectantly at the dark savage face of Kaal. He was a man much feared, this dark one, for his angers, his murderous rages, were entirely unpredictable. He had been known to run from a battle screaming, pleading; then again, he had once killed six Creek fishermen with his own hands, clubbing them until there was nothing of a man about any of them. No one had interfered with Kaal's work that time. His eyes saw only destruction, and any who had

135

crossed before him would have been killed. Only the Raven seemed to have any control over Kaal, who spent weeks at a time alone in the swamps, who returned muddy, naked, covered with leech bites and welts which might have been self-inflicted, to sit by the fire and stare at all around him menacingly.

More than once the council had considered banishing Kaal. Raven had always spoken up for him. The man was evil and filthy, but he had his uses.

"It is as you thought," Kaal said, crouching down. "Yui makes love to the Shawnee girl. When he said there was nothing between them, he lied."

"You saw them!" Raven leaped up exultantly.

"I saw them, Krawsatch. There is no mistake."

"The fool! The idiot, he has let me overtake him. To throw it away for the sake of a woman!" Raven laughed and clapped his hands together gleefully. Kaal stared up at him with morose eyes.

"You will be war leader?" Kaal asked.

"I will, Kaal. And you, my friend, will be subchief, as I have promised you."

Kaal beamed. He shuddered like an expectant hound, his jaw dropping as his vacant eyes stared at Raven. "I will lead us into many good battles."

"Yes, Kaal." Krawsatch started to place his hand on Kaal's shoulder, and remembering just in time that Kaal could not stand to be touched by another human being he made an indefinite gesture with that hand.

"Now shall we kill Yui?" the man asked, and again Raven was struck by how unlike human speech Kaal's voice could be, how childlike and yet malevolent his thoughts were.

"No, Kaal. That is not the way. Not yet. When it is time you may kill Yui." Kaal beamed. "Now, however, I have a more important task for you. You must find Potaqua. Can you do that?" Raven asked.

"Yes," Kaal nodded again, his dull, childish mind reaching the slow decision.

"Very well. You must find Potaqua. You must tell him that we wish an alliance with him. You must tell him that we wish to do whatever Potaqua wishes—do not mention the

Spanish men. Potaqua imagines himself to be independent of them."

"No, Raven."

"Tell him only that we wish to be his allies. Tell him that Yui is no friend of ours, no leader. If he agrees to speak with me, ask him to give you a musket. That will be the bond of our alliance."

"A musket."

"Yes. And if the alliance is sealed, then it will be the musket which kills Yui. And you, Kaal, may be the one to use this weapon."

"I will do as you say. I will begin when it is dark."

"Do not forget."

Kaal looked insulted. "I do not forget what is important to me, Raven."

When Kaal had gone, Krawsatch went to the ladder of his chickee and climbed down. All that remained was to speak again to the elders. They would be told that Yui had indeed broken the alliance because he lusted after a slave girl. He could no longer deny it. It could be proved that Yui was not a fit leader. He thought of himself and not of the tribe. Yui must be replaced, and there could only be one man to replace him. The man who had completed an alliance with Potaqua. Raven himself.

He looked around the dusky village, smiling to himself. It would not hurt to have one person who would verify all he said. Not Kaal, certainly. For Kaal was a half-wit, a murderer, a man despised as he was feared.

Raven looked around slowly, saw the slender woman walking toward the river, water jug on her shoulder, and he started after her, calling until Teska turned to him.

Shanna leaned drowsily against Yui. She kissed his shoulder and then turned so that they sat back to back. The sunset was spread across the sky. Brilliant golden veins gleamed among the red clouds.

"Where has the time gone; where did the day go?" she said in wonder.

"Our day has marched away, joining the endless procession of other days. This day, however, my Shanna, will never truly pass away."

137

"No," she agreed quietly, "it will not."

"Come." He stood and helped her to her feet, holding her briefly. The mist in the air was cool now. Shanna hardly noticed.

"Where are we going?"

"We are going into the village to reveal our joy. You must be my wife, you must live with me. They must all know it."

"Yui . . ." Shanna took his hand between her own, kissed the knuckles one by one, and looked up. "You say this will not mean trouble for you, but I know it will."

"And if it does?" He raised an eyebrow. "Shall we let them destroy our love and joy? They will accept you or they will not. They will take away my rank or they will not. This cannot be controlled. We can only control our own destiny in love. I have thought it over carefully, Shanna—look up at me—I have thought it over and I have decided. I will have you. For the rest of it, let it be as it must."

Shanna said no more, but still she was uneasy. Would Yui one day come to resent her? She would not be able to stand that. For now he was happy, and for now she greedily clung to him. They turned, arms around each other, and started back toward the village.

They were still in the forest, far from the camp perimeter, when Yui halted, his head coming up, his eyes narrowing, every sense alert.

"What is it?"

"Something is happening. Can you not hear it?"

They hurried on, Yui's pace lengthening with each stride. There were voices raised excitedly in the Seminole camp. There were no cooking fires lighted. Yui broke into a run, his hand clamped around Shanna's wrist as they hurried on toward the village.

They were still running side by side when they burst into the clearing to see knots of people standing here and there, arguing, shouting, gesturing wildly.

"Over there," Yui said, turning to his right.

Ahead of them stood the elders and a group of warriors, some with guns or bows in their hands. An exhausted runner sat on the ground before Chamtha.

"Yui . . ." Shanna heard one of the warriors say. She wondered why Yui did not release her hand. He clung to her almost desperately.

"What is it?" Yui asked. Heads turned toward him. The runner repeated his report.

"Boggs is coming out of Fort Madison. He has five hundred men and six cannon."

"We must go out to meet them," Krawsatch said. The Raven's eyes swept over Shanna with dark satisfaction. Other eyes were on her as well. Old Chamtha, frowning; Ockawa, appearing confused.

"Go out to meet them?" Yui said. "Five hundred men and six cannon? No. Have the people gather their belongings. We will march to the eagle camp."

"Run from Boggs!" Krawsatch said hotly.

"Do not choose this moment to display your plumage, Raven. It is the time to march, not time to debate." Chamtha was staring at the two young war leaders.

"Who is warlord?" Yui demanded, his voice rough, booming. "Chamtha? Have I been displaced?"

"No, Yui."

"Then do as I say, all of you. Go to your homes and prepare to march!"

The warriors left, trotting toward their chickees where anxious women, curious children waited. In a minute the camp was a beehive. They had been prepared for this; it had all happened before. They packed hurriedly, taking only food and blankets. All else was unnecessary.

"Shanna!" Yui turned as Shanna twisted free of his grip.

"I must get Pamda," she said with urgency.

"Pamda?" He nodded slowly and then turned to instruct his warriors. The elders stared as Shanna ran across the darkened, bustling camp. She cared not at all. Her only thought now was to get to Pamda, to prepare her.

She was in the corner, kneeling. Her wide eyes lifted as Shanna entered the chickee, glancing around for the items they would need.

"I am sleepy. I hoped you would come to sing me to sleep," Pamda said.

"Not tonight, Pamda," Shanna said, snatching up her own blanket. How could she tell her? She was fearful that Pamda would collapse or fall into hysterics. She had to be told; she had to be made ready. There was no time for coaxing, for cajoling.

"We must dress and leave, Pamda. We are marching to a place called eagle camp."

"Now?" Her voice was thin and wavering.

"Yes. Now. Come, get up," Shanna said briskly. She watched Pamda, waiting for panic to set in.

"This is the night then."

Shanna knelt down and brushed back Pamda's hair. Her mind played tricks on her. For a moment she was with Lychma, preparing her for another flight, another march, another battle, the endless war.

"This is the night," she told the girl.

"I thought so," Pamda said with a small sigh, a little shudder. But she would be all right. Shanna could see the activity behind Pamda's eyes. See her struggle with herself and come to an understanding of what must be. The tormenting demons were temporarily banished.

"Are you all right?"

"Yes, Shanna. What shall we need? Blankets and food. Is there time to pack anything else?"

"I am afraid not."

"No. But I must take my trunk. You understand that, do you not, Shanna?"

"I understand it, Pamda."

Her trunk. Her worldly possessions. A scorched rabbit-skin cape, a straw doll without a head, a broken comb.

Shanna helped her to lift the small split-cane trunk, and with blankets thrown around their shoulders, with a small sack filled with the little food they had in the chickee, they climbed down the ladder and walked toward the village, where all was in turmoil.

"Pamda!" Holotok rushed breathlessly to them. "I hoped that Shanna could find you and help you. I was down the river fishing when the news came to us." Holotok stood holding her hand to her massive bosom.

"I am all right. I know it is the night," Pamda said.

Holotok kissed her. "Yes. Can you manage, Shanna? I have others to take care of. Do you know that the fool Krawsatch wants to fight? After the last time? I am glad that

Yui is here, a man of intelligence. If it happened again . . ." Holotok shuddered, perhaps remembering the cannonballs, the musket fire, the screams of the wounded. She recovered herself quickly.

"Do you know which way to go? No, you couldn't. Stay here, Shanna. After I have gathered all the little ones I will come back for you."

With that Mother Holotok was gone, hoisting her skirts as her great thighs propelled her across the camp. Shanna thought at that moment that she had never known such a courageous and quite beautiful woman as Holotok.

"I am weary," Pamda complained, although they had done nothing to exhaust her. She sat down on the ground, legs crossed, hair in her eyes, trunk beside her.

"Shanna!"

It was Yui, carrying a musket, wearing a quiver with a dozen arrows in it and a bow slung across his shoulder. A small pouch filled with food hung from his waistband.

"Yui." She put her arms around his neck and kissed him, pleased to find the same fire, the same affection in his kiss, in his embrace.

"I must leave you for a time," he said quickly. "I am taking twenty men toward the fort. We will slow Boggs down by harrying him."

"Yui." She gripped his shoulders more tightly. Her vision was blurred and her cheeks felt hot.

Yui laughed, and it was a comforting sound. "Do not worry, Shanna. We are only going to disturb the man, to fire arrows into his flank, to drop trees across his line of travel, to shrill from the deep forest to cut the courage out of his soldiers. We shall not face him. We shall not be hurt. Do you think that our love can last but a day? It is the mandate of Manitou, the wish of Eternity, that our love accompany the years to their destination. Nothing can happen. I will it. Manitou wills it."

He kissed her and was gone, and if he tasted the salt of her tears on her lips, he said nothing about it. He simply turned and strode away, tall, competent, muscular, a god among the lesser warriors who crowded around him.

"Shanna?"

"Yes, Mother Holotok."

Holotok was silent, and when Shanna looked at her the woman was smiling broadly. "That is the first time you have called me 'Mother.' It seems that love is good for our Shawnee maiden. It seems that now she is no longer Shawnee, but Seminole with her heart and her mind."

Am I? Shanna wondered. Am I Seminole now? They were a people she did not care for. Potaqua, Tohope, Krawsatch were Seminoles. But so too were Holotok and Pamda and Yui. *I am Seminole*, she thought, and the thought seemed to lighten the burden she had carried for so long.

Behind and around Holotok were a dozen eager, fearful children. They tugged at her skirt and clung to her leg, hollered and leaped around, depending on their inclination.

"Shanna?"

"I am ready, Mother Holotok."

"As am I. Children, do you know Shanna? This is she. She will be a sister to you. If Mother Holotok is not around and you are hungry or lonely or frightened, you must come to Sister Shanna. Do you understand me?"

"Yes, Mother Holotok," they chimed.

"If you . . ." Mother Holotok said, looking again at Shanna.

"They must come to me," Shanna said. She picked up one small and dirty girl who was rubbing the sleep from her eyes with tiny fists. "You must all do as Mother Holotok says. I will be your sister. I will help you."

"Come along!" Chamtha called. The old chief looked at the two women, at the crowd of children around them. "It is time to go. What foolishness is this?"

"We are coming, Chamtha," Mother Holotok said, and she turned and started after the others, who were already filtering into the forest, walking in a long silent rank, dark figures among the darker trees.

Shanna turned, helped Pamda to her feet, and joined the silent procession, clutching the small girl who had thrown her chubby, hot arms around Shanna's neck and now clung to her, looking toward the forest and the mysterious world beyond.

"You're awfully silent, Dawes."

James Dawes turned his head toward the strutting dark

142

figure of Thomas Harkness. "I've found that it pays to be silent in combat, Harkness."

"Combat! This will be nothing but practice for the gunners. Yui will have fled."

"Perhaps."

The long line of soldiers behind the two officers chatted and joked. The caissons rumbled and screeched. Sabers clanked and the horses clomped heavily along the narrow forest trail.

"Maybe you do not want to meet this Yui," Harkness persisted. "Perhaps you still feel he is wronged by Boggs."

"Perhaps," Dawes said emotionlessly. *Wronged.* How could any people be more wronged? To pay for acts they did not commit. To be slaughtered because they were the nearer, the easier to attack. James Dawes bit at his lower lip. Harkness chuckled.

"It's only your Indian blood rebelling," Harkness said. "Tell me, when the Cherokee play their tom-toms does it stir your soul?"

"Shut up, Harkness. Shut up or I'll kill you."

Harkness turned suddenly ugly, laying bare the malevolent roots of his taunts.

"I don't like you, Captain Dawes. I don't like your bastard Indian heart. I don't like you fooling around with a white woman, a decent woman like Julia Trevor. You pass for a white man with your blond hair and blue eyes, but I can smell the Indian about you." Harkness's voice had fallen to a hiss. They marched forward along the dark corridor formed by the towering cedars.

"Let me tell you how it is here, Captain Dawes. From here on I am your commanding officer in a battlefield situation. If you ever repeat a threat such as you made just now I'll have you summarily shot." Harkness stopped and stepped in front of Dawes, his whiskey breath ripe and raw. "You understand me, don't you?"

"I understand you," James Dawes said.

With a sharp laugh Harkness turned away and marched on through the settling gloom, and Captain James Dawes stood breathing curses through his clenched teeth as the files of soldiers marched past him.

"You ain't alone, sir."

143

Dawes turned, frowning. The speaker was Sergeant Nat Culpepper, a brawny, badly scarred Carolinian.

"Were you speaking to me, sergeant?"

"I was," Culpepper said as Dawes started forward again. He realized he had been clenching the butt of his holstered pistol so hard that his hand was cramped. He slowly released his grip on the weapon. Culpepper, seeing this, grinned.

"I am afraid I don't know what you are referring to, Sergeant Culpepper."

"Oh, don't you now, sir?" Culpepper spat. "I'm referring to that son of a bitch Major Thomas Harkness. There's something wrong in his head, you know? He likes to see people squirm. He likes hurting people."

"You are speaking of one of your officers, Culpepper!" Dawes cautioned the sergeant automatically. His own eyes were digging furrows in Harkness's back as they marched.

"Yes, sir, I am. And I'm talkin' about a man who shouldn't be an officer, shouldn't be a soldier—maybe he shouldn't be allowed to live. I've served with Harkness before, captain. He'll never let up once he's taken a dislike to a man. I don't know what's between you two, but I'll tell you this, there's going to be no end to it unless you break and run. Or until he's dead."

Dawes spun toward Culpepper, not believing what he was hearing. "If you're wise, you will not repeat such sentiments, Culpepper."

"Oh, I'll not be repeating them, sir. I just wanted to let you know you're not alone in hating that bastard. Also you might be thinkin'—a lot of things can happen out here. Sometimes a man don't come back. It can happen to anybody." Culpepper spat again and glanced at Major Harkness's back. The look was significant and wolfish. Dawes knew that duty required him to warn Culpepper again, but he couldn't find his voice. He looked ahead to where the major walked at the head of his column, speaking to one of the Cherokee guides. When he turned back, Culpepper had fallen back into ranks, his scarred face expressionless and horrible.

What had prompted the man to come forward like that? Dawes knew very well what Culpepper was suggesting, but what was behind such a murderous proposal? James Dawes shook his thoughts aside. As much as he disliked Harkness

144

and wished him gone, he would not entertain thoughts of violence. It was not only murder, it was traitorous, and James Dawes was not, would never be, either a murderer nor a traitor.

As for Culpepper, who knew what he was? Dawes decided to warn the sergeant off again at the first opportunity.

In the next moment all thoughts of Culpepper and Harkness were violently dissipated. Dawes didn't see the first man. He heard a sort of gurgling, strangled exclamation and looked toward the line of troops. One man was doubled up; the others around him were looking with strained faces toward the forest.

It wasn't until the soldier fell on his face that Dawes saw the arrow in his back. He started to shout a command to disperse, but before he could do so the muskets opened up from all sides and there were men dying, bleeding, crawling toward the trees and shelter; others ran in confusion in a dozen directions, not knowing where the enemy was.

Dawes, holding his saber against his leg, leaped the tongue of the nearest caisson and drew his pistol, crouching beside the two unarmed artillerymen who had taken cover there.

"Where are they?"

"South side, sir," the whiskered artillery man said. The arrow from behind them whished past Dawes's head and buried itself in the caisson's wooden side. The artillery man flattened himself out against the ground. "North side as well," he said with a grin.

In fact they seemed to be surrounded. Dawes was looking for Harkness, awaiting an order. There were half a dozen men down, and the soldiers were firing at ghosts in the twilight. Muskets bellowed indiscriminately.

"Hold your fire!" Dawes commanded. "You're wasting powder!"

Where was Harkness? Dawes moved in a crouch around the caisson, putting a hand on the flank of the wild-eyed horse in the harness. He had his pistol in hand, but Dawes himself saw no targets. The enemy had come and he had struck. Then he had drifted away on the wind.

Or had he? That was the uncertainty which tightened the muscles, caused the blood to pound in the temples, the entrails to knot up.

Were they out there? Were they waiting to pick off any man who moved, or were they already a mile away, congratulating themselves, knowing that they had left fear as a sentry?

Dawes looked left and then right. Nothing. He saw a man down on the ground, writhing in pain, holding his belly, but of the Seminoles there was no sign.

He darted forward, moving toward the head of the column. Darkness was settling fast in the forest. Smoke still hung heavy across the clearing. He passed four men lying side by side in a prone position, their eyes wide, mouths set grimly.

He nearly stepped on Major Thomas Harkness.

He lay sprawled on his back, one leg drawn up, his head turned to one side, a black rivulet of drying blood at the corner of his mouth, his upper lip curled back to reveal uneven, mocking teeth. His tunic was smeared with a spreading dark stain.

"Looks like a musket ball," Sergeant Culpepper said from behind Dawes. "Looks like them Seminole got him. Seems you're in charge now, captain."

"Are you insane?" Dawes stood and turned. "Did you think you were doing me a favor? Or is there something I don't understand? What could he have done to you worth killing him over?"

Culpepper blinked slowly. His crooked fingers reached up and touched his horribly scarred face. His voice was bland and calm. "I really don't know what the captain means. The major took a risk, looks like. Looks like he paid for it."

Then silently, without saying anything more, Culpepper began to reload his musket, tapping powder from his horn into the octagonal barrel of his weapon.

"What happened?" Dawes said hoarsely.

"It's like I said, Captain Dawes. It seems the major took a chance and got himself nailed. You be careful, Captain Dawes. Don't take no risk of your own."

Culpepper had finished reloading, tamping ball and patch into the muzzle of his musket. Now he winked, slowly, evilly, and he turned his back and walked slowly away.

A dozen thoughts flitted through Dawes's mind. He could have the man arrested, but even if he was sure in his own mind what had happened, there was not the slightest bit of evidence, no witness to corroborate anything Culpepper might have said to him. Dawes was in charge of this expedition now. An expedition which he utterly opposed, an expedition which had been sent to mete out punishment to those who were not guilty. An object lesson, a deterrent. How far could he go now in hindering Boggs's plan to level the Seminole village, to indiscriminately murder the Indians? He was glad Harkness was dead. Glad. Had he spoken to Julia? Could suspicion for Harkness's death fall on Dawes himself? His head buzzed.

"Sir?"

Captain James Dawes drew himself up and faced Lieutenant Murchison, the pink-cheeked junior officer who just now looked as if his knees might buckle.

"How many casualties, Murchison?"

"Sixteen wounded, sir. Three dead." He looked at the contorted figure of Major Thomas Harkness. His eyes traveled inadvertently to the pistol in James Dawes's hand.

"Bury the dead. Transport the wounded back to Fort Madison. Send an armed escort along. Six men should do it. Place Sergeant Culpepper in charge. Withdraw into these trees, Murchison. Place sentries about the perimeter, and send the Cherokee scouts to me. No fires!"

"Yes, sir," Murchison answered with a sharp salute. Still he hesitated before he left. His eyes again went to the body of Major Thomas Harkness, again to the face of James Dawes, who still held the pistol in his hand. Murchison saluted again and was gone. Dawes heard him calling out commands to the men; he saw the caissons being pulled off the road, saw the sentries receiving their instructions.

He looked down, seeing the boot. Highly polished with a thin overlayer of light dust. Unmoving, still. It shamed him, but he felt no sorrow, no grief, no regret. Holstering his sidearm, Captain James Dawes walked toward the camp which was springing up in the forest, waving his arm to hurry the Cherokee scout, Camp Fox, who was jogging toward him from the rear of the column.

They heard the shots from the north and they halted, looking back as sunset bled across the skies above the endless ranks of dark mangroves.

The child clung to Shanna's neck. Pamda gripped her arm.

147

"Hurry along," Mother Holotok said. "The shots are not a bad sign, but a good one. Now the soldiers will come more slowly. Now Yui has shown them that the Seminole are aware of their presence, that the Seminole will fight."

"Yes, Mother Holotok," Shanna said. What the Seminole woman said was true. Once Yui's band of warriors began to strike against the Americans, the soldiers would hesitate, would slow their march, would move cautiously through the forest. Mother Holotok spoke with wisdom. But Holotok did not have a man back there. She did not have the first man she had ever loved making more war, war upon war, the musket balls and arrows flying past him, heedless, blind, heartless missiles of death. She did not have Yui and know that wherever he was the war and death were close by.

They hurried on, and the night closed around them, hiding them from all eyes but the eyes of the war gods who looked down and smiled with contentment. They would have their bloody offering.

The camp was dark and cold and the night winds howled through the endless forest. Across the swamps a panther roared with triumph or disappointment. Children snored softly and the old tossed restlessly in their sleep, muttering in unhappy dreams.

The ground was hard beneath them and the skies were becoming empty of stars as the low clouds swept in from off the ocean. All was still and empty, solemn and barren. Shanna lay awake, her heart pounding too rapidly, too insistently, beneath her breast.

Yui was there. He slipped beneath her blanket, and she rolled to him, gasping with relief. He was kissing her and petting her hair, laughing softly.

"Did you think I would not be back, did you think I did not love you? Did you think anything can happen to me as long as you love me? I know it cannot."

His hand cupped her shoulder and drew her nearer. He drew the blanket higher protectively and she snuggled against him. He was close and warm and reassuring in the night. Shanna threw her leg up over his, trying to get closer, to belong to him. He laughed again beneath his breath, and it was a warming sound, one to thrill the spirits and drive away the darkness.

The camp slept and only they were awake, alive, aware of the highly charged atmosphere of the night. It was like the moment before lightning strikes. The back of Shanna's neck tingled, a slow shudder moved down her thighs, a warm glow spread slowly across her abdomen.

Yui's hand was on her hip, and he rolled to her, his lips going to her breasts. She held his head there, gazing past him at the long and empty night. She felt the heat of his breath against her flesh. She ran a finger around his ear, down the line of his jaw to his lips, and he kissed the finger.

Her hand ran down the length of his muscular back to the uptilt of his buttocks, feeling the clenching and lifting of his body. She gripped him tightly for a moment, clinging to him like a drowning swimmer, letting him lift her higher for that moment before he plunged with her into the depths of the sea, the warm and turgid sea which flowed through her body and threatened to overwhelm, to destroy. She struggled briefly and then gave it up. One can only surrender to an intense and avid, limitless sea, to its strength and waves of sensation, to its sinewy vigor, to its lapping currents which touch the loins and ripple across breasts in teasing rivulets, which swells and drives against flesh and soul alike, opening secret channels, flowing warmly in and as warmly out, a great energetic, muscular sea which raises hips and twists them in a maelstrom motion, a sea of stamina and endless resolution, of tenacity which makes a whirlpool of the body, a flowing, heated reservoir which must spill over or burst, which struggles not in opposition, but in acquiescence, in demanding submission.

Her fingers raked his shoulders and she breathed into his ear, speaking small, meaningless, muddled syllables as he raged against her as he tore her apart, reassembled her ripe, swollen, sated components and ripped her apart again.

It was not enough, she thought; it could never be enough, and suddenly it was. It was more—surfeit, a sweet, overwhelming glut of sensation, a slow, majestic triumph and a slow settling, residual ripples of rich texture, a deep and satisfying glow as Yui kissed her lips.

As Yui kissed her eyes and his fingers ran across her throat and breasts, as his eyes met hers, and his lips, softened and pliant now, met her kiss and held it as his body trembled and she held him, stroking his back as the night ran away to the empty, lonely places where there was no love.

Morning was humid heat, a fiery ball of crimson sun, the crying of a distant loon, a long and endless path through magnolia forests, empty, fetid bogs, strange interludes of almost mystical beauty where poinsettia trees in full, flaming bloom grew among sabal palm, and waist-high luxurious fern flourished across endless stretches of slime-clad swamp where sulphurous springs appeared to be the only source of water.

Shanna had Pamda clinging to one hand, a small child holding fast to the other. The going was treacherous and boggy. At every third step the girl sank to her knees, and without fail she cried out each time it happened, and the adults turned their heads and shushed her until Shanna had to hoist the girl to her shoulders where she rode quite happily, her sticky fingers in Shanna's eyes or pulling at her hair.

Pamda was bearing up well, although she had a tendency to wander from the trail. She spoke of swamp spirits and sky spirits and of those who lived in the bubbling sulphur springs, and of those who clung to her hair and those who dogged her heels, but she trudged on, wide-eyed, gabbling, fearful, trusting, and lost.

Yui was gone again; the day was an empty ominous thing.

He had gone again to his war, and Shanna had not been able to look at his calm, purposeful face, look into those dark, loving eyes when he left. He had kissed the top of her head and had gone. She had watched his shadow depart, waited until she was sure she could see him no more, then lifted her head, wiped her eyes, and gone on.

How could she look at him? How could she look at him and love him and know that she might not see him again, know that he might be killed, that his fine, resilient skin might dry to leather around his bones? That the sinew and muscles, the blood and fluids of his body might be desiccated by the angry sun of war? That what was fine and strong and good might be transformed to moldering waste? That was war, and that was what Shanna despised.

There had been war, always war! It had killed her grandfather and grandmother, it had swept away Cara, her mother, it had taken Lychma from her. It had come in with great stamping, heedless, malevolent feet and crushed all it saw that was good or worthy, reducing the world to loveless rubble. She would not have it happen again!

She would not lose Yui.

War was a serpent to be loathed and crushed, and yet each time it was cut two more grew, each time it was crushed and buried it sprouted from a dozen places, scattering seed everywhere, the issue of a mad and lascivious god.

"It is only another mile to the eagle camp," Mother Holotok said. She had been beside Shanna for some time, but Shanna hadn't even noticed her.

"Fine. Thank you, Mother Holotok. Pamda is tired, I think."

The shots came from a great distance, echoing through the swamps, and the column stopped, turning their heads back toward the north. The war was not so far behind; it stalked them assiduously, with its special cunning and malevolent determination. It laughed and killed and laughed again.

Shanna hurried on, humming to herself loudly, trying to banish the intractable, intimidating ghosts of horror which swarmed about her unguarded thoughts.

They would go to this eagle camp, and there they would rest. And what then? To expect anything but the worst had proved to be folly. One night the alarm would come again. One night they would rise again and again rush into the darkness, hearing the heavy footsteps of war, seeing its dark shadow fall across them. Endless. All was endless and futile and obscene.

Since the day he came.

Since the day the white foot touched the white sand. That day Manitou had turned his face away from his people, perhaps so that they would not see the divine tears shed.

Not that Shanna believed war would end if every white departed. There would aways be Potaquas. But once war had been an infant, a creeping, petty thing. A moment of disruption; a fierce night raid; a horse stolen; a maiden taken away.

With the dawn of the white man it had matured. The infant terror had gotten to unsteady feet and begun to march across the land, growing stronger with each stride, and with each man killed its blood lust increased.

"I despise the war!" Shanna said. It was a moment before she realized she had halted, the child still on her shoulders, her face uplifted, her hands clenched, that she had roared her complaint to the white, heedless skies. Palliated, she walked on, following the tracks of the Seminoles.

Captain James Dawes surveyed the empty, abandoned Seminole camp with vacant blue eyes. Murchison was awaiting his directives. The artillery stood at the ready. The men had been formed into a double rank, muskets primed.

"Sir?" Murchison looked curiously at his captain.

Dawes, standing, put his hands on his hips and stared out at the miserable collection of straw huts, of empty drying racks, corncribs, fishing baskets, neglected gardens. "What shall we do, Murchison? Make war upon this poor collection? This residue of life, this primitive, pathetic community? Shall we bombard these straw huts, set fire to the dry cornfield? I saw a spotted dog. Must have been out hunting when they pulled out. He's sleeping in the shade of that hut. See him? Head on his paws. Shall I send a sniper in or hope the cannon fire eliminates the threat he poses?"

"Sir?" Murchison cast dubious eyes upon his senior officer. The captain's eyes seemed glazed. His mouth was only a thin line sketched finely across his face.

"I say, what should we do, Murchison? Let us consult. Major Harkness is dead. I'm sure he would know what to do in this situation. I, unfortunately, do not. Shall we view this as an opportunity for gunnery practice? Or perhaps a chance to intimidate the Seminoles, to show them that we have cannon and they should not dare to attack us? Of course these people are not the ones who assaulted the Cherokee anyway . . . so perhaps," he muttered, "the lesson would be lost."

"Sir," said Murchison, who was very young and ambitious, and a little self-important, "it was the order of General Boggs that this village be leveled and all inhabitants who would surrender made prisoner."

"Ah." Dawes rocked on his toes. He nodded and looked toward the village again. "In that case, Lieutenant Murchison, we shall bombard the village. It is for you to go down and discover if its sole inhabitant will surrender or fight to the death."

"Sir?" Murchison blinked with incomprehension.

"The dog, Murchison! Attach a white flag to your saber, enter the village, and ask the dog if he will surrender or fight to the death." Dawes gripped the lieutenant's arm below the shoulder and said soberly, "Advise him that we have cannon in position, and that he is surely outnumbered."

Murchison stood staring blankly at Captain Dawes for another moment, wondering if the fever or the heat had taken another man. Was he deranged? Murchison wondered. The memory of James Dawes standing over Major Thomas Harkness returned, and Murchison turned away sharply, nascent terror rising into his mind.

He was mad. At the least bizarre, this Dawes. Murchison had been warned. Harkness had warned him. The man was an Indian.

Murchison, now fearing for his own life, tied a white handkerchief onto his saber tip and advanced upon the camp. Dawes put his hand to his forehead in disbelief. Behind him the men were murmuring, laughing, staring with narrowed eyes.

"Arm your weapons, gentlemen," Dawes said to the gunners. "It is possible the enemy may not surrender."

A pale young Georgian dared to take a step forward and salute. He haltingly asked, "Beg pardon, sir, but what is the target? Which way should the guns be facing?"

"It doesn't matter, does it, corporal? Fire your weapons on command. Burn up your powder. Somewhere the ball will strike and something will be destroyed. Fire at your discretion."

The corporal backed away, his eyes as wide as Murchison's had been. Murchison, meanwhile, was running toward their position, a dog fast on his heels.

"It seems the enemy has torn the seat out of the lieutenant's trousers," Dawes said to the sergeant on the other side. "An act of aggression, blatant and cowardly. Fire at will."

"Sir?" The sergeant had seen some fighting. He had also seen mockery. "Do you truthfully want us to fire?"

"Sergeant, I am afraid that if I do not fire I shall find myself facing a court-martial. By all means, fire."

Yui stood in the forest. From the low sandy knoll he could see the blue-jacketed gunners priming their cannon. He saw the puff of smoke from the muzzle of a thunder gun and the following boom, saw the cannonball strike a chickee and splash its components high into the air in a fountain of kindling and straw.

"Yui." Pohoy touched his shoulder, but the Seminole war leader shook him away.

"Be still, Pohoy, and watch madness at its play."

The day was filled with the roar of cannon fire; the clearing below was obscured by blue-gray smoke. The ground beneath them trembled. The gods of war laughed loud and long.

It was a long run back to eagle camp, but Yui ran the distance gladly, knowing that he would find Shanna at the end of his run. His nostrils still burned with the acrid residue of gunpowder; his ears still rang.

"We had them," Raven said as he jogged. "We had them, but our war leader was too cowardly to attack. We had them, but Yui thinks only of the woman he will bed this night and not of the war.

To the Raven, Yui's cowardice was complete and obvious. In the Raven's view the entire white contingent could have been attacked successfully that afternoon. Their cannon had been discharged indiscriminately. A few chickees were hit. The infantry soldiers stood carelessly about watching the futile gesture. The men were in disarray; their officers behaved as fools. One had gone into the camp and gotten himself bitten by a camp dog—the bravest Seminole on that day.

"Now will you admit that something has gone wrong with Yui?" Raven asked the elders that evening in secret council. "Now do you see that his heart has been taken and squeezed to misshapen cowardice by this Shawnee woman?"

"Because Yui did not choose to attack this day?" Chamtha asked. "Perhaps his spirits told him it was not the time for war."

Raven ignored this weak protest. "You have heard the other men. Yui could have struck terror in their hearts this day, could have brought death to the white man. But we did not attack. We ran and will run again."

"He speaks of joining Osceola."

"Osceola!" Raven laughed. Osceola was in the far south fighting against Jackson in the everglades. "We would be running for months. Before we reached Osceola Yui would have changed his mind again. Why do we run?" Raven bent forward, slapping his chest angrily. "Our war is here, our lands are here, our enemy is here."

"We are too weak to make another kind of war than we have been making," Chamtha protested. "Yui is right. We must be a dog at the white man's heels. Nipping him here and then there."

"Succeeding only in angering him, not in defeating him!

155

Why are we weak? Everyone knows that. Because Yui insulted Potaqua. Because Yui stole Potaqua's property.''

''Nothing can be done about that.''

''I think it can,'' Raven said slyly. Reaching beneath the blanket at his feet, he withdrew a musket. It was new and had been decorated with brass nails driven into the stock. Three feathers were tied to the muzzle of the weapon. ''This is a sign between myself and Potaqua,'' Raven said, his eyes glittering.

''What sign, Raven?''

''It is the sign that Potaqua will ally himself with us. He will help us drive the American invaders from our land—if Yui is replaced. If Raven is made war leader.''

Raven leaned back triumphantly, his legs crossed, his back erect, his foxlike eyes shining. He looked across the fire ring, studying the faces of the elders. They looked confused and hopeful and weary. Ockawa stared at the musket and said:

''It is the right thing.''

''I do not know. But we cannot run forever. When will our homeland be beneath our feet again?'' Chamtha shook his head. ''A man is not made to run like a dog, to fight like one. I want to live long enough to see our land returned, but if I must die to see it''—he sighed and looked at Raven—''then I will die. You are right, Raven. Yui was a great warrior once. I fear this Shawnee girl is a witch. At least a woman of great cunning, one who has the wiles to cut a warrior's manhood away. Yui deceived us when he said he cared nothing for her.''

Still there was distaste in Chamtha's eyes as he looked at the lean, hollow-cheeked young warrior opposite him. Raven was too hard. He was flint. He was too devious and too eager to kill. Yet he was a strong warrior, no one could deny that.

''It is Raven who has made a pact with Potaqua,'' Ockawa said, as if he had been inside his friend's thoughts. ''It is Raven we must confirm as war leader, or it makes no sense.''

There was no dissent. Chamtha's last question hung in the air: ''Who will tell Yui?''

Pohoy waited until Yui was finished bathing in the green, slow-running river. He walked to where Shanna sat watching her man from the shade of the overhanging, moss-laden oaks.

156

He sat beside her and she smiled at him. There was the light of love in her eyes, and Pohoy was glad for that.

"What is it, Pohoy?" Yui walked naked from the river, letting the warm wind whip the drops of water from him as he wrapped his loincloth around his narrow waist. "Have you come to try taking my woman from me?"

"No, Yui," Pohoy answered. He did not return his leader's smile.

"Well then?" Yui sat down beside Shanna, resting a hand on her thigh. Both of them looked expectantly at Pohoy, who sat rubbing his big belly, looking out at the green river.

"Raven has displaced you," Pohoy said. Yui laughed. "I mean it, Yui! He has convinced the elders. Soon Chamtha will tell you."

"Pohoy, you must be making an evil joke," Shanna said. But the big man was not joking. They could read the sorrow in his eyes.

"How?" Yui had been stunned at first. Now a slow anger was building. Shanna covered his hand with her own, feeling the tenseness in him. "How could Raven convince the elders to do such a thing? They know Yui. They know Raven. Why would they make such a choice? How has he brought me down, Pohoy? Tell me this!"

"He has made a pact with Potaqua," Pohoy told him.

"Potaqua!" Yui sprang to his feet. He paced back and forth along the riverbank, looking to the sky. Then, slowly shaking his head, he squatted down, facing Shanna but speaking to Pohoy.

"This will be the end of us, Pohoy. A madman allied with a war lover. Are you sure? You must be sure."

"I am sure. It is so."

"Then," Yui said with resignation, "it is so." He knelt down beside Shanna and she gave him the reassurance of her smile. All was as they had feared. Their love had caused this. Their love had deprived the Seminoles of a wise leader.

"It is as Manitou wishes it," Yui said. "Therefore it is as it must be. Thank you, Pohoy, for telling me."

"It was no happy task. Nor," he said, grunting as he lifted his bulk, rising to his feet, "will this war be a happy task. Raven will want to prove immediately that he is a great leader. There will be recklessness and lives lost. The young men will follow him eagerly. He will give them Spanish muskets and Spanish rum."

"And you, Pohoy?" Shanna asked, "will you follow Raven willingly."

"I will follow Raven," Pohoy said.

"As will I," Yui said. There was no longer bitterness in his words, only resignation. Pohoy left them, and they sat close together, Yui's arm around Shanna, her cheek on his chest.

"How can you follow him?" she asked at last.

"How can I not? These are my people. He is my leader as I was his. Raven followed one whom he despised. I must follow him now."

"Into a bad war."

"So it seems."

"With Potaqua."

"Potaqua will be our true war leader, yes."

"Must you fight?" She tilted her head back and looked up into his eyes. A single drop of moisture clung to his eyebrow, and it sparkled there like a jewel.

"I do not understand you, Shanna."

"Must you fight? Must you die? Must we be unhappy for the sake of a people who have cast you out? Must we fight and die for men like Raven and Potaqua?"

"I still do not understand. Of course I must fight. I am a warrior. Born to fight, I will fight."

"I could not bear to lose you," Shanna said. "I could not, Yui."

"I will not be killed." He smiled and kissed her lightly. "I will fight and our land will be regained. Perhaps they were right to replace me," he said with a small shrug.

"You know they were not."

"No. But things are as they are. So I will fight."

"What difference does one more warrior make?" Shanna pushed away from him in exasperation. He was watching her with warmth and with perplexity.

"What is it you would have me do, Shanna? I cannot displace Raven."

"That is not what I wish. I wish to go." Her eyes searched his hopefully. She placed her hand on his dark knee. "I wish us to leave now, before the war comes again."

158

"Go?" Yui shook his head in confusion. "Go where, Shanna?"

"To where there is peace!" She rose and turned her back to him. She smoothed the front of her linen skirt absently as she stared at the face of the green river, watching an oak leaf swirl past. She faced Yui. "There are places where the Indian and the American live in peace, Yui. I have seen them."

"The Cherokee settlement!" He laughed.

"Yes."

"No. Never."

"Why?"

"They are slaves, Shanna." He was to her, gripping her hands tightly. "They are slaves. A woman who has lived as you have must understand that life. It costs a man his dignity, it costs him his soul. It costs him his freedom, his manhood, his eyes and heart. I will never be a slave. I cannot even consider what you suggest."

"It is not slavery, Yui. Please, listen! They have their land as always."

"They are farmers! The men as well as the women. Once they were warriors, now they are nothing. Neither women nor men."

"They are free!"

"They are slaves! Slaves to the land they pierce with their white tools, slaves to the laws of the white man, slaves to fear."

"And what are we," Shanna asked quietly, "if we are not slaves to this war?"

Raven's anticipated counterattack did not come immediately. The reason for that decision was obvious. They were awaiting the great one. The madman. Potaqua.

Day by day the men prepared their weapons as the camp was held in uneasy stasis.

A week after the impotent attack upon the Seminole camp, the army force had withdrawn, returning to the fort without further contact. Raven was crestfallen. He had wanted to attack the American contingent in the field, wanted to break them and crush them into the ground.

"What does it mean, Yui?" Shanna asked. "Were you

right after all? Could we return now to the camp on the river?"

"I do not know. I do not. The white chiefs are incomprehensible to me."

"Perhaps they need not be," Shanna suggested. She and Yui were working side by side, constructing a small, temporary chickee. The land here was not marshy and there was no need to build on stilts, and so the work was easy. It was also a joy. This, Shanna thought, would be their first home. Rough and temporary as it was, it represented the permanence of their love.

"I do not understand you, Shanna. What do you mean they need not be incomprehensible to us?"

"I have a suggestion, Yui. It may be that I understand nothing of war. Having seen only the results, I imagine my knowledge of its conduct and causes to be limited."

"There is no need to be ironic, my Shanna. Say what it is you have to say and hand me that sheaf of straw or we shall have a wet corner in our home when the rains come."

Shanna went on. "My idea is this, Yui: I have seen this war. I have seen the people suffering. I have watched as we ran, watched as we attacked, watched as we died. But never have I heard talk of peace."

"Peace again!"

"You speak as if it were shameful, but that is not all of my idea. We have heard talk only of war and not of peace because there is no basis for a just peace."

"That is correct, my Shanna."

"But why must that be so? I think it must be so because we do not know what the aim of the Americans is. I think it is because we find them incomprehensible. I think that they must find us equally incomprehensible."

"Yes."

"My idea, Yui, is this: Why do we not speak to the Americans? Why do we not find out if peace can be made? Why do we fight endlessly when there may be a just settlement to be found?"

"The whites are devils!"

"Perhaps they see us as devils."

"Boggs is a madman."

"We have our Potaqua."

"We do not even speak their devilish language."

"I do," Shanna said.

Yui's eyes narrowed. He stared at his wife, astonished at this revelation. "How could you, Shanna?"

"I learned it from my mother, who was a wise and valiant woman, one who believed she must understand the other side in a conflict. I speak English and Dutch. Perhaps my knowledge of the languages is weak, since I listened to my lessons with a child's ear, but I have a knowledge of the tongues. I also have a little French."

"What, no Spanish?"

"No." Shanna's mouth tightened, and Yui was immediately sorry he had mentioned the Spanish. If Shanna was capable of hatred, it was toward the Spanish that her hatred was directed. They had taken her Lychma away onto the vast sea. They had done her a harm beyond forgiveness and restitution.

"I do not know what to say to your proposal, Shanna. Perhaps there is some merit to what you say. However"—he shrugged—"it is no longer my place to make such decisions."

"It could be suggested to the elders."

"Yes."

"What is it, Yui? Do I trouble you?"

"No, Shanna." He sighed and put his straw aside, resting hands on knees. "I am only wondering at myself. A month ago I would never have considered peace on any terms. I would have never considered speaking to the white men. Something has changed me. Perhaps it is you, perhaps it is the memory of the dead, the knowledge that our war from here on will not be so just. We will have our Raven and our Potaqua, they their Boggs, and as you say, what is the difference between them? A just war is a war which must be fought; an unjust war is a war fought for the glory of the war leaders. This, I fear, will be an unjust war."

"Perhaps we can halt it, Yui." Shanna spoke with rising excitement. "We do not know until we have tried. What can it cost us to speak to Boggs or whoever is the white leader? What can it cost us compared to what will be saved?"

"I will think about this, Shanna. I can promise nothing. Understand—it does no good for us to speak to Boggs if we

161

haven't the agreement of the elders that peace should be made.''

"Of course."

"I could propose this meeting, but those who have the power want war. Raven will not consent. And Potaqua . . ." Yui just shook his head. He said nothing else, but began working furiously on the hut once more.

He came that evening. He was astride a tall white horse, a useless creature in a swamp war, but Potaqua did not ride the horse because it was useful. It was a Spanish horse, proud and sleek, powerful. The horse placed him above his followers; it demonstrated his strength, his wealth. He came that evening.

When he came there were six priests before him, thumping muffled drums. When he came there were six hundred men behind him, all armed, all tattooed and fierce, looking with disdain upon their cousins, those who had been forced to beg Potaqua for his help to free themselves of the white man's yoke, those who cowered miserably in this bog, awaiting rescue, a leader, competent soldiers.

"Does he infect them all?" Yui said angrily. He stood glaring at Potaqua's men, seeing the contempt in their faces.

Their chickee was in Potaqua's line of march. They watched as the priests came, and Shanna saw a familiar face among them—Apopkakee, the boy who would be a warrior. He had been initiated into their ranks. Now he marched solemnly behind Tukakee, his father, who appeared now so withered and old that Shanna at first did not recognize him.

Apopkakee seemed to have grown taller, and in his paint and feathers, his topknot carefully groomed, he appeared mature, no longer a boy. His eyes, sweeping the faces of the gathered Seminoles, met those of Shanna, and he nearly stumbled, missing a beat on his drum. He recovered and walked on.

"Look at him," Yui said with disgust. He spoke of Potaqua. Potaqua who had lifted his white horse into a prancing, sideways gait. Potaqua who wore two pistols stuck into the waist of his loincloth, Potaqua who wore a long feathered cape and gold bracelets, who had painted his face demonically, bright-green with circles of black around the eyes, with a crimson smear across his mouth. Potaqua who held his musket over his head and laughed mirthlessly as his horse chased onlookers from his path with its slashing hooves.

"Come along, Shanna. I must see a part of this."

Together they walked through the throng, Yui shouldering his way through the Seminole soldiers, one of whom started to object, then saw who it was who had nudged him and fell silent.

Yui had halted. "Yes," he said with both amusement and bitterness. "Look, Shanna."

Raven had come forth from out of his hut. He was dressed in all of his finery—clamshell necklaces, bone earrings, three black streaks of paint running vertically across his face, an egret cape, and in his hand the symbolic musket. Raven lifted a hand in greeting to Potaqua, but the great one, the madman, did not respond.

Slowly Chamtha and Ockawa, Hepth and Torkol appeared. The elders came forward to stand beside and behind Raven, weapons in their hands. Potaqua laughed out loud.

"Where is the war leader, Yui?" Potaqua asked.

"We have no war leader called Yui," Raven said.

"Is this so, elders?"

"It is so, Potaqua," Chamtha answered.

Potaqua laughed again. He handed his musket to Immokallee, his lieutenant, slid from his horse's back, and walked forward to greet his cousins. As he came the elders placed their weapons upon the ground and stood, arms folded, watching.

"Who is war leader?" Potaqua asked Chamtha.

"The man before you, Krawsatch," the elder answered, and Potaqua embraced Raven.

"Shall we council, cousins?" Potaqua said.

"Come into my poor hut," said Chamtha. "There is food and drink. We shall fill the pipe and talk of what must be."

Potaqua nodded. He was still laughing as he turned in a slow circle, studying the villagers around him. He was laughing until his eyes settled on Yui and Shanna, who stood together near the stamping white horse. Then Potaqua's face set into a stone mask. His body seemed to go rigid. He seemed about to say something, but he changed his mind and turned, laughing again, to Raven. "Let us smoke a pipe, my brother. Let us drink the rum I have brought with me. Let us speak of the death of the white dogs."

163

"He hasn't forgotten or forgiven," Yui said to Shanna. He squeezed her shoulder. "To his mind it was the grossest treachery, my taking you from that Spanish ship. He will never forget. His is a brooding mind and a vengeful one."

"Yui." Shanna turned to him and gripped his arms. "I do not want to be here. I do not want to be a Seminole. I do not want anything to happen. Let us go! We can. We can travel anywhere."

"And what of your peace, Shanna? What shall we do— leave the people in the hands of Potaqua?"

"I don't care! Let us go north or west, away from all of this war, this madness."

He would not look at her. His eyes went to the council hut, and in his eyes was an angry fire. Yui would not leave his people. He would do anything else for her, Shanna thought, but he would never abandon his people to the leadership of men like Raven and Potaqua; and Shanna, watching Yui, felt the first dark foreboding stir in her breast. A sleeping, ominous presentiment, it now awakened, its slumber disturbed by the man who had come. He. The madman.

❋ 10 ❋

"This is an informal hearing, gentlemen. No charges have been brought against anyone. It is simply an attempt to establish the facts surrounding the death of Major Harkness, to examine the ineffectual and abortive expedition against the Seminole Yui."

And to skewer me, James Dawes thought bitterly. General George Boggs even managed to smile as he propped himself behind his desk and began trimming the cigar he had taken from a desktop cedar box.

Present in the general's office were Dawes, Murchison, Lieutenant Taylor, Sergeant Major Lewis Raleigh, Sergeant Nathan Culpepper, Corporal David T. Caulderman, and two private soldiers, one of whom acted as company clerk and recorder.

The general lit his cigar meticulously, turning the tip of it through the flame of his match, taking gentle puffs until he had the ember exactly as he wanted it. Then he waved out the match and sat back, staring expectantly at Dawes.

"Do you want to again briefly summarize the incidents in question, Captain Dawes? For the official records," he said, indicating with a nod that the secretary should begin recording this interview.

"In the face of a perceived threat against the army contingent at Fort Madison by the Seminole Yui and his warriors, General George Boggs—"

"It doesn't have to be so formal, Captain Dawes. As I've emphasized, this is only an informal hearing. Something went wrong; let's discover what it was and take preventative measure to ensure that it doesn't occur again. We're all on the same side of this conflict, after all."

"Yes, sir." Dawes rubbed his eyes wearily. "We were

within ten miles of Yui's camp when we were hit by Seminole raiders. They set upon us from all sides. They presented no targets to our soldiers. We immediately sought any available cover. Shots were exchanged, although most of our bullets must have been fired ineffectively, as there were no Indian warriors visible at any time. We suffered three fatalities and sixteen wounded—I believe two of these have since perished."

"Unfortunately." Boggs waved his cigar-burdened hand. "Go on, Captain Dawes."

"I waited until there was a lull in the firing and then sought out Major Harkness, wishing to ascertain his intentions. I found the major dead. I assumed command."

"One minute, Captain Dawes." The general leaned forward, forearms on his desk. "Did anyone actually see Major Harkness die?"

"Not to my knowledge, sir."

"What was the cause of death?"

"A musket ball had struck his heart, general."

"I see. Go on, please."

"Assuming command, I dispatched the wounded to Fort Madison and then proceeded with the column toward Yui's camp."

"Instead of pursuing the raiders."

"There seemed little hope of effective pursuit in that country, sir. The Seminoles are like ghosts in the forest. I decided to follow your prime directive and push on to the Seminole camp."

"Which you found in what condition?" Boggs asked.

"It was apparently abandoned."

"Apparently?"

"At first sight I could not be certain, but it appeared to be abandoned. I instructed Lieutenant Murchison to make an inspection of the village to discover if there were any inhabitants in fact. If he met with anyone he was instructed to ask them to surrender or inform them that we had cannon and the village would be shelled."

"Lieutenant Murchison met with no resistance?"

Boggs looked at Murchison, who shifted uneasily on his haunches.

"He found no Seminole people."

166

"You then proceeded to level the village."

"That is correct, sir. That was a directive of yours and one which I followed to the letter. As, if I may say so, I followed each directive and proceeded as I believed Major Harkness intended."

"No one is trying to fault your conduct, Dawes. From what you have told us, it appears that you have followed directives to the letter." Boggs smiled thinly. "However, certain questions remain unanswered."

Damn the man, Dawes thought, he's enjoying this. Toying with me, slowly squeezing.

Boggs said, "Rest easy, Captain Dawes. I'll proceed to interview the other witnesses. You see, gentlemen, although the campaign indeed may have been properly conducted as far as the literal interpretation of my orders went, there are still major questions concerning field discretion and competence."

"It is not my duty to interpret orders, sir," Dawes objected.

"It is your duty to use common sense and not make a mockery of my directives, sir!" Boggs flared up briefly and then settled back. "Rest easy, captain," he said again, no more sincerely. "This is only an attempt to discover the truth."

Boggs had to relight his cigar. "Now then. This investigation is concerning itself with two separate points. One, the death of Major Harkness; two, the conduct of the campaign against Yui.

"Let us first concentrate on the death of Major Thomas Harkness. Lieutenant Taylor?"

"Sir!" Taylor who was young, fair-haired, and diffident, nearly came out of his seat as Boggs's attention suddenly focused on him.

"How would you describe the relations between Major Harkness and Captain Dawes?"

"Just a minute!" James Dawes rose from his seat, his face reddening.

"Sit down, Captain Dawes!"

"What sort of turn is this inquiry taking? What in the devil difference is there how I got along with Tom Harkness?"

"Sit down, captain." Boggs was no longer smiling. "Sit down if you wish to remain present."

Dawes did so, running a hand across his forehead. He looked at young Taylor, who was clearly unnerved, torn between duty and friendship.

"I'm waiting, Taylor," the general said.

"They worked well together, I thought."

"How did they get along personally?"

"They used to fish together, sir, sometimes ride on their off-duty hours."

"Lately?"

"Lately was different," Taylor admitted.

"How?"

"Sir?"

"How was it different lately between these two men who had gone fishing together, riding together?"

"I couldn't say, sir," Taylor said helplessly.

"Sir, you had better say."

"Well, there seemed to be a certain amount of friction."

"What amount?"

"Sir?" Taylor goggled at his commanding officer.

"I said, Lieutenant Taylor, what amount of friction was there between Major Harkness and Captain Dawes?"

"There was quite a bit I should say, sir," Taylor said, hanging his head.

"Murchison?"

"There was constant friction, sir."

"And the cause?"

"I would rather not say, sir."

"You had damned well better say, lieutenant."

"It seemed to center around Miss Julia Trevor, sir," Murchison said.

"I won't have Julia's name brought into this," Dawes said, coming to his feet.

"I appreciate your gentlemanly concern, captain," Boggs said with the deepest irony. "However, if Julia Trevor has a bearing on this episode, we shall have to hear of it. May I remind you that you have been warned, captain; sit silently or I will have you removed."

Murchison was staring at the general. He realized that Boggs wanted him to go on. "As I say, it seemed to center around Miss Julia Trevor, sir."

"A romantic rivalry?" Boggs asked.

"I'm sure I couldn't say, sir," Murchison replied.

"You have no idea?"

"I have no firsthand knowledge," Murchison said.

"But there have been rumors?"

"Yes, sir." Murchison sighed and glanced quickly at James Dawes. "There have been rumors that Major Harkness was deeply interested in Julia Trevor."

"Isn't Miss Trevor engaged to Captain Dawes?"

"That is my understanding, sir."

"Harkness intended to ply his love for Miss Trevor in the face of this engagement?"

"He did, sir. So the rumor goes. It is said that he intended to make certain facts about Captain Dawes evident to Miss Trevor in order to discredit the captain."

"Certain facts?" Now Boggs was on his feet. He moved around his desk to face Lieutenant Murchison. Dawes sat staring at the wall beyond the general, knowing what was coming, not caring so much any longer. "What facts, Lieutenant?"

"That Captain Dawes is part Indian," Murchison muttered.

"Excuse me? I did not hear you, Murchison. Speak up!"

"I said that Captain Dawes is part Indian! Sir!"

"Ah." The general returned to his seat. "Knowing Miss Trevor's background as we do, we can assume that such information would have been highly damaging to the relationship between Miss Trevor and the captain." His eyes shuttled to Dawes. "Did you know about this, captain?"

"Sir?"

"Did you know that Harkness was about to reveal to Julia Trevor the fact that you are part Indian?"

"I knew it."

"What was your reaction, Dawes?"

"Anger."

"Did you threaten Harkness?"

"I may have."

"You were overheard."

"All right! I threatened him. He made me angry with his devious intimations, with his callousness, and I threatened him."

"I see." General Boggs rubbed his chin. "Now then, we

have the background, I believe. Let us proceed to the actual incident. Murchison?"

"Sir?" Murchison asked, himself a little weary now.

"You came upon Major Harkness's body soon after he had been shot."

"Yes, sir, I did."

"Will you describe that?"

"After the Seminole attack," Murchison said slowly, "I too went looking for my commanding officer to see what his orders were. I found him dead."

"Alone?"

"Sir?"

"Was he alone when you found him?"

"Captain Dawes had reached the body first. I found him standing over the body. He had a pistol in his hand," Murchison said, nearly choking.

"A pistol?"

"Yes, sir."

"It had not been discharged!" Dawes said, enraged by the turn of the investigation.

"Had it, Murchison?"

"I could not say with any degree of certainty, sir."

"Very well. Let it lie. You then proceeded to the Seminole camp under the command of Captain Dawes."

"Yes, sir," Murchison said, leaning back with some relief. Although he had his own suspicions, he had not wanted to be put into the position of actually accusing Dawes of having killed Harkness.

"Describe the events, Murchison. You have already heard Captain Dawes's recollections. Would you say he was accurate in his narration?"

"Oh, yes, sir," Murchison said hastily. He appeared wilted and confused. He looked again at James Dawes, who had resumed a rigid sitting position.

"In all details."

"Yes, sir. Of course . . ."

"Of course what, Murchison? Dammit, man, I am asking you—no, ordering you—to relate the events as they happened. As *you* saw them."

"We found the Seminole camp empty of inhabitants, sir,"

Murchison said, speaking so rapidly that his words were scarcely separated. "There was, however, a dog in the camp."

"A dog!" Boggs bellowed.

"A dog, sir. The captain requested that I tie a flag of truce to my saber and proceed into the camp . . ." now Murchison's words came hesitantly, heavily; he looked again at Dawes and shook his head in apology. "The captain instructed me to ask the dog if it would surrender and to warn the animal that we had cannon in position."

"Did you?" Boggs asked, his lips hardly parting, his face growing crimson. Nat Culpepper choked off a laugh, and the general's eyes flickered that way.

"It was an order, sir. I proceeded to do as the captain had instructed me."

"With the result being?"

"I had inflicted upon my person a painful injury which had to be attended by the company physician."

Boggs stood again, hands clasped behind his back. He stared at the floor. "Did this request, this order, not seem odd to you, Murchison?"

"Extremely so, sir."

"Extremely odd. Is that how you would characterize the captain's order?"

"Yes, sir."

"Bizarre?"

"Yes, sir."

"Incomprehensible?" Boggs walked behind his secretary, reading the notes over the soldier's shoulder to make sure of the record. "Incomprehensible, Murchison."

"Yes, sir. Incomprehensible."

"Sergeant Major Raleigh. You were in charge of the artillery detachment, were you not?"

"Yes, sir," Raleigh said, standing at full attention, his chest out, his chin drawn into his throat.

"At this point I believe Captain Dawes ordered a bombardment of the Seminole camp."

"He did, sir."

"You complied?"

"He was the officer in command, sir," Raleigh said, as if his own behavior were being unjustly questioned.

"What were your primary targets?"

"The captain did not say, sir. The corporal here asked where our fire should be directed and I heard the captain respond that it didn't matter to him, just to fire whether we hit anything or not."

"And you didn't question the order?"

"Sir, I have never questioned an order. We set powder and ball and began firing, making a lot of noise and smoke. I believe some of the Indian huts were hit."

"And the captain?"

"Sir?" Raleigh cocked his head as if that would help him to comprehend.

"What was Captain Dawes doing during this time?"

"Oh, I see what you mean, sir. He was just standing there, as it were. Rocking on his toes."

"What were your thoughts, Raleigh? No, let me put it another way." Boggs tilted toward the sergeant. "Would you be eager to serve under Captain Dawes during a battlefield engagement after the events you have described?"

"Sir," Raleigh said thoughtfully, "Without prejudice, I believe I should be a little chary of serving under the captin in battle."

"So should we all, Sergeant Major Raleigh," Boggs said. "So should we all."

There was a little more. Boggs ran the corporal through his story, which was substantially the same as Raleigh's, then interviewed the private soldier and asked Lieutenant Taylor a little more about the rancor between Harkness and Dawes, but in effect the probe had ended after Raleigh's statement. No, he wouldn't serve under Dawes if he had the choice. That was what Boggs wanted to establish.

To establish that Dawes was incompetent, incomprehensible, unable to lead, possibly dangerous, not fit to command.

It was another hour before Dawes and the general were left alone. The others had filed out solemnly, none of them looking at Dawes. The door had closed behind them, leaving Dawes and Boggs in a vast, heavy silence.

"I have to relieve you of command, Dawes."

"Yes, sir."

"That doesn't surprise you or anger you?"

"No, sir."

172

Boggs pursed his lips, shaking his head as if with great sorrow. Dawes couldn't guess what his true emotions were.

"You know that this is the end of your military career, don't you?"

"Is it?" It didn't seem to matter much just then. The only thing that mattered was Julia, and already Dawes knew that this was the end of that as well.

"Oh, you could hang on for quite some time," Boggs said, spreading his arms as he yawned. "Until retirement, possibly. But you'll never rise above your present rank. You must know that now."

"I do," he said indifferently.

"This"—he slapped the notes left by the secretary—"will become a permanent part of your record. I couldn't court-martial you, Dawes. There just isn't enough proof of anything. You're the only one who will ever know what happened between you and Harkness. As for the rest of it—well, as you say, you followed orders. But I won't have you in my command!" His fist fell against the desktop. "No, sir, I'll be damned if I'll have a lunatic, murdering Indian under me." Boggs was trembling as he spoke, the anger rising. Dawes watched him dispassionately. "You'll resign, of course?"

"I haven't decided," Dawes said.

"No? I thought it was obvious that that is your only course. If you won't, you won't, I suppose. I have duty for you then." Boggs actually grinned. "You'll remove yourself from Fort Madison proper and establish yourself as adjudicant on the Cherokee reservation. You'll settle things when a Cherokee's pig eats his neighbor's corn. You'll decide who the father of a baby is. You'll decide who has stepped on whose ancestor's bones. And you'll stay there until you resign or rot away, sir. You may take a tent or establish yourself in the disused grain shed. You will not return to this post for any reason whatever. You shall send a man with your report on conditions in the settlement to me each Friday morning.

"Maybe you'll be happier there, who knows. With your own people. You are dismissed, sir."

Outside sunset was flushing the skies above Fort Madison. A hundred gulls from the nearby beaches swirled and darted, squawking loudly overhead as the garbage was taken from the post kitchen to be buried. The few soldiers Dawes saw seemed distant, but that might have been imagination. Damned fool, he thought angrily. Why not resign? Why not turn around and do it at this moment, get out of this stinking fort, this stinking Florida where they all look at me as if I'm hydrophobic?

Yet he did not turn back. He walked toward the barracks to pick up his personal belongings, followed by the jeering of the gulls.

When he again stepped out onto the plankwalk before the barracks the skies were purple, the shadows deep. The birds had flown.

He was still standing there, his duffel beside him, when there was a cry and the gate of the fort opened. The wagon rolled toward it and through it, the gates closing behind it, and James Dawes hefted his duffel and walked on. He had gotten only the briefest look at the girl who rode in the wagon box. It was to be his last look. He would never see Julia Trevor again.

He would have only that moment. That moment when she sat beside the driver and her mother, her hands folded on her lap, her eyes staring straight ahead, her back rigid, unyielding, her face flushed by the dim light of the dusky skies. And then the gate had closed. She was gone. Harkness must have chuckled from his grave.

The evening skies were alight with the glow of the bonfires. The trees surrounding the Seminole camp seemed to sway and move in the light of the flames. There was the playing of drums and cymbals, the thin high wail of a flute, the chants of drunken dancers as they moved in uneven rhythm, their legs withered by rum, their faces flushed and joyous.

Yui turned away in disgust.

"You see how simple it is to be a great war leader, my Shanna. One buys the allegiance of warriors with gifts and rum."

"Have you thought about my plan, Yui?" Shanna asked.

Yui was preoccupied. It was a moment before he turned to her and said: "Your plan for peace? Do you know what kind of mood these men are in now, to what pitch Potaqua has prodded them? They are ready to war, they are ready to kill, willing to be killed. They are convinced of their destiny. No,

I did not approach the elders with your plan. They will speak to no white man now."

"If you spoke to them perhaps they would wait. They know you, Yui. They loved you, worshiped you."

"No more," he said without rancor. "No more, Shanna. That day is past. I am nothing to them, nothing at all."

"If they try to storm that fort many will die."

"Do you not think I see that? Tell them, Shanna!" He waved a hand toward the painted, dancing warriors. "Tell them it is madness."

He turned away, both hands raised. Shanna could see the tension in his back, the tendons standing out on his neck. Slowly he relaxed, slowly he conceded to fact. He took her hand briefly without looking at her face.

"I cannot watch this, Shanna. I cannot think, I cannot sleep. Let me walk alone for a time. Let me go out into the silence, somewhere where I cannot see the fires of madness and hear the song of folly."

She let his hand slip away, let him go, her eyes following him until the shadows covered him. She turned back toward the fire, watching the dancers. The warrior Kaal was watching her. No, he was watching the path where Yui had disappeared. Shanna looked behind her, but Yui was gone. What did the man want?

He held a new musket, one with brass studs in the stock, decorated with feathers. Kaal's mouth hung slightly open. His body was tilted forward as if he were about to spring into motion, but he simply turned and walked away, leaving Shanna to frown and speculate about this mad one, this animal, Kaal.

She returned to her chickee, but it was empty and cold without Yui. Walking around the camp, she came to the hut where Mother Holotok and her brood slept. Entering, she found Holotok telling the transfixed children the tale of Wakechee, the storm maker. Pamda sat with them, hand on her chin, eyes as bright as any child's. Holotok motioned to Shanna, but she shook her head and went out again.

The drums pounded incessantly, maddeningly. The drums pounded and the men danced. The drums pounded and the warlords plotted death. Shanna put her hand to her forehead and walked swiftly away, entering the dark forest.

175

She walked along the river trail, hoping to meet Yui, although she knew that Yui wished to be alone for a time.

The moon was rising, and it silvered the slowly flowing river. The tips of the trees held moonlight. An owl swooped low across the river. The man was suddenly before her.

"Yui?" Shanna halted abruptly, knowing it was not Yui.

"It is I, Shanna," Apopkakee said. "I am sorry I cannot be Yui."

"What are you doing out here, Apopkakee?"

"I followed you. I wished to speak with you."

"What have we to speak about?"

"Shanna, please tell me you are not angry with me still." Apopkakee came nearer to her, and she could see the anguish on his moonlit, boyish face.

She smiled. "No, I am not angry. After all, if it had not been for your failure to guide us north that night I would never have found Yui."

"Does he mean so much to you?" Apopkakee asked, almost with distress.

"Yes. He does."

"I see." He was silent a moment. "That night, Shanna . . . I wanted to come!"

"Do not explain, Apopkakee. You did not come. We walked north alone. Yui captured us."

"Lychma—that too was my fault." Apopkakee shook his head and looked upon the river. "I cannot tell you what my sorrow was like. She is gone to the far lands, and it was my fault, it was my cowardice, which caused it."

"Let us speak of it no more," Shanna said sharply. She did not wish to think of Lychma, to imagine what had befallen her. "Let us walk a little way, Apopkakee." She took his arm. "You have grown tall!"

"Yes. Tall and in a small way important." He helped Shanna across a fallen log. "But still my heart is troubled. I am not a priest despite the visions."

"The visions?"

"Yes. After you had gone with Yui they began to come. One night I saw a fiery rain falling from a white sky. I rose from my bed and under some compulsion I do not understand I went to Potaqua."

"What happened?"

"I told him of my dream and he asked me, 'Are you not a priest? The son of Tukakee?' I said that it was so, and he rose from his bed. The entire camp was awakened and we marched through the night. In the morning a runner brought the news that an American army force had destroyed our camp."

"And so your vision was true?"

"Yes. But I almost wish it had not been so. I was initiated the following day. Potaqua has kept me by his side ever since."

"It is an honor," Shanna said. They had stopped beneath a twisted, moon-lacquered oak, and Apopkakee leaned against the tree. In his paint and wearing his feathered cape, he looked like a child wearied of playing grown-up.

"It is an honor," Apopkakee said with a sigh.

"But you do not care for it?"

"Shanna," he blurted out, "I have cared for nothing since you left!" He smiled and leaned back, the moonlight on half of his face. "When I knew you, I had life. When you left there was nothing, it seemed, but preparing for death. I know—" He held up a hand. "Do not say I am young, there are good things ahead, there will be another woman. I tell myself these things, but I know inside that it cannot be so. There was you; then there was life. . . . Well, you do not wish to hear my shameful confessions. I must embarrass you."

"You flatter me, Apopkakee."

"A child's flattery." He smiled ruefully. "I should have gone north with you to become a Shawnee warrior."

"Perhaps. How do we know what should be done? The longer I live, the more I accept the view that there is nothing which is not preordained. We struggle against our destinies, but it is useless."

"Yet you struggle, Shanna."

"Yes. One must struggle." Shanna came to a decision. "You say you care for me, Apopkakee; what if I were to ask you a great favor?"

"I would do anything," he said immediately, sincerely.

"It might be dangerous."

"Anything," he repeated.

"It has been in my mind to speak to the white men to discover if peace cannot be made. I would go now—Yui

177

would go with me—except that now is the time when Potaqua sings his war songs, when he listens to no one, when the warriors have been told they must spill blood. I would go to Fort Madison, Apopkakee, I would speak to the whites and discover what they want, but I cannot go while Potaqua is waging war.''

"What is it you are asking of me, Shanna?"

"This.'' She moved nearer, her voice lowering. "What you have told me of your visions, of Potaqua trusting to your prophecies, has given me hope.''

"I did not mean that he obeys my wishes!"

Apopkakee was trembling. Shanna looked at him and thought, He is still the boy who was frightened to leave his tribe. She spun away, her hands falling against her hips.

"Shanna.'' She felt his hand on her neck. "Tell me what it is you want. I have failed you. Perhaps now I can make amends.''

"I have told you it is dangerous,'' Shanna said. "I see that you have no wish to do it. I cannot blame you, Apopkakee. I still am your friend. I was asking the impossible.''

"Tell me what it is, Shanna. Turn to me. Look at me. I am not a boy. Yes, I fear Potaqua, but so do many men. Tell me what it is you want.''

She turned toward him uncertainly. Could he do it? It was not right to endanger him, to use him. Yet many lives might be saved if Apopkakee could accomplish what she had in mind.

"If you went to Potaqua and told him you had had a new vision, would he listen?"

"Yes, of course.''

"If you told him . . . that in your vision you saw him being crushed by the whites. If you told him that in your vision Manitou had come and said to you that the moon was not right, that Potaqua must fight no battle until the moon was full again, what then?''

"I do not know, Shanna!'' Apopkakee was aghast.

"You would not be going against his will, Apopkakee. You would simply be telling him to wait a little while. A little while during which I could go to the fort and perhaps discover a means for peace! You could save the lives of many people.''

178

"It might not work, this plan of yours. Who is to say they will speak with you and Yui? Who is to say the elders will listen to any proposal you might return with? Who is to say there will be peace?"

"I am not speaking of certainty, Apopkakee. I am speaking of a chance. A chance for peace, a chance to keep alive those friends of ours who now walk this earth. A chance!"

The young priest was silent. He looked at the ground beneath his feet and then at his hands. Finally his gaze returned to Shanna's face.

"I will do it," he said, his voice muffled and uncertain. "I will do what you ask. I will not fail you again, Shànna."

Then before she could thank him he walked swiftly away, breaking into a run as he reached the trees and Shanna felt pity for him. She pushed the pity aside, however, and turned westward, following the river. She must find Yui and tell him that there might be a chance for a period of grace, a chance to prevent the unleashing of the dogs of war.

He watched her go, and then he silently turned away. He watched her go, and his eyes glittered in the moonlight. His chest rose and fell with exultation. It was rare to see the Raven smile, but he did so now. He had taken a dozen steps when he heard the musket touched off. Then the Raven laughed out loud, looking over his shoulder toward the west.

Shanna halted abruptly. The musket report still rang in her ears. She frowned and started slowly on.

"A drunken warrior, testing his new weapon," she told herself, but already her feet were hurrying forward, and soon she was running breathlessly along the river's edge, leaping obstructions, her hair flying, the moon lighting her way.

She rounded the river bend, heard the rustling in the underbrush beside her and turned quickly that way. She fought her way through the tangle of vines and scrub oak and was suddenly into the clearing.

"Yui!"

He sat slumped against the trunk of an oak, his eyes staring blankly at Shanna. She was to him, stroking his hair, searching his body for wounds, and Yui laughed.

"You're all right!"

"Too much rum, I think." Yui lifted an arm, and Shanna looked behind her to see the sprawled figure of Kaal lying against the dark earth, his face covered with leaves and blood. Yui's knife was in his throat.

"Here, let me up," Yui said, and he rose to cling to Shanna, who was shaking violently.

"I thought he had killed you. It is Kaal, is it not? I saw him earlier. I should have known. He was wolfish. I should have known what it meant when I saw him watching you."

"He is dead. It does not matter. Be still, my Shanna." He held her, stroking her hair, and her tears ran down across his chest. He held her away and smiled, looking into her damp eyes. "Do you love me so much?"

"I cannot even say how much I love you, Yui. And I thought you were dead." She wiped the tears away with a knuckle.

"Very nearly," Yui said slowly. He walked to where Kaal lay, the musket beside him, just out of reach of his curled, still fingers. "He came to kill me. I was beside the tree. He fired and missed. Kaal was too eager to do his work, too eager to kill. He missed, and I killed him. Then, forgive me, I sat down to rest against the tree. I sat down to rest and to look at Kaal and decide what this meant."

"Raven sent him! Raven and Potaqua."

"Perhaps. With Kaal, who is to know? He was a mad child. A dangerous coward, a brutal innocent. What he did he frequently had no reason for doing. He came and tried to kill. Perhaps he thought I was a demon from some personal hell of his. Perhaps he thought I was Mish-sha-shak, come to take him to my underworld."

"Perhaps he thought you were Yui," Shanna said, unconvinced by any of Yui's speculation.

"Perhaps so," Yui said with a thin smile. "Come. I do not wish to stay beside the dead."

Nor did Shanna. Yui picked up the musket and hurled it toward the river. Then, looping his arm around Shanna's waist, he walked with her toward the village, where still the fires raged, where still the drums thumped, where still the men drank the poisonous white rum.

They walked through the camp, heedless of the eyes which followed them. They saw Pohoy sitting alone over a small cooking fire and spoke briefly to him.

"This is bad, Yui. My heart is a stone. Soon Potaqua will want to war and I will go with him, but the joy of battle is gone forever. It will never be as it was when you and I were together, when we went willingly to test our arms against those of the enemy."

"Perhaps you are growing old," Yui said in a joking tone. There was no humor in Pohoy's answer.

"Perhaps I am."

They left the giant brooding beside his small fire and returned to their chickee. Yui, amazingly, was able to fall asleep. Shanna was not.

She lay awake listening to the drums, the whoops, the quieter sounds of Yui breathing, watching the moon rise higher into a tortured sky.

"Shanna."

The whispered sound of her own name being spoken reached her. She sat up, confused and dazed. She had somehow finally fallen to sleep and wandered through a series of broken, frightening dreams filled with bloody Kaals and wolflike creatures with wings, with small annoying spirits no bigger than her thumb, with faceless men who pretended to be Yui.

Shanna looked around in the darkness, thinking at first it must have been Yui who had called her name, that he wished to hold her in his arms and make love to her, but he still slept peacefully.

Who then? She slipped from her bed and peered out of the chickee.

"Shanna."

She heard or thought she heard her name whispered again. Apopkakee. It must be. She dressed quickly and stepped out into the darkened camp, seeing no one but here and there a drunken warrior asleep on the bare ground.

She hesitated. Nothing moved across the camp. A slow, thin mist was drifting across the sky. Had she been dreaming after all? One of those persistent dreams which obtrudes into the waking minutes which follow sleep?

There was a sound. Shanna turned her head. A small, indistinct sound like someone again whispering. Was it imagination?

If it was Apopkakee he would not be able to speak to her in

the camp. He would be silent and wary. And if it was Apopkakee, then she must speak to him. She sheathed herself in determination and walked toward the dark forest beyond the camp clearing, watched only by a yellow dog.

She moved along the path which had its beginning near where she had believed the sound to come from. She paused frequently, listening, calling out herself softly:

"Apopkakee?"

There was no answer. A small animal, possibly a fox, dashed away from nearly underfoot, and Shanna went on. The mist was cool, the moon veiled by it, the trees were dark and still. She could smell the river nearby.

"Apopkakee?" she whispered again.

"Shanna."

The voice was so faint that she could hardly be sure it was her name which had been spoken. She leaned forward, peering into the darkness, seeing nothing.

"Where are you?"

There was no answer. Shanna went on, turning toward the river, which she could see now glimmering dully in the moonlight.

Apopkakee was standing beside a tree, his mouth open, blood smearing his chest. A lance had been driven through his chest and into the tree, and it alone was holding him up. He was dead, and his sightless eyes still held terror.

Shanna leaped back in horror; her heel struck a tree root and she fell to the ground, scrambling up to run blindly through the forest, her heart pulsing in her throat, her head spinning crazily, the loud mocking laughter of Raven in her ears.

❀ 11 ❀

Camp Fox lay in the long, sun-warmed swamp grass, watching the grasshopper which gnawed scallops along the side of the blade of grass it was climbing. The sun was warm on Camp Fox's back. He was thirsty. He yawned heavily, bringing tears to his eyes.

Camp Fox was a Cherokee. The Seminoles had killed his wife and his small son. He did not like the white men, but he hated the Seminoles more, and seeing that the Americans had the strength to fight against the Seminole nation and intended to do so, Camp Fox had joined them as a scout.

It was good work. He did not have to live with the whites. He did not have to put on their uniforms and boots. He simply had to find the Seminole and tell the Americans where they could be found.

Usually the Seminoles were gone before the clomping, careless Americans reached their position. But at times they came up unseen upon the Seminoles, and those were times of joy for Camp Fox, for he was allowed to join the battle and kill the Seminole devils.

The grasshopper moved again, and Camp Fox prodded it with his fingertip.

He felt something beneath him, and Camp Fox was suddenly still, as still as a dead man. The earth was moving, and it spoke to Camp Fox.

He slithered forward slightly and slowly lifted his head so that his eyes could see above the swamp grass which covered the knoll where he had taken up a position.

For a long time he saw nothing. Still he did not move, and his patience was rewarded. He saw a shadow move through the trees along the creek, saw a flash of color. Camp Fox held his position. Although he was expressionless, inside he was laughing as he watched them approach.

Potaqua!

Potaqua and many warriors moving toward Fort Madison. A hundred, five hundred, perhaps a thousand men. The war party must be a combination of Potaqua's and Yui's men, Camp Fox thought.

He waited to see no more. Moving cautiously, he slid back down the knoll, hardly disturbing the swamp grass as he passed, his breath stilled, his eyes alert.

Then he was behind the knoll and out of sight, and Camp Fox broke into a trot. Before long he was running, running with all of his strength, his heart racing exultantly.

"We have him, by the Lord God!" General George Boggs slammed his fist against his desktop and rose. He turned to Murchison. "I want every man who can walk in formation within fifteen minutes. I am taking personal command of this expedition." His eyes were gleeful, bordering on maniacal. Murchison by comparison looked shrunken and small.

"Well," Boggs roared, "have at it, lieutenant! Have at it!"

Murchison stammered a reply and was gone, leaving General Boggs to belt on his saber as he hummed a tuneless song, his face flushed with optimistic excitement.

Potaqua still rode the white horse. He carried a Spanish lance in his hand, and the warrior jogging beside him carried his Spanish musket. Raven was to his left at the head of his own column of warriors. He had bathed and prepared himself with a sweat bath, oiled his body to a mahogany gloss, tied his feathers of rank into his hair. He too carried a musket. He too anticipated the glory that this battle would bring. He too had his eyes on the yellow-blue horizon beyond the swamps where stood the fort of the white general, Boggs. Boggs who had proved himself to be inefficient and cowardly, Boggs who was no warrior but an administrator. Boggs whose scalp would hang from Raven's musket by nightfall if he did not run away, his tail between his legs, his fort abandoned and pillaged. This was to be the day which would crush the Americans forever, driving them from Florida.

Yui was among them. Yui with his face painted half red, half blue. Yui with the heavy heart whose thoughts ran constantly back to the small, beautiful woman he had left behind, to her revelation. Apopkakee had been murdered. Murdered by the men who would have no vision of peace.

Now and then Raven would look at Yui, and his head, thrown back, sheltered eyes which shone with triumph and arrogant pride.

Pohoy, the faithful one, jogged beside Yui. They ran in silence. This was no time for conversation, but their eyes met and they knew each other's thoughts. To serve Potaqua, to follow Raven, was a disgrace. Not to follow the war leaders, however, was unthinkable. They were Seminole warriors. When the drums stopped and the men gathered, their paint masking their faces, when the cry went up to Manitou asking for victory or brave death, they could not stand aside.

It did not matter if your woman clung to your arm and her great deep-brown eyes fixed themselves on you, if her lips trembled with unspoken pleas. One went; one fought; if necessary one died. This was the way of a warrior. This was what a man was born for, and if he shied away from the moment of truth then he had no right to exist.

Potaqua's hand went up.

"What is it?" Pohoy turned his head from side to side, searching the horizon.

"There." Yui's eyes were turned to the north. Then Pohoy too saw them. Ranks of blue-clad Americans standing in neat ranks and files. Before them a dozen cannon, at their head a man in blue and gold, sitting a black horse. Boggs.

"The fools," Pohoy muttered. Potaqua would tear them to pieces if they insisted on fighting this way. Standing together, moving only on order, each man a cog in a strange, unwieldy machine.

They could hear Raven's voice. "Is he mad? Does he expect us to attack from the front? Does he expect us to march into his cannon fire?"

Potaqua was expressionless. He did not like this. Why, he did not know, but he did not like it. The wind was in his face and he could scent the salt of the ocean. His horse pranced beneath him. He did not answer Raven. He simply stared across the long, swamp-grass-covered flat.

"Well?" Raven demanded.

"Be still!" Potaqua turned his hard eyes on Raven.

"Why do we not attack?"

"Can even Boggs be such a fool?" Potaqua asked himself. "What is he doing?"

The Seminole had only to disperse, to flank the American contingent, to cut them off from the fort. Raven ground his teeth together impatiently. The stiff wind shifted the feathers in his hair. It was hot and dry. His paint felt sticky. The dry grass crunched beneath his moccasined feet as he moved around, imploring Potaqua: "Now is the time! Now. We have him!"

"Do we?"

Potaqua still did not move. His warriors were bunched behind him. They should be dispersing, Raven thought angrily, forming a pincer around Boggs, filtering into the woods.

"What does this mean?" Pohoy asked Yui. Boggs might be inept, mad, but not to this extent. His men stood bunched together. True they were protected by cannon, but as of now Potaqua's advancing force was out of range. Even were the cannon loaded with murderous grapeshot and touched off at exactly the right moment, still before they could be reloaded, Potaqua's warriors could be past them and into the ranks of soldiers.

Boggs had to have learned from hard experience that men fighting in a box formation, in ranks of three, could not be effective against the American Indian's guerrilla brand of warfare, and yet that was exactly how Boggs had formed his men, in rigid boxes, stiff ranks where no man could break, run, use initiative, fire unless ordered.

"What does this mean?" Pohoy said again.

Yui shook his head. He looked at Potaqua and Raven, seeing that Potaqua was uneasy. Raven, however, hopped around like a boy in his first battle, eager to die.

Suddenly, as they watched, a dozen soldiers broke ranks. Boggs, sitting his black horse, stared straight ahead, across the long-grass marsh toward Potaqua.

"What are they doing?" Raven demanded. "Now! Let us attack now, Potaqua. It is time!"

Potaqua, motivated more by impatience than tactical considerations, nodded his head. Raven turned toward the massed warriors and raised his arms in ebullience. "Now!" he screamed, and those nearest him cheered.

They pressed forward, and soon they were running wildly across the dry-grass marsh, weapons raised to the sun, war cries filling their throats, trilling skyward, muscular bodies sleek and purposeful, eyes bright, hearts thumping solidly, strong hands clenching muskets and bows, feet flashing as they ran, their leaders urging them on, the Americans standing stolidly behind their cannon, their tight ranks unwavering, their brass buttons gleaming in the sunlight, their general with his arm upraised.

Yui saw Boggs's arm lowered, saw the sharp gesture repeated. He flinched slightly, expecting the air to be filled with cannonballs, grapeshot, gunsmoke, and cannon thunder.

There was nothing. No response at all to the gestures of Boggs but an ominous silence somehow more terrible than the expected explosion would have been.

It was Pohoy who first realized what was happening. The Seminole were drawing nearer to the cannon, still filling the air with their exultant war cries, still feeling the surge of euphoric energy which struck the common soul at this moment of commencement.

"There!" Pohoy was running beside Yui, and he nearly stumbled as he reached out to touch his shoulder. "Over there as well!"

Yui also saw them, and it struck terror into his heart. A soldier had ignited a torch, and now he ran northward, touching the torch to the tinder-dry grass. Black smoke billowed up, and writhing orange flames leaped forward to devour the grass.

To the south another man did the same, and between them others touched fire to the grass. The wind was stiff out of the east, the grass brown and parched. It accepted the conquest of the flames eagerly.

Within minutes the flames were ten feet high, roaring toward the Seminole warriors, stretching out embracing, deadly arms; and the cannon roared.

The day was alive with heat and the air filled with the sudden death of grapeshot. The Seminoles under Potaqua's command paused, looking to their leader. Yui too looked that way. Potaqua had gone berserk.

187

He turned his white horse in a circle, waving his Spanish lance in the air. His mouth frothed, his voice was a roaring madness above the crackling of the onrushing flames. Yui was near enough to hear him, but his words made no sense.

Raven was shouting: "Onward, onward! Through the flames! Go through the fire!"

The flames closed toward them rapidly, forming a giant U, sending waves of heat into the sky, clouds of smoke and ash, and still Raven shouted, urging his men forward.

If they had broken and run at that moment they still might have succeeded in turning the tide of battle, but they hesitated, listening to their leader, and the fire swept forward. By the time it reached them it was an inferno, sending showers of golden sparks and black columns of smoke skyward, and there was nowhere left to run.

The day was black and crimson, the lungs of the warriors clotted with smoke, their eyes filled with tears, their bodies scorched and feeble before the onslaught of flames.

They ran. Yui grabbed Pohoy's arm, and they set off at a dead run. Yui leaped a patch of fire, started by sparks from the conflagration behind them, turned in time to see Pohoy go down and lurch to his feet, his hair and clothes afire.

Yui rushed to the giant and rolled him to the ground, slapping out the flames. The fire had already eaten away at Pohoy's face. His chest was burned terribly. Smoke obscured all vision now. Yellow-red sheets of flame encircled them, and all around were the screams of the dying as the fire, like an angry sea, surged over them.

Potaqua's horse was lying on its side, legs kicking futilely as its hair burned away, as the smoke did its deadly work. Potaqua, his prized Spanish lance still in his hand, lay beneath the horse, hairless, eyes open, his flesh blackened, dead.

A man appeared from out of the sheet of flames before Yui, screaming for help, crying to Manitou for mercy, but there was no mercy for him. Yui could not even recognize the charred warrior.

He held Pohoy up by main force, his arm beneath the giant's. Their weapons lay abandoned behind them. Flames lashed out at them, their heat enough to singe the eyebrows away, to burn the flesh from fifty feet away.

There was no sky, but only a black, rolling, suffocating mass which repelled the lungs, cut out the light of the sun, stung the eyes, coated men's bodies black, sifted down slowly to be hurled skyward again by the rising columns of heat from the still-vigorous, angry flames.

"We have to go through," Yui panted. His mouth was dry, throat constricted. His tongue felt as if it were afire, his lungs were dry and airless. Pohoy nodded, his terrible, burned face remarkably placid. Perhaps he could feel no more.

Yui took a deep breath and propelled them both forward, ducking low as they rushed into the wall of flames. His body was overwhelmed by waves of heat, his flesh was torn by fiery fingers.

Pohoy groaned, bucked in Yui's arms, and slumped. Yui wrapped his arms around his friend and dragged him onward. There were no sounds but the blustering of the flames, the cries of agony; there were no realities apart from the reality of heat and flame and exhaustion, the weight of Pohoy's slack body, the damnable sky. Yui was a swimmer through a crimson sea; above the ocean there was the light of a black and withered sun. He was drowning slowly. And Pohoy was dragging him down.

They stepped on something rubbery, something super heated, and fell. Yui found himself face to face with a scorched, unrecognizable corpse.

"Pohoy! Pohoy!" He called twice, the effort filling his lungs with fire, with grating chips of flint, but there was no answer.

He would not leave Pohoy. He rose again, slapping at his own hair, burning his hands on the sparks which had lain smoldering against his scalp. He lifted the giant to his feet, shouldered him, stepped across the body of the unknown Seminole warrior, and plunged ahead.

Suddenly he was free of the flames. It seemed incredible, unreal. The sky was smoky, dull, but the grass ahead of him was unburned. Yui tried to run and went to one knee, staggering beneath the weight of Pohoy, who lay slack and unmoving across his shoulder.

He was free of the flames, but not out of danger. From the safety of the woods beyond the Americans fired at those few Seminoles who had been lucky enough to escape the fire.

Yui saw Immokallee lying dead on the ground, his arms twisted beneath him, his head thrown back, eyes staring blankly. Yui ran on, Pohoy's weight burdening him. He did not even know if Pohoy was still alive.

He was within fifty feet of the woods when the bullet hit his leg and he fell, Pohoy crushing him to the ground. Yui clutched his leg, gritting his teeth. When he took his hands away from his thigh the blood flowed out in hot rivulets. He tore away a part of his loincloth and tied it over the wound, keeping himself low so that another sniper's musket ball would not find him.

Looking back, he saw the smoke-filled sky, the tongues of darting orange flame, saw the field which had already been burned over littered with bodies. He looked at Pohoy then and shook his head. The big man was dead.

"Faithful one," Yui said, putting a hand on Pohoy's arm. "Walk the bright trail on the far side. Walk in peace." Then, looking around cautiously, Yui began crawling toward the woods.

The guns still fired a constant barrage. Yui crept forward, believing he could make his escape if he could reach the trees. True, the Americans were positioned there, but Yui had spent his life hunting and warring in these swamps. There were none who had eyes sharp enough to follow him through the trees.

He forced himself to crawl slowly forward, keeping his head below the grass. He concentrated only on the line of trees ahead of him and fought back the terrible thoughts of what lay behind.

For back there was the end. The end of a people, of hundreds of lives, of aspirations and mad dreams. Yui froze his motion.

He could hear the boots upon the long grass. Peering to his left, he could see the dull shine of polished leather. Sweat trickled into his eyes, stinging them. His leg throbbed and spasmed with angry pain. The sun was hot, the smoke from the fire was a pall across the green and brown land, a black veil tugged across the blue sky.

"You there, get up!"

Yui did not understand the words. He sighed and sat up, wrapping his arms around his upraised knees. The younger soldier had a thin blond mustache. His face was sooty. He gestured with the muzzle of his musket, and Yui pointed at his leg wound.

"I cannot get up," he said to the uncomprehending soldier. He thought he could rise, thought that if he found himself unguarded for a moment he could still make a dash for the trees.

He watched the uncertain young soldier. For a moment he thought the man was going to shoot him, but perhaps this young one had seen enough slaughter today. He simply stood there, the gun trained on Yui.

"I got a prisoner," the soldier called out. He waved his arm, and two others came running. Yui was lifted to his feet and led away to their camp. The fire roared on, but the sound of muskets was rapidly fading away. It was ended. All of it.

"By God," General Boggs said, "it's Yui!" He crouched down beside the wounded Seminole war leader and, smiling, he said, "Don't you worry, Yui. We'll see to your wound. You'll live long enough to swing from the gibbet as an example to the others."

Yui did not understand, but then he did not have to. He could read the man's eyes, and what he saw there was a promise of death.

"Bind him and stand watch over him. I don't want this man unguarded for a minute!" Then Boggs, with a last satisfied nod, turned and was gone. The Seminole prisoners sat quietly together. There was nothing to say. It was over and Boggs was their master. It was over and they were only the remnants of a nation, the living dead. They offered no resistance when the soldiers prodded them to their feet, tied their ankles with short lengths of rope, and started marching them toward Fort Madison and imprisonment.

"What has happened?" Mother Holotok kept asking. "Someone should have returned with some news."

"I saw smoke. I saw fire. I heard a death song," Pamda said over and over.

Shanna simply stood and watched the trails, the forest verge, the sky where smoky clouds drifted. She shared Pamda's sense of doom. She could not explain it—she had never been particularly prescient, although that gift was said to run in her family—but she knew. She knew as well as Pamda did. Pamda, who stood with tears tracking across her face, rolling from her large, luminous eyes, repeating:

"I saw smoke. I saw fire. I heard a death song."

The runner burst into the camp from the east, and Shanna felt her heart leap. Holotok clutched her breast and Pamda cried out.

They knew already; yet what the man had to relate was worse than anything they could have imagined. "All dead. The fire . . ." The man shook his head, tried to catch his breath, and went on rapidly. "All dead. Potaqua, Raven, Chamtha, Ockawa, Immokallee . . ."

"Yui?" Shanna asked, trying to fight back the nausea which swept over her, knotted her stomach, blurred her vision. The faces around her seemed unfamiliar. The day began to spin and the earth beneath her to sink away.

"Yui is a prisoner," the runner answered, and Shanna felt her life begin again. Her knees buckled, and Holotok had to hold her up.

"He is alive?" Shanna asked. She had to be sure.

"He is alive. I saw the prisoners being taken away. I could not run until they were all past. Yui was among them. Wounded, but alive."

A woman across the camp screamed, and they turned that way. The soldiers were already into the camp, encircling them. Women and children picked up stones and sticks and tried to fight. Shanna saw a woman clubbed down, saw a child kicked aside.

"Do not resist!" she called. "Do not fight back!"

"I saw smoke," Pamda chanted, her hands clenched tightly, her face turned up to the skies. "I saw fire. I heard a death song."

Shanna put her arm around Pamda and squeezed her, watching defiantly as the soldiers approached.

They were not allowed to enter their chickees to gather their possessions. The straw huts were put to the torch, and fresh clouds of smoke billowed up above the swampland.

They were herded together and guarded by armed men. They had to stand and watch the conflagration until the last of the flames had died down and nothing but sad heaps of smoking ash were left to mark the eagle camp.

"I cannot understand it," Pamda said."It is not night. Are we to have no days now either? Are we to have nothing?"

The march to Fort Madison was long and wearying. Shanna shared the general sense of desolation, but she did not wail as did those who had lost loved ones, nor did she feel the utter trembling despair of others. Yui was at the end of this trail.

She would be reunited with him, and perhaps they would somehow begin a new life, perhaps a better one. They might live as the Cherokees did. The sorrow would not pass quickly away, but in time perhaps they would find a good life.

Teska walked at the head of this ragged column, and Shanna saw the proud, jealous woman speaking to a soldier. Both heads turned toward her, but Shanna gave it no significance.

It was sundown when they reached the fort. Shanna immediately began searching with her eyes. But she could not discover where Yui was being kept. She saw no Indian faces but those of the Creek and Cherokee scouts. The other faces were pale, alien, arrogant.

They were herded into a compound beyond the fort. Hastily constructed, it was watched over by dozens of armed men. The sky darkened and the children wailed. They were hungry and weary and frightened. No food was to come that evening, and they lay down to sleep upon the barren earth.

There were no sounds, no conversation, nothing but the soft chanting of Pamda: "I saw smoke. I saw fire. I heard a death song."

❈ 12 ❈

In the morning they were fed. It was only a corn porridge, cold by the time it reached them, but Shanna had eaten many poor meals in her lifetime, and this was no worse than most.

After they had breakfasted, when the sun was a rising red ball emerging from the silver sea, the soldiers came again. Boggs himself was among them and he stood before them as if they were his subjects. Perhaps they were. He spoke, and the Cherokee at his side translated. Shanna, who spoke some English, realized that the Indian translator was softening some of the general's language, and she respected the Cherokee for that.

"The war is over," Boggs began, "and you are a defeated people. We do not wish to deal with you harshly, but we will if we must. Do not forget that. You have been led into a bad war by bad leaders. Men who did not understand what peace meant. You will not be punished for what your leaders did. Those of you who have husbands will be reunited with them in time. You will be given food and blankets. You will be settled on the land to the south of the fort. There you will practice agriculture as the Cherokee and Creek do. We will help you. But God help you if you try to run or entertain any idea of resistance. That will not be tolerated.

"Your leaders are criminals. All of them will be executed. When you see them hanging in the sun, look closely and remember that this can be the fate of any of you who is not willing to live peacefully."

There was more, but Shanna did not hear the droning words.

Executed. Did that mean Yui? She stepped forward and was prodded back by a soldier with a red beard.

"Yui!" she cried out. In halting English she demanded: "Will Yui be killed? Will Yui be murdered? Will Yui die?"

194

Boggs's eyes flickered toward her, but he did not respond. Shanna tried to push the guard aside and was shoved back into the crowd.

She immediately went forward again, but her way was barred by the guard, who held his musket across his chest. Shanna gripped his musket and looked toward Boggs, still shouting.

"Will Yui be killed? Will you murder him?"

He did not answer. In another minute Boggs was gone and the gate to the makeshift compound was closed, and Shanna was left to stand against it, her forehead pressed to the wooden staves.

She did not even hear what Mother Holotok said as she tried to comfort her, she did not feel her hand resting on her shoulder, nor the persistent tugging of the small girl at her skirt.

The sun rose higher and still Shanna did not move. What was there to move for? They were going to kill Yui, the finest of men, these soldiers who were not fit to walk on his shadow.

She straightened a little, a new thought coming to her. Perhaps she could speak for Yui, tell them that he had not wanted this last battle, that he had been asking his people to make peace.

If she only had the opportunity to speak to General Boggs, perhaps he could be made to listen. That thought buoyed her slightly.

How could she win an interview? There must be a way.

No sooner had that thought entered her mind than the gate opened and the soldiers came into the compound. Teska, inexplicably, was with them.

Shanna began speaking rapidly: "I must see General Boggs. Please, I beg you! I have important information. You must let me speak to Boggs."

"That is the one," Teska said. "She is Yui's woman."

"Yes, I am Yui's woman. Please let me speak to General Boggs." It was a moment before she realized by the look of savage triumph on Teska's face, by the grim expressions of the soldiers, that she had been identified for quite a different reason.

"She's dangerous," Teska said, her words rapidly trans-

195

lated by a dubious-appearing Cherokee. "She always urged Yui on to war. Now she wishes to bring an uprising to set Yui free."

Shanna could only stare for a long minute. Finally she managed to say, "Teska, I did not know you hated me so much."

"Didn't you?" Teska sneered. "Then you were a fool. This is all your doing, don't you see that? You brought Yui down. You started this battle by removing him from his position as war leader. You took my man away and deprived me of my rightful rank! You. You have caused it all, Shanna. She is the one," she said again, and the soldiers stepped forward to take Shanna's arms.

"What does this woman say about me?" Shanna wanted to know. "What am I accused of? Where are you taking me?"

"Shanna!" Pamda screamed, and Shanna had a last glimpse of her, arms outstretched, a grim Mother Holotok holding her back. Then the soldiers had Shanna out the gate of the compound and she was being hurried across a clearing toward a great wooden building.

Shanna looked around frantically. Teska stood, hands on hips, head thrown back to reveal her teeth, laughing. Beyond the clearing, Cherokee and Creek Indians worked in their peaceful fields. Above the stockade wall, Shanna saw two soldiers fastening a rope to a gibbet. Ahead and to her left, a young blond captain stood on the porch of the barnlike building, watching. The images blurred together, tangled, and spun around. She felt rough hands at her armpits, smelled white soap, white sweat, white scent, saw the green eyes of one of the soldiers, the frowning young officer's face . . . and the gibbet.

Always her eyes returned to the gibbet; it drew her attention magnetically. It was a horrible, fascinating thing. She had a last glimpse of it before she was led into the grainshed which was empty but for a few stored odds and ends—bits of harness, old saddles, a few unmarked crates. The floor was packed earth, the walls of graying unpainted lumber. Shanna was hurried through the building, where the air was close and musty.

At the far end was a locked room with a heavy door, and she waited as it was unlocked.

"Here," the Cherokee said. He handed her a blanket and a sack of water. Then the door opened and she stepped inside, listening as they closed and locked the door behind her, listening as their footsteps receded.

She looked around at the bare walls, at the wisps of straw scattered across the floor, at the rusted harrow, the leather-bottomed chair, the high barred window too narrow for anyone to crawl through, and she sighed. She stood, head hanging, her hand against her forehead. Then, angrily, she threw down the blanket and walked toward the window. She had to get onto tiptoes and grip the bars to lift herself high enough to see out; and when she did so she was rewarded only by a perfect view of the stockade wall and the gibbet with its looped rope hanging in readiness from its boom.

She turned away, sickened and angry and desperate in turn. She walked to the door and pounded on it until her fists hurt.

"I want to see General Boggs! I must see him!"

There was no answer.

She was alone in the world. She could not bear to look out the window where the gallows stood ready. She paced the room for an hour, finally from exhaustion lying down, her blanket over her, watching the changing light, watching as the sunlight beaming through the window crawled across the floor and up the gray wall of the old grainshed, marking time. She lay there and stared at the ceiling, listening to a scuttling rat, a persistently peeping sparrow, feeling the small movement inside her body, feeling the small being there stir and stretch within her womb.

Someone came at dusk and opened the door to put a bowl of food inside. Shanna saw him only as a dim silhouette. He was there for a moment, being still, watching her, and then he was gone. The silence, the emptiness, returned. Later she could see a single bright star drifting past the window, beaming silver-blue light into the room where she lay alone and defeated.

Always before she had willed herself to fight back, convinced herself that there was something to live for, to attempt. Now she could not believe it anymore. The night would pass, life would pass, and it had all been for nothing. There had been only Lychma and Yui. Lychma the war had taken; Yui the war would kill.

Lychma had been taken away on a boat, far away across the dark sea to a southern island where she could not have survived. She was too frail, too dependent on Shanna. She would have withered away, died, not understanding what had happened to her. Now it was as if Yui were slowly sailing away. Across another dark and endless sea.

Had she slept? She did not know. She was aware that the sky was gradually graying outside her window. She heard a clattering sound, a creak, a shout, the muttering of other voices.

She leaped from her bed and went to the window. She drew herself up by the bars and peered out into the predawn grayness. Beyond her window were the Seminole people, ringed by armed soldiers. Their eyes were raised toward the stockade wall, and Shanna's gaze followed theirs.

There was nothing to be seen. Two bulky white men stood beside the gallows, hands clasped behind their backs, staring out at the gray skies.

The wind was cool through the window. Shanna shivered. The first ray of golden sunlight pierced the grayness and gilded the trees to the east. The drums began.

A long rolling sound, unlike the drums of the Seminole, but telling the same message. Death.

The men on the gibbet platform came to attention, and Shanna went rigid. Her throat constricted so that she could barely breathe. The wall of the grainshed seemed to tremble and sway. Her hands were clamped around the iron bars, bloodless and cramped. Her mouth hung open. The drum roll continued, and now the others appeared on the platform. Boggs in gold and blue, two other officers.

Yui.

The wind was in his loose hair. His hands were tied behind his back. He stood erect, looking down at the Seminoles, who were being forced to watch this. His eyes must have been seeking Shanna, but he could not find her. She saw him toss his head and say something to Boggs, saw Boggs stiffen and give the order to the man nearest the dangling rope.

The rope was around Yui's neck, and still he stood straight and unmoving.

The gate was tripped. And then there was nothing.

The gate was tripped, and Yui plunged downward. Shanna

198

screamed. She stretched a hand through the window bars and fell herself. She clambered up quickly. She could see nothing. Only Boggs standing on the platform, only the taut length of rope, only the gray sky cold and shifting, struck through by a single band of sunlight. Only the distant gray of the ocean. Nothing.

It counted for nothing. Why did the sun rise? Why did the sea roll on? Shanna slumped to the floor of the shed, trembling and ill. She had bitten through her lip, and blood trickled down across her chin. She was unaware of it. The floor beneath her seemed to be quicksand. She was sinking slowly into it, suffocating, and she did not care. She heard the sparrow peeping in the rafters. Then there was only darkness.

She awoke to full sunlight. Shanna staggered to her bed, her hand over her eyes. Someone had brought a fresh bowl of food. It nauseated her to think of it. She lay down, her haunted eyes staring at the ceiling. A grain rat scuttled past her, eyes beady and glittering. She paid no attention to it as it crossed to her bowl and clambered in, its claws making tiny scratching sounds.

A bugle sounded. A horse clopped by beneath the window. A man laughed. All of it was unreal. This was a different world, a limbo where one waited to die. She looked at the window, seeing only blue sky. She turned her eyes away, wanting to sleep when she could not. Shanna rolled onto her side and drew her knees up, clutching her belly tightly.

The world had ended and she had survived. It was the most exquisite torture yet devised. To remove one's heart, one's soul, leaving only a sheath of flesh.

The sunlight was a mockery. Why did the clouds not storm past?

Hours passed, or days. There was a hazy sameness about the hours. Shanna would open her eyes and see the sunlight, twist uncomfortably in her bed and find that the night had settled in, that the patch of sky beyond the window was blue-black, star-speckled. Twice she saw Yui's face in the window; but only the first time did she rush breathlessly to it, strange, strangled murmurs escaping her lips. She had clambered up, feeling the weakness in her arms, and pressed her face to the cold iron bars to find nothing. Outside it was as empty and as cold as it was within the cell. As futile, desolate and evil.

She ate. It was a repulsive, pasty mass in her mouth. Her stomach fought against the food, but she ate finally, on that third day. There was a small one inside of her, and it was Yui's. It must not die. It must be fed and nurtured. It must be strong and healthy. And free.

"And you shall be. I swear it," she whispered. "You shall be free to walk this land as your father did."

For another week Shanna saw no one, and she was grateful for that. The stunning shock had passed, but in its place a leaden bitterness had settled. She did not want to see another human being.

When the key turned in the heavy lock and the massive door creaked open, Shanna was sitting on the floor, her back against the wall, simply staring.

She had seen him before, but she did not know where. The young captain was blond and tall. His eyes were blue, his shoulders carried squarely.

He simply stood there, looking at her. Hesitantly he took another step.

"Would you like to go out into the sunshine? Would you like some fresh air?"

Shanna did not answer. He repeated the question in the Cherokee language. She looked away, her lips tightening.

The captain came forward, his forehead furrowed. He looked more closely at Shanna, touched by the thinness of her body, the proud tilt of her head, the challenging eyes, the sorrowful mouth.

"You're not Seminole, are you?" he asked, crouching down. "If I didn't know better . . ." He spoke to her again, and the tongue was that of the Shawnee Indians. "Would you like to go out into the sunshine and fresh air for a while?"

"No," she snapped.

"You are Shawnee."

She did not answer. She stared at the tiny window.

"I want to help you. I can be a friend of yours. I don't want to see you treated like this."

"No white man is a friend of the Indians!" She turned toward him, her eyes virulent, her lip curled back.

"Perhaps not. I can try," the captain said quietly. "You

see, I am part Indian. My father also was. He fought for a time on the side of the Shawnee people.''

Shanna's expression softened. She studied the man crouched before her. A slow knowledge was budding. Her eyes narrowed. ''What is your name?''

''Dawes. Captain James Dawes.''

She touched her breast. ''I am Shanna,'' she said.

''Shanna? Shanna the daughter of Cara, the granddaughter of Crenna, the Oneida woman?''

''Yes, it is I.''

''Crenna was my grandmother. My father was your mother's brother.''

''Yes.'' The old antagonism returned. What did it matter if this white soldier was related to her by blood? He was still a killing man, one who had destroyed Yui.

''Let me help you.''

''I need no help.''

''You must get out of this place. You will grow ill.'' He smiled. ''The baby will grow ill.''

She gaped at him. Her hand rested on her rounded abdomen. She glanced down. She had not known it showed. She looked again at Dawes deliberately and said, ''I do not want your help, James Dawes. Leave me to myself. Leave me here.''

He rose and turned away, walking out the door, locking it behind him. Shanna simply stared. And then the tears began again and she buried her face in her hands.

James Dawes went out of the grainshed into the cool sunlight. He watched the nearby fields being worked, watched the ''civilized'' Indians plant their corn and beans, watched the platoon of soldiers drilling across the parade ground.

He wondered again why he hung on here. What earthly good was he doing himself, his country, the Indians? Julia was gone; he had never heard from her again, nor had he expected to. His ''duty'' was just a form of punishment. He would never be promoted, never be given a position of responsibility. He could not even talk the young Shawnee woman into coming out into the sunlight. His cousin, Shanna. His own cousin mistrusted him; all the Indians must. The army mistrusted him. Why, when there were millions of square miles to the west, did he hang on here, withering away as surely as Shanna was?

His mother was still alive. Presumably the family still owned land in Ohio. Why not take a turn at farming? Why not wander westward toward this Mississippi everyone talked about? Beyond the Mississippi, it was said, was only desert. No white man would ever live there. But who knew? *Why am I hanging on?*

"I must be insane," he said aloud.

"That's the general opinion, James."

Dawes turned to find Lieutenant Taylor behind him. Although, as Taylor was diligently trying to have Dawes discover, he was no longer a lieutenant. A captain's insignia glittered on his epaulettes.

"Congratulations," Dawes said, trying to sound hearty.

"Necessary, James. Can't have a lieutenant in command at Fort Madison."

"In command!"

"Yes." Taylor smiled and suggested, "Let's take a walk, James. I'd like to talk to you."

"All right."

They started toward the Cherokee settlement, veering off toward the forest. It was a pleasant day, cooled by a sea breeze. Larks sang across the fields.

"It was announced at commander's call this morning," Taylor said. "The general is going south to relieve Andrew Jackson. Osceola is still raising hell, and Boggs is champing at the bit, dreaming of succeeding where Jackson failed."

"Where's Jackson going? Ohio?"

"You mean you haven't heard? What hole have you been hiding in, James? Jackson's running for president!"

"I hadn't heard. I don't get much conversation," Dawes said with some rancor.

"No. I know that." Taylor stopped abruptly, removed his hat, and wiped his thin pale hair. "That's what I wanted to talk to you about, James. To my way of thinking you've gotten a raw deal—don't stop me—and to my mind, I had a part in doing this to you."

"You couldn't help testifying honestly."

"No, but someone should have spoken up, done something."

"There was nothing to be done, Taylor. Not with a man like Boggs."

"Maybe not, but there's something I can do now. After a

decent interval I plan on reinstating you. I'd like to bring you back into the fold. I always thought you were a good officer, James."

"You're unique in that estimation," Dawes said wryly.

"Maybe so. But it's going to be my decision, James. Murchison is going south with Boggs. I'd like to have you back."

"Maybe."

"Maybe!" Taylor shook his head. "What earthly good are you doing where you are? What exactly do you accomplish in a day? Do you even have any duties?"

"No," Dawes said honestly. "I talk to the Cherokee settlers. I weigh bags of seed, I distribute supplies. That's about it."

"Then why . . . ?"

"Because I don't know if I want it anymore, Taylor. I just don't know if I can soldier anymore. Assuming I would be an effective leader, and I doubt that, knowing what the gossip must be."

"I'm trying to make amends, James."

"I know you are. But I don't want to ruin your career as well, Taylor."

"You'll think about it, though?"

"Yes. I'll think about it. And I'll be around—after a decent interval—to ask you for a favor."

"Oh?" Taylor frowned.

"It's Yui's wife," Dawes said. "That woman has done nothing, and Boggs knows it. The woman who gave evidence against her was a jealous hen who had wanted Yui for herself. What are we holding her for? What has she done? She's going to die in that shed, Taylor. If you want to do something for me to make up for the injustice I might have suffered, let her go. That is a greater injustice by far."

It was only four days later when Dawes again spoke to Shanna. He found her looking thin, shrunken. Bright eyes looking up at him out of a skull which had lost flesh through deprivation and anguish.

"Up."

She simply looked at him.

"Up," he repeated. He snatched up her blanket and looked around the shed.

"I still do not wish to go out and take exercise," Shanna

said, and the faltering thinness of her voice shocked Dawes. He forced himself to be stern.

"You are being moved. Get up, Shanna. This is not a request. You will follow me or be carried out."

She rose and immediately staggered so that she had to throw her hand out and brace herself against the wall. Dawes winced mentally.

"Come." He handed her the blanket, careful to keep his face turned away from Shanna's eyes.

She followed meekly. It did not matter where she was taken; it did not matter if she were taken to the gibbet herself.

The sunlight was overpowering. Brilliant and piercing, it seemed to strike through to her brain. Without intending to she clutched James Dawes's arm for support. It was only a brief, thoughtless gesture, however, and she released it immediately. Dawes's heart sank.

I am the enemy, he thought.

Ahead was the wagon, and Shanna was helped aboard. Dawes clambered up into the box, unwound the reins from the brake, and put the horses into motion. Shanna sat unmoving on the wagon bench, distant and withdrawn.

Dawes clamped his jaw shut. None of what he had intended to say now seemed suitable. He watched the road between the ears of the horses and turned the wagon toward the Three Tree house. Long before they pulled into the yard before the pole-and-mud house, Dawes saw the Three Tree clan begin to gather on the porch.

They had wanted none of this initially. The woman was not Cherokee. What did they know about a Shawnee woman? But Dawes had coaxed and cajoled, falling just short of making it an order, and in the end the Three Tree clan had agreed to accept Shanna into their home.

The clan, a sort of subtribe group, was made up of three families which shared the small but growing house. In the back of the house Dawes could make out yet another addition which was being constructed in their spare time.

The patriarch of the clan was Jonathan Three Tree—he who had once been named Ha-tha-Shone and who had led General Armstrong on a merry chase in Georgia. He had two sons, both married, Tom and George Three Tree. Jonathan Three Tree's cousin, Mary Three Tree, was a big, gregarious woman with an unmarried daughter of her own to look after. Then there was Young John Three Tree, who was actually a second cousin of Jonathan's. He was unmarried and lived alone as he had since his mother, father, and brothers were killed in the shelling at their home camp in South Carolina.

These stood on the porch of the poor house watching as James Dawes slowed the wagon and team.

Dawes reined in and greeted Jonathan Three Tree. The old man responded, ''Hello, James Dawes, captain,'' in his halting but improving English. ''This is the Shawnee woman. Sad eyes, I think. Well, and we all have sad eyes, do we not, James Dawes, captain?''

''Yes, Jonathan Three Tree,'' Dawes answered, wishing again that he had not introduced himself to Jonathan as ''James Dawes, captain,'' since the old man had taken his rank to be part of his name.

''Step down, step down, young Shawnee with the sad eyes. Here is home. Does she speak English, James Dawes, captain?''

''Yes, Jonathan, but her heart is burdened. She does not speak much.''

''We shall lighten her heart. Step down, Shawnee woman. Here.'' He took her elbow, and Shanna stepped to the ground heavily. ''Too thin, James Dawes, captain. You must feed these Seminole women.''

''Yes, Jonathan, but she does not wish to eat.''

''Do you hear that, Mary Three Tree?'' the old man said, turning to the enormous Cherokee woman behind him. ''She does not wish to eat. Well, she must eat here. Mary is offended by a guest who does not eat. Come, Shawnee woman, come in and rest. Eat and rest.''

Shanna was taken into the small dark house and shown a room where she would sleep. There was nothing at all in it but a tick mattress on the floor. There was a window on the eastern wall, and a blanket hung across the door. Shanna placed her blanket on the bed.

She was taken then to the largest room in the house, one in which a table and chairs stood. It seemed odd to see chairs in an Indian's home, Shanna thought.

''Sit down,'' Mary Three Tree said in a rumbling voice

205

which seemed on the verge of laughter. "Sit down and eat, Shawnee woman."

She was served venison and hominy, wild potatoes and beans, in massive quantities. Shanna sat looking at the steaming food as Mary urged her: "Eat, child, eat."

Through the front door she saw Dawes and Jonathan in conversation, then saw the captain drive off, turning the team in the wide yard. She saw Jonathan lift a hand. Two younger women stood outside with him, glancing at Shanna from time to time, trying to pretend they were not. Both wore white-made cotton dresses.

"Eat." The admonition was repeated, and Shanna poked some of the food into her mouth with her fingers. It made her mouth water, but her stomach still rebelled. She ate something for the sake of the baby and for the sake of Mary Three Tree, who stood arms folded across her massive bosom, watching.

Someone else was watching. From the corner near the stone fireplace the young man—was it John?—watched. He was crouched, eyes lifted. When Shanna's eyes met his, he rose and turned away.

"I must see to the hogs," he said to no one in particular, and then he was gone, pausing at the doorway for one quick backward glance.

"Now," Mary said when Shanna was through with her meal, "I think you must rest again."

Shanna rose automatically. She looked at Mary Three Tree without really seeing her, turned the wrong way, and finally found her room. She lay down on the mattress, hearing the murmurings of conversation in the other room.

She thought someone said the word "free," and she realized that she was in fact free, that she had found her "peace," a world where there was no fear of being rousted in the middle of the night, of seeing the village burn, of hearing the cries of pain.

She had found her world of peace, that longed-for world where war had been banished. It was not so very much different from slavery.

She slept until the next morning, and when she went out conversation around the table stopped. She was seated and introduced again to the family. Tom and George, Sarah and

206

Paula, the young couples, old Jonathan and bustling, bubbly Mary, and Mary's daughter, Edith. And John.

He was small, serious-appearing, shy. The antithesis of a warrior, Shanna thought, but he fitted this new world.

"If you are strong enough you might wish to go out and see our farm," George said. He was a big man, round in the face, affable.

"I am strong enough to work," Shanna said.

"I didn't mean for you to work."

"I must pay my way. I have always worked."

"All right," Tom said, "if you will stop when you grow tired."

Shanna nodded. She bent her head to her bowl and ate. She would work, she would eat, she would breathe in and out, but none of it would have meaning; there would be no joy in it.

They kept destroying her worlds.

She had lived with her mother and Lychma, with brother Kokii, with her father, the warrior Ousa. It had been a good world, but something had happened. They had come. The war, the white man, the devils. It had all been cut away from beneath her feet. She had never thought to find happiness again, but she had eventually found Yui. That had been the beginning of a good life, the best of lives, loving and being loved. But they had come in their greed and their malevolence and they had destroyed the world.

She had not the strength to build another world for them to crush. She would only eat, breathe, work, and pray that war would stay away from her child. Perhaps this was the way the Cherokee felt; she did not know.

When the meal was finished they went out into the fields, all but Mary, who would come after cleaning the bowls and storing the food away.

They rode on a cart drawn by an ancient gray horse, all of them holding an unnatural silence which Shanna guessed was because of her presence.

Old Jonathan did speak after a time. They had crossed a thin, oak-lined creek and were emerging onto a cultivated flat plain.

"Now all the land this side is mine. All belongs to Jonathan and the family. You see there. For a half day's walk to the edge of the forest all is mine. Ours. We are very wealthy now, Shanna. You see we have fine clothes to wear." He was in fact wearing a pair of black jeans, a red-and-white cotton shirt, a black felt hat. "We have this horse and one other. Lame now. When the crops come in we have much more and we buy what we wish at the fort."

Shanna nodded. It was a good life, she supposed. For those who had someone to share it with. The young corn was to her knees. Pumpkins grew in a large patch along the bottom. Cotton had been planted on the drier upland areas.

There were no white faces in view, no soldiers. It did not matter. These people were not free. That was what Yui had meant. They were not free to be *Indian*, they were free to be red Americans.

They climbed down from the cart and were given tools. Shanna was given a hoe and a section of corn to weed. She got dutifully to work, finding a release from her thoughts in the mechanical task which demanded the concentration of eyes and hands, muscles and fiber, but not of the mind. The mind was free to empty itself and lay dormant beneath the warm sun.

"Please stop when you grow weary," the voice beside her said. She turned, wiping her forehead with the back of her hand, to find John Three Tree watching her anxiously.

"I am not weary," she snapped.

She continued to work, noticing with irritation that the young man still watched her. "What do you want?"

"Nothing, Shawnee woman."

"My name is Shanna."

"I want nothing, Shanna. I am concerned for you."

"Do not waste your concern."

"I am concerned for your baby."

"The baby is my concern alone," Shanna said bitterly. The young man looked hurt. He nodded then and turned away. Shanna started to call after him, to apologize. Instead she only sighed and returned to her work.

In the middle of the afternoon they met beneath the oaks to sit in the shade and eat while the sun was high. Mary had brought sweetcakes, and Shanna suspected they were for her benefit. She ate most of one, tasting the honey, the yeast.

The others were silent for the most part. "Excuse me," Shanna said, rising. She would walk for a time. Let them have their conversation without the stranger among them. She went down to the narrow creek, watching the blue dragonflies dart and hover above its silver surface. The day had grown humid, excessively so, and Shanna glanced toward the skies. Long white skies barren, oppressive. The skies, like the land, had belonged to the Seminoles. This had been their world, every tree and blade of grass, each rain drop and sparrow. Yes, and the poisonous denizens of the swamps, the terrible wide-mouthed alligators, the stalking panthers, had been theirs as well. They had been pushed aside so that those more docile, those more willing to become white, might have their land as the whites had taken the Cherokee lands to the north.

Now they were all gone. All. In the south Osceola fought on, but it was a symbolic war. The Seminole had already been defeated. And who had been right in the end—these who had taken up the hoe or the Seminole who would not lay down his war club and had died, leaving nothing but the blank and limitless sky which would pour down rains to wash away his footprints from the earth?

"We are going to work again," John Three Tree said.

Shanna turned toward him. He stood turning his hat in his hands.

"All right."

"Tom is going back to the house. If you wish to stop now you may ride with him."

"No."

"Are you sure?"

"Why do you speak English?" Shanna asked sharply, abruptly.

"It is better to practice," John Three Tree said hesitantly. "It is our tongue now."

"And forget the old ways."

He looked stung. He licked his lips. "The old ways were the way of war, Shanna. We have much land now. The Seminoles have only the ground they lie in. Do not scorn us for wanting peace."

Then he was gone, jamming his hat onto his head. Shanna stood there by the creek a moment and then followed.

They worked through the afternoon until sunset was flooding the skies a deep crimson. No one had spoken to Shanna the remainder of the day, and truthfully she could not blame them. She had been snappish and rude. Somehow she did not care. Perhaps in time they would come to be as her own people. Perhaps in time she would come to appreciate this peace. Perhaps in time she would forget the bloodshed and the pain. She rode homeward in silence, looking at the flourishing fields, at the quiet settlement, at the empty Seminole skies.

It was harder these mornings to rise. Shanna's back ached
constantly, and her extremeties were frequently swollen. She
could never eat breakfast. She walked heavily to the cart and
was taken to the fields. She was left to work alone, and she
preferred it. Even Mary Three Tree no longer tried to cheer
her. None of them spoke to Shanna unless it was absolutely
necessary.

None of them but John Three Tree.

She had rebuffed him and ignored him, but it did no good.
He sat with her at meals—not beside her, but near her—and
when there was heavy work to be done he made it a point to
help Shanna.

"Why are you doing this?" she had asked him, but he had
looked so hurt that Shanna felt a twinge of pity for this shy
Cherokee farmer. Thereafter she accepted his help, welcome
or not, and let him come near, although she had no wish to
speak to him. Often she caught him standing, leaning on his
hoe, looking at her with dark, nearly pleading eyes.

She had been with the Cherokees a month when he asked
her for the first time:

"Shanna, will you marry me?" He was looking at the
ground, hat in hands as it always was when he dared to speak
to her.

"No."

"Why not?"

"No."

"A woman needs a husband here. How will you survive?"

"No."

"I need you."

"I have answered you."

"A child needs a father, Shanna."

"My child has a father," she said, and John Three Tree said no more. Since then he had asked her a dozen times, each time as shyly, as hopefully as before. The answer was always the same, and he would go away for a time, becoming gloomy and silent for a few days or weeks. But he always returned. Finally Shanna had to tell him:

"John Three Tree, let us make a bargain. I will agree to be your friend, your sister. But you must stop asking me to marry you. I will not marry another man. If you persist in asking me, I shall go away."

"Go away!"

"Yes. Away. I shall birth the baby in the wilderness. I am not afraid. That is where I was born. I shall take my baby and go somewhere, I do not know where."

"Don't leave us, Shanna." He stretched out a hand which never quite reached Shanna's shoulder.

"Then you must stop asking me to marry you."

"I will. I promise it."

He was true to his word, although his attentions increased rather than decreasing after that. He was constantly at hand, helping her even when she did not want or need help, watching her with sincere, sad eyes.

The rains came early, and they were forced to stay in the house for day upon day. Lightning filled the skies and the storms off of the sea rolled into shore, one on the heels of the other.

It had been raining continuously for a week when they heard the horse in the yard, heard the porch squeak beneath booted feet, heard the rap at the door, and James Dawes was admitted.

"Hello, Jonathan Three Tree," Dawes said.

"Hello, James Dawes, captain."

"Not 'captain' anymore, Jonathan Three Tree." Dawes looked around. "May I sit down?"

"Yes. My lodge is yours." Jonathan waved an arm. "Would you like some tea or a pipe?"

"Tea."

Dawes took off his dark rain slicker, and they saw that underneath it he wore a gray civilian suit, white shirt, and string tie.

Shanna edged into the room, and James smiled. "Hello, Shanna. How are you?"

"I am healthy."

"Good." He smiled wanly and crossed his legs. No one said anything for a time except for Tom, who noted that it was still raining and probably would for a time.

Mary brought a cup of sycamore tea to Dawes, and he sipped it, nodding his thanks. Jonathan Three Tree, forgetting himself, sat cross-legged on the floor before Dawes.

"You have come for a reason, James Dawes," Jonathan said finally. "I read that in your eyes. We see that you no longer wear a white army uniform. Does that mean you are not a soldier anymore?"

"That is what it means, Jonathan."

"You are going home? To Ohio?"

"To Ohio, or farther west, I don't know yet. I only know that I cannot be a soldier any longer. I have seen enough of soldiering."

"Yes." Jonathan nodded sympathetically, his old eyes growing distant. "I understand this, James Dawes. I too have seen enough of a warrior's life."

"He has something else to say," Shanna put in. She moved into the center of the room, her arms folded above her rounded belly, and she stared at Dawes. "He has come with some news."

"Yes," Dawes admitted, "Shanna is right. I have come with some news. Bad news."

"What sort of news, James Dawes?" Jonathan asked.

"I don't know how to approach this. I suppose the best way is just to show you."

From his coat he took a folded piece of paper. "In the morning this will be posted everywhere. In the trading post, on your houses."

"What is it?" John Three Tree asked, concern growing in his eyes.

"It is notification to the settled tribes of a new piece of legislation which has been passed by Congress and signed by the President of the United States." Dawes shook his head and turned his eyes to the paper.

"Read this legislation," Jonathan said, and his voice was as cold as anytime in Dawes's memory.

213

"It is a law, Jonathan Three Tree." He could not look the old man in the eye. "It is called the Indian Removal Act."

"The Indian Removal Act?" John Three Tree spoke, wagging his head as he came nearer to Dawes. "What does it mean? Read it to us."

"I won't read the whole thing," Dawes said. "I will tell you the gist of it. It says this: The government does not want Indians to live on the land in Florida and Georgia. The land must be sold to white settlers. The Indians, the Cherokee, the Seminole, the Creek, the Chickasaw, the Choctaw, must move to the land beyond the Mississippi River."

"We must sell our lands?" Jonathan said in confusion. "It cannot be." He laughed. "We were promised that if we laid down our weapons we would be allowed to live forever in peace, forever upon this land. I have a piece of paper with this treaty written on it!" Jonathan started to rise.

"The treaty is no good."

"It was signed by the president!"

"That president is no longer in Washington. The treaty is ended."

"Forever is ended!" Jonathan said, rising angrily. He stalked the room, trembling with rage. "Forever has come and gone? Forever we kept this land. Forever we pledged peace."

Dawes couldn't answer the old man. He was aware of a muffled, half-hysterical sound, and he looked up to see Shanna laughing.

"What did you expect?" she blurted out, hiccoughing as she spoke through the tears and the harsh laughter. "Peace! There is no peace ever with the white man. Only those like Yui understood what the white man wanted. Everything! Forever!"

"Shanna . . ." John tried to comfort her, but she spun away, turning her back to all of them.

"The Mississippi," Mary Three Tree said in wonder. She had only heard of that river. It was said to be at the edge of the world. It was said that the strongest warrior would take many weeks to walk there. "What then?"

"They say that an Indian nation is being created there, north of Texas. There you will live in peace."

"Here we live in peace!" Jonathan said.

"Are there not other Indians already living in this Indian nation? What of them? Will they kill us?"

"It will take a hundred days to walk there."

"Why must we sell our land? We have cleared it and planted it as we were told to do. We have made it rich."

Dawes could answer none of their questions. He sat with his head hanging, feeling antipathy growing around him.

"I will take my rifle against any man who wishes to remove me from my home," Jonathan said quietly.

"Please don't, Jonathan!" Dawes came to his feet. "I beg you, do not do this. You will all be killed."

"Go, Dawes," Jonathan said slowly. "I know you meant well by coming here, but I cannot stand to look upon your white face any longer. Leave my home."

Dawes nodded. He placed the bulletin on the table, and Jonathan's hand angrily swept it to the floor.

"Shanna," Dawes said, speaking to her back, "I am going to Ohio. If you wish to go with me, you may."

She did not even answer, and Dawes, picking up his rain slicker, nodded again and opened the door upon a stormy, dark day. He went out and closed the door behind him, leaving a patch of dampness on the door.

John Three Tree stood looking at the bulletin he had picked up from the floor. He blinked at the others. "There must be a mistake."

"Yes," Jonathan said. "There was a mistake made, and now it is too late to remedy that mistake. We should have fought. We should have killed every one of them."

"We shall have much money," Sarah Three Tree said, trying to lighten their mood. "After we sell the farm we shall have much. We can buy a wagon. We shall ride west to the new land. Perhaps it is rich and beautiful."

"This is my land," Jonathan said. He swung the door open again and watched the rain beat down, watched the jagged forks of lightning blaze their way across the rolling skies. Then, without closing the door, he stumbled from the porch and walked away, disappearing into the rain.

"Captain Taylor?"

Sergeant Major Lewis Raleigh rapped on the doorframe of the commanding officer's office and waited to be summoned.

"What is it, Raleigh?"

"The council leaders are here, sir."

Taylor pulled out his watch and glanced at it. They were early. "Have them wait a minute, sergeant."

"Yes, sir."

Taylor squinted tiredly, pushed the pile of papers on his desk aside, reached into the bottom drawer of his desk, and quickly poured and drank a glass of whiskey. Damn those men in Washington. The president, the war secretary, the Department of the Interior—all of them. Did they know what kind of operation this was going to be?

The Indians were in an uproar. Taylor was glad the relief company had arrived the evening before. The more uniforms he saw around him these days, the better he felt about it.

"Send them in, sergeant!"

Taylor rose, perched on the corner of his desk, and waited for the representatives of the civilized tribes to enter his office.

They were all grim men, wearing white clothes, some with beads. He tried to recall all of their names but could not, with the exception of the Choctaw Silver Fish and the Cherokee Three Tree.

"Good morning," Taylor said. He received a deep silence in response. A silence and six pair of angry black eyes staring at him. Taylor felt ashamed for a moment, but then anger swept over him. Damn them! What right did they have to complain? They were going to be paid for their land, then escorted to a land farther west where they could live as they liked, apart from the white man as they had always wished. It saved friction, would cost them only a little time. They did not want to go any more than they had wished to be relocated to this settlement years ago, but they had done all right here, hadn't they?

"Who will speak for you?" Taylor asked dryly.

"I will speak," Silver Fish said. "We ask why our treaty has been violated. We ask why we must go to a distant world. We ask to speak to the president."

"The president is far away."

"So is this Indian nation. We will go."

Intractable, as always. "There isn't time, Silver Fish. According to my orders you must be on your way within thirty

216

days. There is no time to go to Washington. Even if you could, the president, by himself, could not alter this law, which was passed by both houses of Congress.''

"We wish to speak to Congress," Silver Fish said.

"I have explained," Taylor said with waning patience, "there is no time for you to go to Washington and speak to anyone about this. Besides, it is extremely doubtful that anything would be changed. The law has been passed. White settlers are already en route. I hardly think Congress would dare rescind this bill. The furor it would cause among those who are counting on establishing themselves here would be overwhelming.''

"Taylor, captain," Three Tree said. "When our land was given to us there was a treaty. We signed this. We agreed to this. Now when they wish to take it away there is no treaty, we did not agree to it. How can it be? Before we were told, 'You must sign this treaty so that we can give you land.' How can we sign nothing and have it taken?''

Taylor sighed. "Jonathan Three Tree, we have discussed this over and over.''

"It still does not make just sense! We can discuss it one hundred times, it does not make just sense! We signed nothing!''

"Nevertheless, it is the law! It will be carried out. You must move.''

"Then we can say nothing else?''

"No.''

"We have sick people, young children. How can they walk so far?''

"Provisions are being made, I assure you. There will be wagons and horses, food. Gentlemen, I have no more time. You are making far too much of this. In the Indian nation there will be no white army, no white police. You will have your tribal laws again; you will govern yourself. The land is fair . . .''

"You have seen it?''

"I have been assured that it is good land.''

"We have been assured of many things," Silver Fish said. He looked at the others and slowly shook his head. "There is nothing more to be said here. The captain is right.''

Taylor watched them file out. Then, feeling uneasy, he

217

returned to his desk chair, where he automatically reached for the whiskey bottle, wondering if he was beginning to rely too much on that bottle.

He gulped a second glass down and called out loudly for Sergeant Major Raleigh.

"Sir?"

"Find Lieutenant Fortune and have him double the standing guard."

"Yes, sir." Raleigh saluted and went out, and Captain Taylor returned to his paperwork.

The first of the civilian land buyers arrived not by wagon, bonneted wife and children beside him, but by the last of three fast horses which had been purchased in preparation for this day in Savannah. Two of the horses had been run into the ground. The last, a leggy, lathered black gelding, was barely able to walk when Mr. Jacob Lattimer, formerly of Charleston, swung down in front of the commanding officer's office at Fort Madison.

"Do you wish to see a Jake Lattimer, civilian, sir?" Sergeant Major Raleigh asked. He frowned. The captain must be halfway through his first bottle already. His eyes were bloodshot, cheeks flushed deeply.

"Who?"

"Jake Lattimer, civilian land buyer, sir."

"All right," Taylor said indifferently. Minutes later the tall, hawk-nosed Lattimer, still trail-dusty, perspiring, was shown in.

"The harbinger," Taylor said, his voice slurred.

"What?"

"Never mind. What is it, sir?"

"Jake Lattimer, Georgia Eastern Land Company." He placed a greasy card on the captain's desk.

"Yes?"

"I want to see the Indian land that's for sale. Maybe you could have one of your men show me around."

"Land companies are excluded from this sale," Taylor said. "The Indian land is intended for white families. Individuals."

"Now, sir, that's an interesting point. The thing is, however, as my boss, Mr. Greaves, who is an attorney, has discovered, no matter what the intent of the Indian Removal Act is, it's

218

not specifically stated in that act that a company can't buy this land so long as it's passed on to individual farmers in the end.''

"You want to buy up all the land you can and resell it," Taylor said. Liquor might have dulled his senses, but it hadn't deprived him of all of his intelligence.

"That's it in a nutshell." Lattimer went on quickly, setting the hook, "Point of fact is, we could use a local representative, a man who could show us the good land, give us a hand dealing with the Indians."

"You are offering a bribe?"

"I offered a business proposal. If you know someone who might be able to help the company out," Lattimer said. Both men were smiling, and Taylor was reaching for the bottle and another glass.

"How much were you thinking of offering this representative, Mr. Lattimer?"

"Whatever's fair, Captain Taylor," Lattimer said, accepting the glass of whiskey. "Whatever's fair."

Shanna heard the men arguing in the yard. She hobbled toward the door, holding the small of her back. She was full with child now. In a month the small one would be into this world, looking around with frightened curious eyes. And what would he see?

The front door was open. Two white men, one in uniform, stood talking to Jonathan Three Tree in the muddy yard. Mary stood on the porch off to one side.

"Five cents an acre seems fair to me, Three Tree," Taylor said.

Jonathan was so angry he could barely sputter an answer. "Five dollars. Five dollars."

"This land cost you nothing, Three Tree," the tall civilian said.

"The labor of a thousand days is in this land."

"That won't help you in the Indian nation, will it? Cash money will."

"My crops . . ."

"You won't be here when them crops come in," Lattimer said.

"I cannot sell for what you offer! I was told you would give a fair price!"

"It is a fair price, Three Tree. The going price. Hell, this land won't go for much anytime. Can't raise cotton or tobacco."

"You can grow food."

"Corn ain't exactly a high-return crop, Three Tree."

"I cannot sell for what you offer. It is an insult. It is thievery." He looked around hopefully. "What about my house? It is a good house. It does not let in the wind and rain."

"That?" Lattimer looked at the pole-and-mud house. "Won't even make firewood. You don't think a white man's going to live in a place like that, do you?"

"I will not sell."

"All right." Lattimer took up the reins to his horse. "I'll file on this place then."

"What do you mean?"

"Just that. I'll file, and when it's abandoned, I'll claim it. You ain't goin' to be here in three weeks, chief, remember? When you're gone, I'll move in. Of course," he said, swinging slowly into the saddle, "you'll have nothing then, will you?"

Then with a nod the two men were gone. Shanna stood on the porch, watching them go, and she thought: These are worse than warriors. Worse than murderers. They are the carrion birds.

Mary turned her broad face toward Shanna. Her habitual smile had been washed away by grief. "It is not fair," she said. "It is not fair." She wiped her eyes with her apron and went back into the house, still murmuring.

Jonathan Three Tree stood in the middle of his yard, to his ankles in mud. He was stunned, defeated. There was no longer any talk of arming themselves, of fighting back. It would mean mass suicide, and they knew it. He slowly turned toward the porch, his eyes hollow, his thin white hair drifting in the wind.

"Tell Mary I have gone," Jonathan said.

"Where, Jonathan Three Tree? Where do you go?"

"To sell my land." His voice was broken with emotion,

and he turned quickly away, plodding off through the deep mud toward the fort, and Shanna could do nothing but stand and watch, feeling the anger rise.

It was a cool gray morning, the skies flattened by the mist which hung overhead. The sun had risen, but it showed only as a leaden ball behind the clouds over the Atlantic. The Indians were gathered to the west of Fort Madison, assembled under armed guard. Now they waited in silent bitterness, in fear, in hopelessness as their houses were searched for any who might have stayed behind.

There had been two shooting incidents that Shanna knew of. One was an older woman shot by mistake, the other a son of hers who had tried to avenge her death and been cut down mercilessly.

Shanna stood against the wheel of a wagon, John Three Tree holding his protective position beside her. The Three Tree clan had been "fortunate." They had actually received the wagon promised them by the army. Most had received nothing. There were few blankets. Many, more obstinate than Jonathan Three Tree, had not even been able to pocket the few dollars the land company had offered them.

"Look at them," John Three Tree muttered.

Shanna lifted her head to study the soldiers. There were many more of them than necessary, she thought. Their leader, a man called Fortune who seemed afraid to meet their eyes, had spoken to them all that morning, telling them that he was their friend, that they must endure for a little while, that beyond the forests, beyond the distant Mississippi, was their promised Indian nation and a rich, comfortable life.

No one believed any of it.

They waited until the search was completed. To the north, someone had said, an army of white settlers waited as well. Jonathan Three Tree spoke to no one; he simply stood and stared at his land, perhaps, Shanna thought, remembering the mighty warrior named Ha-tha-Shone who would have fought to the death before suffering this indignity.

But Ha-tha-Shone had become Jonathan Three Tree, and the courage of the old warrior was gone, traded for a few acres of land, for the safety of his clansmen. He must have been wondering if it was worth it—those few years of peace and comparative prosperity.

As for Shanna, she considered herself a slave again. It was curious, but she had never known freedom, except as a very young girl. Nor had she known happiness. Except in the arms of Yui, the enchanter, the warrior who if he were alive now would look around with astonishment at the weary, beaten Indians surrounding him.

The Cherokee were here, the Choctaw, the Creek, the Chickasaw, and the Seminole. Shanna had spoken to Mother Holotok earlier. That proud woman still bore up, comforting the children, loving them, looking ahead with strength and dignity. Pamda had appeared frail, but happy in the manner of one whose spirit does not dwell in this world.

Shanna had no emotions.

She could not even hate the whites; she could not mourn the loss of a land which had never been hers; she did not rebel against the long march—when had she not been marching, fleeing war and its residue?

"You will not have to walk," John Three Tree said. "You must ride in the wagon."

"I can walk," Shanna snapped, and then for the first time, John Three Tree drew himself up and commanded her:

"You will not walk! You will ride in this wagon. You are carrying the child of the man you loved. This child may be injured if you try to walk. You have your pride, and I understand this. You will always have your pride, but do not let its influence extend to injuring a tiny innocent. You will ride in the wagon."

She would have argued, but the concern in his eyes was overpowering. Shanna looked him up and down and said finally, "Yes, John Three Tree. I will do as you say," and even the smile on her lips could not tarnish the relief the young Cherokee felt at that moment.

Shanna was helped up onto the wagon bench, where Mary, eyes straight ahead, face wooden, sat holding the reins to the horses.

To their left the Seminoles, most afoot, lined up to begin the long march, and to the rear the Cherokee, the Chickasaw, the Creek waited with their bundles in their hands, with fading hope in their eyes. Shanna saw the young lieutenant who was in charge of this expedition lift his hand as he studied the gold watch in his other hand.

At the proper time, on that proper day, beneath a gray and lowering sky, the lieutenant's arm fell, Mary Three Tree snapped the reins, and the wagon lurched forward.

The long procession moved out forlornly toward the distant promised land.

❀ 14 ❀

The long trail stretched out endlessly. Their numbers constantly swelled as they passed into the homelands of the Choctaw and of the Chickasaw to the west. The newcomers, waiting dutifully beside the trail, would fall into the line of weary Indians which stretched now for miles. Everywhere they saw white settlers waiting. Soon there would be no Indians in the South. None in Alabama or Mississippi. Only in the far south of Florida where Osceola fought his dream war would there be any of Manitou's people living as they always had.

Shanna watched it all. Watched the dusty and broken-hearted people trudge westward, their chins lifted, their eyes shining, hoping still. Hoping that this would bring the final peace, hoping that this time the white man had not lied and that the Indian nation beyond the great river was fertile and good.

The caravan rolled on, and it stopped for nothing. There was a schedule to be met. The man in charge of the white soldiers was called Lieutenant Fortune. He was uncertain and, Shanna thought, frightened. He was badly outnumbered. If this had been a battlefield he would have turned and run, but the Indians carried no weapons.

He had been given a man named Culpepper as his sergeant. This one, Shanna decided, would welcome war. He had eyes like those of Kaal. He was a killing man, and Shanna turned her head when Nat Culpepper rode past their group of wagons, searching their faces.

They camped in a pretty beech and pine forest beside a small silver creek. At sunset the skies put on a brilliant display. Crimson and gold, deep purple and deeper blue. One old Choctaw said: "Manitou bids his people farewell."

Already they had named this trek the Trail of Tears. Already it deserved that name. The day before a young girl had bounced off a wagon seat and been run over by the heavy wheels of the following wagon. Already several of the old ones had died. Some said it was from broken hearts, and Shanna knew that it could be so. She had suffered a torn and ravaged heart herself and it had nearly killed her.

John Three Tree came walking swiftly to the low campfire where Shanna sat with the family.

"They say there is no more food."

"That cannot be. I saw the soldiers eating their meal!" Tom Three Tree said angrily. His small daughter was hungry. His wife, Sarah, was ill with a fever.

"They say it is not our food. Tomorrow, Culpepper told me. Tomorrow there will be a supply wagon to meet us."

"What of those who must suffer tonight?" Tom said. He picked up his daughter and tried to quiet her. "I will speak to Culpepper."

John grabbed his arm. "Don't, my cousin. It will only lead to trouble. Culpepper is very bad and eager to kill, I think. Shanna?"

"It is true. Culpepper will kill. I think he must have killed many times. John is right."

"How can he kill me for asking for food?" Tom asked in anguish. He pondered his own question. "He cannot."

"We are in a land where only the guns of the soldiers rule," Shanna said. "If a man is killed the soldier must only say: 'He attacked me.' Who will judge him? Who will extract revenge? Who will care? You must stay alive, Tom. Do not approach Culpepper alone."

"My family is hungry."

"Perhaps the supply wagon will catch up tomorrow."

"Perhaps it will not! Shall we start believing those men now?" Tom asked.

"Your family needs a strong warrior, a good husband and hunter, more than it needs a meal this night," Shanna said quietly. She too took Tom's arm, feeling the tension there. "Come. We still have a little jerky, a little porridge. We will share it."

"If there were time to set snares . . . if they would let us

rest for one day . . . if they would let us have one hunt . . ."
Tom wandered off, his head hanging.

"He will do something dangerous, Shanna," John Three Tree said.

"Not if we watch him."

"Leave him." The voice was Jonathan Three Tree's. "Leave the man to do what he must do. He is a warrior, a proud man. He sees injustice, he sees his family suffering. A man must do something."

"Not if he dies, Jonathan Three Tree," Shanna said, crouching beside the old man, her hand on his arm, her fecund belly against his back. The old man sat staring into the golden embers of the fire. He sprinkled a little more water onto the embers to raise smoke against the swarms of mosquitoes. His eyes turned to Shanna and he said:

"Yes, small one. Even if he dies. You must know that. It is the difference between a man and an animal that walks upright—the willingness to end his own existence for what is right. The ability to love that much."

There was no answer to that, and so Shanna rose, the old man watching her. "John," he said, "you are a wise young man. Wise for wanting this woman to be your wife. Look at her! It is in our time of tribulation that she grows strong again! We falter and grow weak, our spirits fade, but this one—she is a woman to lead a people, to walk beside a man."

The wagon which was supposed to be carrying food for them did not catch up the next morning. They moved on, hungry and weary. Now there was anger as well. Tom's wife was still ill. She lay in the back of the wagon, tossing from side to side. Shanna crouched beside her, dabbing at her forehead with a damp rag, giving her sips of the precious water.

"How is my baby?"

"She is well, Sarah."

"I heard her crying last night."

"This morning she is happier. She is with her father."

The little girl was in fact exhausted and hungry. Perhaps she had a touch of this fever which had infected Sarah. She was riding on Tom's shoulder, a limp, dirty doll whose face had suddenly grown too old for her three-year-old body. Tom

226

himself was angry, too angry. His brother and John took turns walking beside him, trying to calm him.

"I am afraid he may do something and get hurt," Sarah said. Her hand gripped Shanna's.

"We will not let him," Shanna promised, and Sarah managed to form a thin smile. Shanna turned the cloth on her forehead, then stood, walking back to the wagon bench to sit beside John.

"Better?" he asked hopefully.

"A little," Shanna lied.

The length of road they now traveled was treeless. Looking ahead, they could see the long column of Indians stretching, it seemed, to the horizon. Dusty rifle-bearing soldiers rode on either side, an army of men escorting their enemy into hell.

The sun rose higher, and the humidity rose with it. The day was stifling, hot. "Where are we?" Shanna asked.

"The river ahead is called the Alabama after the people who live along it. Outside that, I know not where we are. Somewhere between the old world and the new."

Sarah cried out in pain, and Shanna stepped into the bed of the wagon again, nearly falling as the wagon hit a deep chuck hole. John looked behind him anxiously, saw that Shanna was all right, and returned his gaze to the front.

A people marched toward their destiny, toward a land they had no wish to live in. The sick and the lame marched on awkwardly, helplessly. They could not stop; there was no room for them in the wagons. There had never been enough wagons, not nearly enough, and now there were far fewer. They had lost a dozen moving through the muddy bogs behind them.

"Is she all right?"

Shanna was beside him, and now she sat, hands folded, looking straight ahead with unfocused eyes. "She is at peace."

"Dead!"

"Yes."

"Oh, no." John's voice was quiet, but grief-constricted. "Someone must tell Tom."

"You are his cousin," Shanna said.

"Yes." John handed the reins to Shanna. Then, crouching on the side of the box, he leaped to the earth as the wagon rolled on. Tom was directly behind them, the little girl limp as she sat on his shoulders.

"You will break a leg, John," Tom laughed.

"Let me carry the girl for a time, cousin," John Three Tree said.

"It is not my turn to ride."

"I think you should go to the wagon," John said, and Tom's eyes flickered. He knew suddenly. He stopped, and they quickly transferred the girl. Then Tom took off at a run. John saw him reach the wagon, leap over the tailgate, and disappear into the interior. Then there was a long silence.

It lasted for minutes, and then at last the silence was shattered. John closed his eyes tightly as Tom Three Tree's keening wail broke the stillness. His mourning song rose above the rumble of wagons, the shuffling of thousands of feet, the clopping of horses' hoofs. He cried out in anguish to Manitou, he cursed the white man, the spirit which had invaded his wife's body. He cursed heaven and earth and all of its inhabitants in a breaking, ululating voice. Heads turned toward the wagon. A soldier held his horse up, frowning, shifting his weapon.

"What the hell's all that racket?"

"A man's wife has died," John Three Tree said.

"Oh." The soldier was satisfied that there was no threat to his own life, no uprising underway, and that was all that mattered.

John watched him ride away and meet another soldier, and he heard their conversation.

"What's up?"

"Nothin'. Some squaw died."

John's face lifted slowly. He had never been quick to anger, eager to hate, but at that moment he could have killed them both. He could have torn them apart with his bare hands and left their bodies strewn across the land for the vultures.

"Where is my father?" the small one on his shoulders asked.

"Hush. He is riding in the wagon."

"Where is my mother?" she demanded.

"In the wagon as well."

"Why can I not be in the wagon?"

"Hush, small one."

228

Shanna shuddered as Tom's death song rose into the humid air. She listened as he ranted, as he pleaded, and then listened to the soft sobbing which seemed to go on endlessly.

When she next saw Tom Three Tree he was composed, his face as still as stone. He sat beside her, back rigid, fists clenched. "We must stop, Shanna. We must stop and give her a proper burial. The songs must be sung. She must be sent into the Bright Land in a matter befitting a good woman."

"No one is allowed to halt, Tom Three Tree."

"No one is *allowed*!" Tom said angrily. "We are allowed to grow sick as we enter strange lands where the spirits do not know us, where they infect us with disease. We are allowed to be hungry. We are allowed to die! But not allowed to halt. What should I do, Shanna? She cannot ride through the heat of this day back there. Should I dump her from the wagon to lie upon the road? This woman of mine who did no harm to anyone her entire life?"

"What is it?" John Three Tree was jogging alongside again. He caught at the whipstock and pulled himself up to sit beside Shanna. At Tom's look he told him, "I gave your daughter to Mary. She will let her ride in her wagon for a time. She is weary, Tom, very weary."

"I am weary," Tom muttered. "You must stop, Shanna!"

"It will mean more trouble."

"What is it?" John asked again.

"I must bury Sarah properly. It is right. It is the way. If we have no dignity in life, let us at least have dignity in death. I will not have her pass over into the Bright Land without a song to accompany her."

"Shanna?" John looked automatically to her for advice.

"We have been warned about stopping. There would be trouble. Perhaps if we sought out Lieutenant Fortune and explained that we must stop he would allow it."

"I will find him. I will ask," Tom said resolutely.

"I will go with you," Shanna said.

"Why? I do not need you."

"I will go with you, Tom, and try to explain that we must stop. It is better that you do not go alone."

He started to argue again, but ended by shaking his head. "All right. Let us find this man."

"He will be at the head of the column," John guessed.

229

"We can take Jonathan's horse," Shanna said. Jonathan Three Tree's best horse, a gray four-year-old gelding, was tied to the back of the old warrior's wagon.

"You cannot ride, Shanna!" John said.

"I can do whatever must be done," she said, handing him the reins. "Besides," she added as the wagon hit another hole, "it can be no more formidable than riding on this wagon seat."

John looked at her dubiously and slowed the team, halting it amid the cries of the column behind them, the soldiers on the flanks. Shanna let Tom help her down, and together they waited beside the road for Jonathan Three Tree's wagon to draw abreast.

Tom shouted up his intentions, and Jonathan Three Tree stepped to the rear of his wagon to untether his horse. Tom caught up the reins.

Shanna slipped onto the horse's back. It was hardly easy, hardly comfortable, but she had done many things more difficult.

Tom vaulted up behind her and heeled the horse into a trot. They rode toward the front of the column, which seemed endless now. Shanna saw people she did not know, from tribes she could not identify. Where had they all come from? Legions of plodding, grim-faced, silent people, moving across the raw land. Her heart leaped suddenly.

"Look, Tom!"

Tom's thoughts were elsewhere. He had no idea what Shanna meant by pointing at the Indians they now passed. "You know them?"

"They are. . . Shawnee!" Shanna whispered.

She could not make out their faces as Tom raced the gray gelding past them, but she knew their dress, their jewelry, their feathers. All from a long-ago time, from her childhood.

It was then that she felt the tragedy to its fullest, that she knew the breadth of this victory of the white man. She had somehow imagined that the Shawnee had been victorious or at least undefeated. It had been something to cling to. The thought that to the north was home, that there things were different, sane, peaceful, disrupted by battle, perhaps, but enduring. All of that dissipated now as a child's dream. The Shawnee too had been defeated. All the tribes had been

230

defeated. All. The way of life was gone. Entire peoples were shifting westward. The world had rolled over and become a world where only the white could survive, where all others must go westward. Westward to the great river and beyond it a thousand miles to . . . the end of the world, a place where the Indian could exist in banishment, in shame.

What else could have been done? Brave warriors had stood up against this wave of aggression and led their people by the thousands into death. Others had surrendered, leading their people into slavery. There was no solution, no answer, only the vast tragedy.

"There he is, I think," Tom Three Tree said.

There he was indeed. Lieutenant Fortune, appearing very young, quite haggard. He watched the approaching horse warily, looking around as if to assure himself he had soldiers nearby if necessary.

"Why are you here? Get back in line."

"We wish to speak to you, Fortune," Shanna said. The gray horse walked beside Fortune's bay gelding, tossing its head.

"Get back in line."

"Fortune, we are not prisoners," Shanna said. "We are not a defeated enemy. These people you are supposed to be caring for are called 'civilized tribes,' which means that they have accepted your ways, that they are content to live in peace and farm. They have even allowed themselves to be transported thousands of miles—all to avoid hostilities. But we are not slaves! Not prisoners. We must have the right to speak."

Fortune's lip twitched. His hand rested on the pistol which was thrust into the scarlet sash around his waist. "What is it?" he asked finally.

"My wife is dead. We must stop and bury her. There must be a proper ceremony."

Fortune laughed out loud. "Stop these thousands for one man?"

"For one woman," Shanna corrected coldly. "But," she amended, "we do not wish to halt the march, we only wish permission for the family of the dead woman to stop and perform the rites of the dead."

"Impossible," Fortune answered.

"Impossible!" Tom Three Tree was livid. "Why do you say this, Fortune? It is easy perhaps for you to say 'one woman' as if Sarah were nothing. You did not know her, so perhaps you are the kind of man who feels pity and concern only for those you know, for your own family, for your comrades, but is incapable of broad compassion, of knowing that others suffer as well. This, perhaps, I understand. But I cannot see how you can deny us this right. Do you not have a god, a church, a rite which you follow? Do you not believe that these must be followed if the dead are to arrive safely and quickly in the Bright Land?"

"It's hardly the same," Fortune said. He was growing angry, perhaps at Tom's temerity. Shanna thought it was the sort of anger which rises out of impotence and uncertainty, however.

"We wish only to halt and perform the services," Shanna said. "We will catch up quickly."

"And I'd have to assign soldiers to watch you, to make sure you didn't turn back toward Georgia."

"We will not."

"How can I know that?"

"We will give you our word," Shanna said simply.

"That hardly reassures me," Fortune sniffed.

Tom was furious. "Do you understand nothing of honor and of obligation? I must bury my wife. We have given you our word that we will not turn back."

Fortune seemed to waver, but only briefly. "I have my orders," he said. "If my superiors were to discover that I let some of my group fall out, I would have to offer some sort of explanation, and I'm afraid that compassion wouldn't answer that challenge."

"What does he mean, Shanna? I cannot understand what he is saying."

"He is saying that one woman is not important enough to halt the column. He is saying that our word means nothing to him. He is saying that he is afraid his chief will be angry." Shanna's words were bitter and rapidly spoken. Fortune still watched the two Indians, not ashamed, not challenging, but only fearful.

"He is a small man," Shanna said. "He can do nothing for us."

"He has a chief."

"Yes, but even if this chief would let us speak to him, we would find our words falling on deaf ears. Let us go, Tom. We can do nothing."

"You must listen," Tom said, his hand reaching out toward Fortune. "This must be done! I cannot leave my wife to lie beside the road like a dog.!"

"Tom!" Shanna placed her hand on his and pulled it down. "It does no good to speak to him."

"He must listen!"

"He does not understand. He understands only his regulations."

"No." He shook free of Shanna's grip. He grabbed for the reins to Fortune's horse. Shanna saw him grip the bridle, and saw simultaneously with shock and terror that Fortune, in panic, had drawn his pistol and had it cocked and ready to fire.

"Tom!"

"Fortune!"

But Fortune's answer was a roaring flash of flame. Tom was blasted from the horse's back. The gray went to its hind legs and whirled, pawing at the air. A soldier shouted, and Shanna, clinging to the gray's neck, looked down to see Tom Three Tree lying on the ground, his chest stained crimson, his eyes open to the hard sky, his heart stilled.

"You!" Shanna screamed.

"He was coming after me. He tried to attack me," Fortune babbled. There were other soldiers, some afoot, some mounted, coming at the run. Fortune was speaking to no one as he said, "You saw him. He leaped at me. How did I know what he was going to do? I had to shoot."

Shanna had gotten from her horse, and now she crouched beside Tom Three Tree, looking up at this coward, this Fortune, who sat now surrounded by soldiers.

He had to say something, and so he repeated his lies. Tom had been angry because his wife had died. He had tried to attack the officer when he was told that the column couldn't be halted while he buried her. Fortune had had to shoot. What else could he do?

The Indians plodded by, their faces turned away. Shanna crouched in the dust, looking at the soldier with the still-smoking gun, looking into his heart to see the fear, the smallness there as he rattled off his lies, which must have sounded false even to his soldiers.

Then slowly she rose. She rose and stood in the middle of the road, letting the Indians file past her in an endless stream, her eyes lifted to the far horizon.

❀ 15 ❀

They made camp an hour after sunset in a tangled, over-grown glade which hummed with insect sounds. There, tired and hungry, they crouched around their small fires and stared at each other, saying nothing.

After sharing the small amount of food they had left, the Three Tree clan buried two of its members. Sarah and Tom would lie side by side in this foreign land, waiting for a friendly wandering spirit to lead them home, to take them to the Bright Land beyond.

Shanna watched silently, listening to the prayers. Then, unable to bear it, she walked into the darkness, disobeying the rules against wandering from the camps.

She walked through the deep glade, listening to the small night sounds. Out here, she thought, all was as it had been. Even the white men had not ordered the birds, sought to transplant the oaks and elms, the bullrushes and cattails. She stood in a silent glen for a time, listening, watching, aware of all around her, of the caress of the night breeze against her cheek, of the whispering of the leaves, the eternal song of crickets and cicadas, and she recalled a time when she had been much younger, when she had stood in the swamps of Florida and felt the pulse and whir of life around her, felt the flow of warm blood through her veins, felt the bundles of nerves doing their delicate, unremarked work, and felt that she, Shanna, her soul and heart and body were a part of all of Manitou's vast unity.

Yet on this night there was no sense of unity. She was not free. She alone of all of Manitou's creatures was never meant to have freedom. She alone was not natural, at peace with existence; she alone, a creature who was capable of knowing freedom and longing for it, could not be free.

She left the glade and walked to the top of the low, grassy knoll beyond it. She looked out at the dark plain dotted with hundreds of fires. Red stars against the blackness. A sign, a silent supplication, a plea . . . no, it was only firelight where people huddled and avoided each other's accusing eyes, where, while darkness held, they forgot.

Shanna walked through the camps, now and then taking to the woods to avoid a patrol. She found the Shawnee fires and walked among them, drawing incurious glances. There must be one, surely there must be one face she could recognize, one who would know her.

"What do you want?" an old woman asked. She sat with a very small child beside a dark fire. At first Shanna had not seen her. Now she moved nearer, looking down at the old face which had been cross-hatched by weather, at the eyes which had squinted into many suns and seen war and death, love and hatred.

"I am Kata Shawnee," Shanna told her.

"Kata?"

"Yes."

"No." The old woman shook her head. "There are no more Kata Shawnee. All dead. They fought. They are all dead."

"Not the entire tribe!" Shanna said in disbelief. "Not an entire people!"

"All dead," the old woman repeated. She returned her attention to the child, and Shanna was left to wander off alone through the massive, silent camp.

The Seminoles were farther back, camped on the low ground beside the trail. Shanna found Mother Holotok easily. Her great voice boomed out as she called to the children, her charges. When Shanna called her name she turned happily toward her.

"Our Shawnee girl. Where have you been, Shanna?" When Shanna told her, Mother Holotok said, "You must come and travel with us. Who will help you with your baby?" Smiling, Mother Holotok put her hands on Shanna's belly and was quiet for a minute. "Very soon, I think."

"Very soon. But I cannot travel with you, Mother Holotok. They have their rules, you know. I must stay with the Cherokee. That is where I began the trip."

"You have someone to help you?"

"Yes."

"Then I will not worry about you. Have you seen Pamda?"

"No."

"She looks for you constantly. She loved you so. She is well, Shanna. The new sights occupy her mind. I believe she is healthier than when she would sit and wait, wait for what she knew must come."

"You must tell her that I think of her always," Shanna said. Looking across the camp now she could see a party of white soldiers, and she told Mother Holotok, "I must go now." She paused, threw her arms around Mother Holotok's neck, and scurried back into the shadows, circling wide toward the Cherokee camp.

She was back in the woods, back in the silent world of Manitou, of nature, of the quiet spirits. It lasted only briefly.

John Three Tree rushed to her as she entered the camp. "Where have you been, Shanna? My heart was troubled. I did not know what had happened to you."

Shanna looked at him, looked into those boyish eyes, reading the deep concern there. "I was only visiting friends. I shall not leave again without telling you, John Three Tree. Perhaps . . ." Perhaps, she started to say, we shall come to this Indian nation and find that it is good. Perhaps there will come a time when I shall wish for a man, a father for my baby. But she said nothing. She took John Three Tree's hand and gripped it tightly for a moment and then walked away, leaving him wrapped in confusion.

"Lieutenant wants to see you," Nat Culpepper said.

Teska turned toward him, repelled by the sight of this brawny, scarred white man with the terrible eyes.

"I was taking this water skin to the camp," she said. She leaned against the wagon, her haughty smile fixed, challenging.

"You can do that later," Culpepper said. He spat and wiped his mouth on the back of his sleeve. "The lieutenant wants to see you."

"About what?"

"How the hell do I know? He wants you, you'd best come along."

"All right."

Teska sighed and hung the water bag on an iron hook projecting from the side of the wagon. Culpepper watched her, trying to appear indifferent.

"This way," he said, gesturing with his rifle.

"Through the woods?"

"It's shorter. Come on, Miss Uppity. Get a move on."

Teska tightened her mouth contemptuously. "Lead the way."

"You go first. I'll tell you when to turn."

Teska started off at a fast walk, her fluid hips swaying from side to side, her back erect, her head held proudly. The soldier was a fool. Perhaps he thought Teska feared him, but she had never feared any man, with the exception of Potaqua. A woman has tremendous power over men, and Teska, who had recognized that early in life and had cultivated it so that she had become confident but not agressive, able to obtain what she wished without appearing demanding, knew what she needed to do to soften men's eyes, to quiet the anger in their hearts, to dominate them.

"This'll do," Culpepper said.

"What?" Teska looked around at the dark beech and pine forest and laughed. "Is the lieutenant here?"

"What do you think?" Culpepper sneered.

"I think you are a filthy man."

"Maybe." Culpepper placed his rifle against a tree and walked to her, tossing his hat aside. Teska started to run, but Culpepper dove at her, catching her by the ankles. She fell to the earth, still not afraid—Teska was never afraid—but only angry. She jabbed at the soldier's eyes with her fingers, slapped his cheek so hard that the blows rang. She could hear him puffing, swearing under his breath. Then she saw his hand lift and saw it fall, and Teska's world disappeared in a shower of vanishing sparks.

When Culpepper rose, shaking and flushed, he looked quickly around. The woman was still unconscious. He walked back to where he had left his rifle and returned to Teska.

It's a shame, he thought, looking at her lovely sprawled figure, but that didn't deter him. He wasn't going to risk getting shot or demoted over something like this. He stood over her just a moment longer and then lifted his rifle, striking down violently. It troubled Nat Culpepper so little

238

that he even managed to whistle as he walked through the dark woods toward his guard post.

They were rolling again before first light. Shanna shivered in the gray predawn. The morning sickness and the swelling in her ankles had gotten much worse. She reeled dizzily as John and Mary Three Tree helped her onto the wagon bench. She sat staring at the long trail before them, at the soldiers who yelled and prodded irritably.

"They are alone now in a strange land," John observed. "The soldiers taste fear. They want this over and done with."

"No more than I," Shanna said, and John nodded grimly.

That was the day they finally saw the Mississippi.

They could smell the river for miles. The land was flat, with only scattered oaks and here and there a sycamore. The column halted suddenly, and Shanna's eyes lifted. It was not mealtime. "What is it?"

"I don't know."

Jonathan Three Tree, astride his grey horse, shouted out to them: "The great river. The Mississippi."

Shanna strained ahead, seeing nothing. The column began again, moving jerkily, slowly. Two hours later they finally saw the river and the many thousands clustered along its banks.

The river ran in a muddy torrent. It seemed miles wide. A group of white officers sat their horses, gesturing toward the river.

"It runs too fast."

"How deep is it?" Shanna asked, studying the breadth of the magnificent river. On the far side—was that to be their land, the Indian nation? She received no answer but a shrug from John.

They saw Lieutenant Fortune riding slowly toward them. His arm lifted, and he pointed at Jonathan, who was watering his gray horse at the river's edge.

"You, Three Tree. You have a good horse."

Jonathan turned his eyes slowly on Fortune, the contempt and hatred obvious.

"Three Tree!"

"Yes."

"I am ordering you to take your horse into the river and test the current. I want you to find a crossing."

239

"Send a soldier."

"I am sending you."

"If I refuse?"

"I am ordering you, Jonathan Three Tree. You may not realize it, but there is a severe penalty attached to rebellion."

"Do what you like." Three Tree turned away, folding his arms. He leaned against the shoulder of his horse. Fortune changed tack.

"These people must cross the river by sundown. It is obvious that the river is very high. If someone does not find a decent ford, many lives may be lost."

Jonathan wavered. Finally he said: "I will do it, Fortune. I will do it for you although you are a murderer and a coward. I will do it, but you must not say: I order you, Jonathan Three. You must ask for my help."

Fortune was livid. He started to shout back an answer, then, remembering, he looked upriver to where his superiors sat their horses, watching him. He answered, his voice a dry squawk:

"Jonathan Three Tree, I would like to ask you if you would help us by finding a safe ford."

"I will try," Jonathan said, his face immobile. He swung onto the gray's back and sat looking at the river for a long while, reading the face of the Mississippi, knowing by the white water and the ripples where snags and sandbars lay beneath the reddish surface of the great river.

This was no time to ford. They should camp for a week, let the people rest, let the river calm itself. But the white soldiers had decided to cross today. By sundown. And so they would cross and there was nothing to be done about it, nothing but try to find a safe crossing.

Jonathan eased his reluctant gray horse into the river current. The horse had taken only half a dozen strides before it was to its knees in the swiftly flowing muddy water. Shanna watched Jonathan try to soothe the horse, to quiet it. Its eyes were wild and it tossed its head, not minding the reins well.

But Jonathan had a touch with horses, and this one, young and frightened, calmed so that Three Tree was able to walk it forward until it was up to its belly.

Jonathan's eyes searched the river, and they could see him shake his head. He turned the horse northward, paralleling the bank. Along the edge of the river the Indians stood or squatted on their haunches, watching.

Jonathan's horse was now in shallower water. He had found a sandbar, apparently, and was casting about from side to side, trying to determine its width. Shanna watched him rein the horse westward and walk it farther yet into the river. He was a hundred yards from the bank, his head turned back toward them. He was there and then he was not. The gray horse plunged into the water. They could see its frantic motion, hear it whinny, see Jonathan Three Tree try to raise the horse's head, and then he was gone.

The current, swift and powerful, simply swept him away. Shanna stood, hands to her mouth, watching the muddy river. She saw the horse's head, saw Jonathan Three Tree's uplifted arm, a flash of color, and then there was nothing, nothing but the muddy, seaward-flowing, mammoth river.

Shanna sat down, stunned. John had his arm around her, and it was a time before she realized he was embracing her, trying to comfort her.

"I need another volunteer!" Lieutenant Fortune was calling.

"Damn you!"

It was George Three Tree who had shouted, and now he tore himself out of his wife's grip to rush at Fortune, who was sitting his horse, eyes pale and nearly blank.

"George!"

John Three Tree leaped from the wagon box, dragging his cousin down as George rushed toward Fortune, his mouth torn by anguish, his veins flooded with hot, savage blood.

John collided with his cousin, and they went down in a heap, raising a cloud of dust. Fortune's horse danced away. Paula Three Tree screamed. The others stood silently watching.

George struck out at his cousin, his fist landing on John Three Tree's ear as they rolled across the ground.

"George! George!"

"He killed Jonathan!"

George tried to get to his feet, but John was clinging to him, dragging him down again.

"He killed Jonathan, he killed Tom!"

"And he'll kill you," John Three Tree shouted angrily. "You have a wife. You have Tom's daughter to think of!"

241

"Get off me," George growled.

"No."

George roared and slammed his fists against John's face. John felt the blood spew out of his nose, felt the savage writhing of his cousin as he rushed toward destruction. John drew back his own fist and drove it down into George Three Tree's face.

The Cherokee sighed and lay back, unconscious, dirty, smeared with John's blood. John rose unsteadily, feeling the sudden embrace of Paula Three Tree, who looked down at her husband and repeated again and again, "Thank you, John. Thank you."

Her murmuring was broken only by the strident, clipped voice of Lieutenant Fortune, who continued to say: "I am looking for a volunteer! I need a volunteer to find a crossing."

None was forthcoming. Fortune finally sent an enlisted man into the dangerous current, and the white solder was nearly swept away. He returned and offered his own diffident advice:

"Mebee it's best to let that river go down, sir. I can't see no way across."

There was no choice in the end. The Indians set up night camp and sat down to eat. For most the meal was only parched corn. John had somewhere come by a small venison steak, and he roasted it while George watched morosely, his anger still festering.

It grew dark early along the river, and they sat in the silence, listening to it run, watching the stars roll past against a liquid sky. When Shanna had finished eating she rose.

"I need to walk," she said.

"May I come with you?" John asked, and on this night she accepted his company.

They walked in silence to the river's edge, watching the play of firelight on its broad face. Beyond the river was dark forest, and beyond that somewhere, their home.

Walking downriver, they came to a fallen oak log, and John helped Shanna to sit on it while he stood, leaning against the fallen tree, staring into the darkness of the night. Frogs grumped in the cattails, crickets sang a raucous, methodical song.

"You are silent, John Three Tree," Shanna said. Obeying

a gentle impulse, she placed a hand briefly on his head. He was a long time replying.

"I am silent. The land is silent, Shanna. It is the silence of death. I feel our sorrow this evening. Tom is dead, and Sarah. Jonathan, who was more than a father to me. And they are only swept to the side of the road, forgotten as soon as their last breath has been drawn. Who are these soldiers? I see no regret in their eyes."

There was nothing to say to that, and so Shanna held her silence. After a while John turned to her, his face bright in the starlight, his eyes sincere and gentle as always.

"I could not bear to lose you, Shanna."

"You will not," she said. His remark made her uncomfortable.

"Even if you will not marry me, still you have been a great friend to me, a sister. When we reach the nation I shall build a house. for you. When your child is born I shall be friend and brother to it."

"You don't have to say all of this, John."

"I have to say it. I want you to know. To know that I will always be there. Whenever you need anything, John Three Tree will be there."

He looked expectantly at her, and for a moment it was all she could do to keep from wrapping him in her arms, for she knew that he loved her, knew that he was a kind man, and a strong one beneath his natural gentleness. She could not cling to him, however; memories of the other held her back.

The other, Yui with his dark flashing eyes, with the lusty laugh, with arms of hewn oak, Yui of the gentle ways, the courageous heart. The father of her child.

She was silent too long, and John stretched out his hands to help her from the log. "Come, let us walk a way. We have said all we have to say."

16

It was three days before they could attempt the river crossing. The ford they finally used was four miles upriver. The river was lower, but the current still treacherous.

Shanna clung to the wagon seat as John Three Tree started the team into the river. She felt the wagon slew immediately, felt the wheels lift and shift, felt the wagon rock violently as the muddy river raged past. Ahead men swam the river or walked it with children clinging to their necks. She saw a horse rear up excitedly and spill its rider.

The soldiers shouted constantly, urging them forward, hurrying them, threatening. Children shrieked, men cursed in five languages; the constant rush of the river pummeled them. Shanna saw a hand raised as someone was swept away, saw a horse thrashing madly in the water, sending up silver fans of water.

She was never to know how many were lost during the crossing, but at the night camp that evening the sounds of mourning songs rose from all around her. Manitou's people calling to him for help, pleading for him to find their dead and lost and guide them to the Bright Land. There was no answering voice to be heard, only the shouts and laughter from the soldiers' camp.

They marched on at dawn. Their feet were raw—their moccasins had long ago worn out. The sun was a harsh adversary; the land was strange and wild and dry.

Once they had cleared the forest which grew near to the Mississippi they found themselves traveling a barren, endless land. The Indians marched in a perfectly straight line toward the west, toward their nation, toward peace.

Shanna saw the mothers beside the road wailing, lifting their hands to the dreadful sky, saw the small ones lying against the ground. She heard the tortured voices of those who were thirsty, those who had come out of the swampland behind them with the fever. Many of the old simply sat down and waited. The soldiers ignored them.

Their own wagon was now overloaded with the injured, the weak, the ill. The horses strained against the harness, their backs and sides salt-flecked, their mouths hanging open, their eyes stoic and dull.

The offside horse went down in a heap a little past noon when the sun at its zenith scorched their tragic party and baked the land to hard clay.

"Cut that horse out!" Nathan Culpepper shouted to John. "What in hell are you doing, Indian? Cut that horse out and drag him off to the side. You're in the way."

Grinding his teeth, John got down. Wiping the sweat from his eyes, he got to work on the harness while the second horse, wild-eyed, smelling death, bucked and reared. Shanna held the reins tightly while those in the back of the wagon cried out.

"Are we there? Is this the nation?"

"Why have we stopped?"

She looked at them, a dying people, a worn and defeated race, and the tears welled up in her eyes. She answered them calmly.

"In a minute. In a minute we shall travel on."

She watched as George and John dragged the horse to the side of the road, feeling the perspiration trickle down her breasts and back, feeling the small one kick her angrily.

"You have a right to be angry, small one," she whispered.

The second horse died a mile on.

He went down in his harness, got to his knees and tried to rise, fell and lay kicking against the earth. Shanna looked at John, seeing the lines of sorrow which the trail had etched into his dirt-streaked face.

"Now what shall we do? What shall we tell them?"

Shanna looked into the bed of the wagon, where the old and the injured lay silently. No one asked any questions this time. They knew.

"We will tell them they must walk." Shanna sighed. "It is not so long until dark. We can all walk for a little way."

"You cannot."

"I can," she said defiantly. "I can walk. I can find this promised land. I can birth my child. I can grow crops and raise the child. I can! I am Shanna. I have walked far, John. I have always walked."

She did walk on, with John beside her, with the sun a fierce menace in the white sky. They walked, passing those who could walk no more, passing the dead stock on this endless, waterless plain.

When the sun finally, mercifully, darkened and sank triumphantly into the cradle of the western horizon, Shanna collapsed to sit beside John, leaning against him, now for the first time needing a little of his strength, a little of his comfort. There were only a few fires that evening. There was little to cook, nothing but the dried buffalo chips which lay scattered across the plains to fuel a fire. The land held the heat of the day until well after midnight, but by morning when they rose shakily to face the gray premonition of dawn, the temperature had plummeted so that they stood together in small shivering groups, using each other's body heat.

The sun was a blossoming rose against the eastern horizon when they started out again. Beginning the endless march, the travail, the useless, eternal trek.

Shanna walked on. She was one of thousands of faceless, voiceless upright creatures being herded westward by time and fate, by white warlords. Her tongue stuck to her palate. Heat veils rose off the land before her, wavering and shimmering, bending the figures of men and women, of horses. Dots of red and yellow, of green, danced behind her eyes. Her head felt light, and at times it seemed to lift from her shoulders, to spin madly around, to float high above the long plains, seeing the endless trudging, dark line of people, seeing the uselessness of it all.

She staggered, and John Three Tree caught her arm, holding her up. She shook him off. "I can walk. I have always walked."

He said nothing. All around Shanna there seemed to be a humming, a sound like the buzzing of thousands of summer bees. She shook her head to clear the sound away.

"Shanna?"

"I am all right." But she knew she was not all right. She could barely form the words she spoke. She was barely

246

walking, moving on legs which seemed to have no sinew, no muscle.

"Shanna!"

Why was he shouting at her, annoying her? She shook her head again. She realized suddenly through the fog which had gathered in her brain that she was simply standing, doubled over, holding her abdomen.

Pain swept over her; she felt her abdomen contract; a giant fist clenching and unclenching.

"Oh no, not here," she said to John. Then her legs went from under her and she fell to the ground, clutching at the sleeves of his shirt.

Had she passed out? She was flat on her back, John's folded shirt beneath her head. People were filing past, faceless, nameless people, people who had no eyes to see. And hovering above them was the mocking white sun which, as Shanna watched, exploded against the sky, becoming thousands of flaming petals.

"You there. Get her off the damned road!"

"I cannot move her," John Three Tree said furiously. "Can you not see she is in labor?"

"Move her, dammit!" Nat Culpepper ordered. "We've had enough trouble with your family."

John was kneeling beside Shanna, seeing the perspiration trickle down her face, seeing the convulsing of her abdomen, her fists clenched so tightly that her nails were drawing blood from her palms. He looked up, his eyes anguished.

"I cannot."

"Damn you!" Culpepper's boot slipped out of the stirrup and arced forward, slamming into John Three Tree's jaw, and the Cherokee was jarred backward, his head ringing, his face trickling blood. "I'll do it my own self," Culpepper grunted. He swung down, his horse sidestepping perilously close to Shanna, who saw it only as a menacing black shadow before the white sun.

"No!"

John Three Tree's voice roared out. He lunged at Culpepper, who spun just in time to see the savage intent in John's eyes. The Cherokee hit the soldier with all of his strength, and the two men tumbled to the earth, the horse dancing away in confusion. They rolled off of the road, the file of passing men

247

and women barely looking at them. They kept their heads bowed, their mouths shut. They did not want to see—they had seen too much already on the Trail of Tears.

John and Culpepper rolled over and over, John's screams filling the empty skies, his fists, knees, and feet pummeling Culpepper.

The soldier fought back, jamming the heel of his hand against the point of John's chin, trying to break his neck. But John Three Tree wriggled free. He was all over Nat Culpepper like a mauling beast. Until Culpepper found his pistol with his right hand and shoved it against John's stomach, touching off.

John Three Tree was hurled back by the bullet, and he lay against the ground moaning and twitching, his eyes searching for Shanna, his lips trying to form her name until the great dark veil was drawn shut behind his eyes and he saw no more, heard no more.

Culpepper staggered to his feet and thrust the pistol into his belt. Bending over, he hooked his hands beneath Shanna's arms, dragging her roughly from the trail, leaving her to lie beside John Three Tree.

She was near enough that she could touch his hand. It was bloody, warm, unmoving, and she took it in her own, wishing she had let him love her for that little while.

The spasm of pain washed away all thought. She screamed out, thought she had screamed, but the sound did not come to her own ears. She lifted her head, looking for help, wanting Mary Three Tree or Mother Holotok. Pamda.

There was no one. No one to hold her hand with living fingers, to wipe the perspiration from her eyes. She blinked and rolled her head from side to side. No one. The plains were empty; the sad ones were all gone. There was not even dust to mark their passing. Their shadows had crossed the earth and now were gone. The time had ended. There were no more long trails to walk.

The pain came again, harder, more purposeful. It was time for the child, and there was no one at all to clean it, to feed it, to help it to learn to walk the broad land.

Shanna closed her eyes and clenched her teeth against the pain. When she opened her eyes again they were there.

She could not see them. Why did they not speak, why did

they not move? They sat around her, black figures against the white sky, silent and spectral. She looked up at them, tried to speak, tried to lift her head, but she could not. The child was coming and she hadn't the strength to give it life. This time she heard her scream, high and long, echoing across the empty plains, slowly dying away as the breath leaked from her, as the white sun went black and the distant voices called softly, summoning Shanna to them.

17

The warriors sat perfectly still. There was no sound but the shifting of their ponies' feet, the sounds made by the woman in labor. They only watched.

The Comanche were puzzled. The day had been filled with strange signs.

They had seen a crow attack a coyote, seen blue fire in the northern skies, seen an army of Indians walking with white soldiers, walking westward where nothing lived. It had been a day of omens.

Now they found this woman. She was dying; all of them could see that. Yet she was determined and she clung to life, trying to birth the child which was in her belly. She lay looking up at them with eyes which appeared to see nothing.

The wind was hot and dry off the western plains, lifting the ponies' manes, shifting the feathers in the Comanches' hair. They watched and waited, and after a time the baby emerged.

"She is dead," one of them said, meaning the woman who had ceased her struggle, who had done all she could. "The baby will die."

One of the warriors leaped from his horse. He strode to the baby, wiping it clean, cutting its cord with his knife. Then he raised it squalling to the torpid sun.

"Leave it. We do not know anything about this woman."

"The child may be an omen. It may be a shaman baby, this little one."

"A girl. I do not like it. Leave it—we have too many to feed now."

The younger warrior did not answer. He climbed onto his pony's back, still holding the infant girl. "I have a sister who is nursing her own child. I will give this baby to her."

"It will die before we reach our camp."

"Not this one. There was much strength in its mother. This will be a strong woman. She will live."

The Comanche war party turned northward, riding away from this trail, this evil place, and out onto the broad, free plains, the baby raising its cry of fear, of hunger and determination, to the empty skies.

ABOUT THE AUTHOR

Paul Joseph Lederer was educated at San Diego State University. He now lives in Southern California with his wife, Sandra, and their four children.

His interests include silent films, American folk music and Eastern philosophy.

Mr. Lederer is the publisher and entire staff of his own Cormorant Press, which releases literary efforts outside the mainstream "when funds are available."